About the Author

Writing has always been my escape. Whenever life gets too busy or frustrating, I love the prospect of escaping into a world that didn't exist until I thought about it…

Broken Bonds

To Emma
Lots of love,

Becky
x

Rebecca Spinks

Broken Bonds

Olympia Publishers
London

www.olympiapublishers.com
OLYMPIA PAPERBACK EDITION

A CIP catalogue record for this title is
available from the British Library.

ISBN: 978-1-80074-526-1

This is a work of fiction.
Names, characters, places and incidents originate from the writer's
imagination. Any resemblance to actual persons, living or dead, is
purely coincidental.

First Published in 2022

Olympia Publishers
Tallis House
2 Tallis Street
London
EC4Y 0AB

Printed in Great Britain

Dedication

This book is for the greatest grandparents in the world, The King and Queen of the clan. I would be nowhere without you.

Acknowledgements

Thank you to my family whose faith in me has never wavered, not even for a second.

Chapter One

As Lina Simons watched her clothes being wrenched around the confines of the large metal chamber within the washing machine, her patience began to wear thin. She was twenty-one, *supposedly* in the prime of her life, living for the moment, doing the kind of things that she would later have the time to regret. Yet there she was, stuck in the relative confines of the prison-like household that was her life. The house was big, airy, and more spacious than any one person could ever need but unfortunately living in this dragon's den disguised as a castle was a reminder of everything that she wanted to forget. This house wasn't hers, never would be, in fact if she curled up in a corner for even half an hour, all the other residents would likely forget that she existed. Lina sighed, it's what you get from being the child of the second wife — officially part of the family but realistically just a hindrance. Her mother didn't care and that made it so much worse. The only thing she seemed to love was finding a man with a bigger bank balance than the last and although it was difficult to admit, Lina knew that her life would probably just follow suit of the only role model she had ever had.

As Lina contemplated her current situation, she could feel her lower body losing all feeling. She slapped both of her hands against the hard tile floor that she was sitting on and lifted herself slowly. She stretched and felt her bones sigh in relief as she grabbed the washing basket she had just emptied, her bare feet padding through the vast house like an echo. In the distance Lina could hear her mother talking on the phone, a phone that was simply pointless as she neither knew how to use it or earn the money to pay for it. As Lina's thoughts overtook her senses, she found herself walking straight into a tall, solid figure. As she looked up, she was relieved to see it was Harrold, her stepfather.

Although she hated the situation she was currently forced to live in, Lina couldn't help but smile slightly. Harrold, or 'Harry' as he reminded her every time she misspoke, had always made her feel welcome and included in his family. With him she felt special, as if she really was someone worth loving. The problem was high-powered men with high-powered jobs were hardly ever home.

"Lina!" Harry jerked slightly as they collided, the laundry basket falling to the ground in the scuffle.

"Hi, Harry," Lina said, slightly distractedly as she bent to pick up the basket from the floor.

"Just the girl I was looking for. Do you remember Peter Torne?" Harry looked expectant and slightly excited.

So much so Lina had to focus on him once more and take in a large indrawn breath to respond half-heartedly, "Vaguely, I think."

Harry continued, not being able to detect the slight hopelessness that had invaded into Lina's tone of voice recently. "Well, he just called to say that he has an opening for a trainee journalist on one of his smaller papers and remembers me mentioning your interest in the field."

Lina's ears perked up. Finally, a chance to get out of this house and start building a life for herself that could enable her to be her own woman not just a younger version of her mother! "That would be…" Lina felt herself begin to hyperventilate.

Harry put his hands on her shoulders and bent slightly to look her directly in the eyes and smiled. It was infectious and altogether completely charming. "Lina, I get it, this is a big deal and you deserve a shot at this great opportunity. Don't worry, I understand it can be a bit emotional," he said, pulling her into his arms and patting her back affectionately.

Harry ended the ever so slightly awkward embrace, gave her a small smile, and jogged back up the long twisting staircase. Lina just stood where he had left her with a shy half smile stuck to her face. She hated the way her mother had forced her to live, and yes, she felt awkward sometimes not really being in the inner circle of the Ryker 'clan', but Harry had become her safe place, a paternal figure she could trust. With this small act of kindness, he had given her life purpose and a way forward. Lina was still smiling as she wandered into the spacious kitchen. Her mother looked at her for a few seconds with a mix of disinterest and annoyance and then continued with her call.

Lina heard a rustle from the refrigerator and suddenly remembered what the day was. She snuck around to the other side of the fridge and went for the intruder. The small squeaky laugh that followed was exactly the effect Lina had intended. Rory was home. Although he was only her half-brother, Rory was the main source of her happiness, they'd been each other's rocks since he was born. As part of the custody agreement, declared by a judge, Rory had to spend most of the year with his father. It was still a mystery to Lina, why her mother had fought so hard to keep Rory with her for any of the year at all. Melinda, her mother, cared as much about Rory as she did

Lina, but housing Rory and officially 'taking care of him' meant she could keep claiming child support and that gave Melinda more of the one thing she cared about the most. Money.

Hours later, sitting on one of the large sleek stools that eloquently matched the kitchen island, Lina sat and watched as her brother dug into his favourite meal rambunctiously, whilst still trying to find the time to speak about the amazing adventures he'd conjured up about his time away from her. In a way Lina envied Rory. He had the one thing she didn't — a parent that cared enough to acknowledge her existence. Rory's father Dominic wasn't the world's greatest person, but he loved his son, spent time with him and made sure Rory knew just how much he was wanted. The six-year-old had come along just before her mother had married Harry but had barely spent more than six weeks a year in the house his mother had taken over.

"Zebras, rhinos, lions, penguins and..." As Rory continued to explain the many animals he had seen, Lina reached over and wiped a small amount of pasta sauce from the corner of his mouth and sadly smiled at him while his eyes gleamed as if he was reliving his adventure all over again. In a way it was upsetting that Rory couldn't feel his father's love all year round, but Lina was guiltily aware that she was somewhat relieved that he was able to be her saving grace in a house that would never be considered their home. As Rory rattled on, the sharp click of a woman's stiletto heels came from the adjoining corridor made of stone. Her mother continued to plough her way through the kitchen as if her own flesh and blood weren't even there and then stopped.

"Rory! My love." Melinda wrapped her dainty couture-drenched arm awkwardly around Rory's tiny shoulders. Her forced show of affection was evident to her, however she knew Rory saw it as a great privilege, so she kept her sharp retorts, the ones she had imagined herself saying, every day and night for as long as she could remember, to herself. As she sat venomously loathing the parent in front of her, she became consumed by her own thoughts and missed the question that was being directed at her. "Lina, I am getting sick of your air-headed attitude to life. When your mother speaks to you — YOU LISTEN!" With a roll of her eyes and a flick of her bleach-blonde and horrifically dyed hair, Melinda stormed off.

"Obviously couldn't have been that important then," Lina muttered under her breath.

Chapter Two

The heap of colour lining every inch of her bedroom floor represented failure to Lina. The many items of clothing she had tried on, liked, and then discarded was growing by the second. Without a doubt the people interviewing her wouldn't care about the exact image she portrayed only that she looked smart and presentable, however, this didn't seem to make any difference in Lina's mind. She needed the right top — the one that said 'here I am ready to start my amazing career' and the trousers that outlined her need for success in the field that she craved to be a part of. Lina glanced at the clock beside her and read the large luminous red numbers that flashed every second it counted She needed to be in bed, asleep, because after all what good is a perfect outfit when the wearer has bags under her eyes that run all the way down to her cheekbones? With a sigh and a roll of her eyes she swiped the clothes that had tried to overtake and imprison her bed onto the floor and not then so elegantly flopped under the covers.

Sleep wasn't easy. Especially with an altogether scary yet excitingly life-altering opportunity looming over the very sheep that Lina was endeavouring to count. The sad part was that Lina knew that even if all her luck came in and she managed to land this job, nothing would really change in the day to day, she'd be busier, sure, but she'd still be pedalling through a life that existed in a world which really didn't care about her minute life. Sighing into her pillow Lina took a few deep breathes and slowly fell into a deep yet tormented sleep.

Chapter Three

The slow drip of the water droplets forming at the end of the tap's faucet echoed through the kitchen. Melinda sat on one of the tall kitchen stalls, her body drenched in silk and her hands gripping her long hair. She sat staring, no feeling in her eyes, nothing to indicate the storm that was brewing within her mind. Melinda's knuckles turned almost transparently white as she gripped the roots of her hair. She didn't hear the footsteps approaching. "Ermmmm... Hi." Rory stood shuffling from bare foot to bare foot on the hard granite floors. Some would say he looked adorable all kitted out in his superhero-themed pyjama jersey and trousers, but she couldn't see it. It sounded stupid even to her, he was her son, her baby, her child and yet every time she looked at Rory, she became instantly uninterested.

"Rory, what are you doing up?" Melinda tried, as she always did, to show somewhat of a caring nature towards the child that she had birthed but, on this occasion, she fell horrifically short. Rory paled and looked quickly behind himself almost as if he was looking for an escape. With an agitated sigh Melinda motioned for Rory to go back towards his bedroom. It wasn't the boy's fault, she thought. By the time he came along her life had already been disrupted beyond repair. Lina, she thought, now there was a person she could blame. Seventeen, pregnant and penniless Melinda couldn't even afford to abort the baby that would become the deciding factor in whether her life would become something epic or something dull and joyless. She could have done something with her life, she could have created her own path but here she was, two kids that depended on her multiple spouses' fortunes with a body, that in a few years' time, would not give her enough leverage to trade in her current husband for one of a better monetary value. Some would say that the term 'gold digger' applied to Melinda but in her mind, it was simply scouting out men who could deliver her what she was owed by the universe. She had been through a teenage pregnancy and had practically no one from the minute she came into the wretched world, so why shouldn't she be entitled to a bit of relaxation and money.

Melinda padded her way to the large double-doored fridge and opened it, grabbed a bottle of chilled chardonnay, and reached for a large crystal glass from the accompanying cabinet. As Melinda placed the glass on the worktop it 'clinked' against smooth stone. As the liquid poured from the bottle in a smooth almost orderly fashion, the glug of the wine falling through the lip of the bottle broke the deafening silence that encased the dimly lit kitchen. Melinda retuned the bottle to the fridge and went back to her space on the island. The un-ladylike gulp that she swallowed summed up her last few years, they were years of drinking, spending money and loathing — all in a tortuous cycle that she feared would never be broken. Every time Melinda drank, she thought and every time she thought she loathed, thus expanding her feeling of hatred towards her own child. What had she done? Nothing, but she knew things and the knowledge of what she could do with those things was worse than any opportunities she'd missed because of her seventeen-year-old pregnancy.

She felt horrible, of course, Lina was her child, her first born and deep down she knew it really wasn't all her fault, but she needed someone to blame, or else she'd be forced to rectify herself with the fact that she was the one that deserved a reckoning. She was the one that was to blame for so many more things than just one ruined life.

With that piercing thought, Melinda became vaguely aware of a sharp smashing sound, and then slowly she felt the pain that accompanied the sound. Melinda opened her palm as a mix of glass and droplets of blood fell to the counter beneath her. For a moment she sat just staring at the pile of sharp edges and crimson liquid. She squeezed her fist together and more fell through the gaps in her fingers. Finally, Melinda let out a long sigh, got up and mindlessly walked over to the tap and rinsed off what she could. Draping a dish cloth over her sliced hand, she reached for a large dressing from the cupboard beneath the sink and clumsily wrapped it around her palm. Melinda put both her hands on the edge of the counter that surrounded the sink and hung her head. She looked through the window facing her, and her own reflection stared back at her, the darkness illuminated her features in magnified detail. How had she got it all so wrong?

Chapter Four

The hiss and chopping sound that was iconic for a coffee shop of this size was like a welcoming hug for Riya. She thrived on the liveliness of a hustle and bustle lifestyle — it's what came from living in a house full of men. Her father, Harry, and her two brothers, Logan and Thomas, were her guide posts in everything. After her mother, Victoria, had died, her family unified, it became a unit that had un-breakable bond after un-breakable bond which she often thought of as their saving grace when their initial grief had hit after the funeral, it is what had made the process of beginning to heal remotely possible. No matter what her family had looked like over the years they remained a family and for that, she would be forever grateful for every day she spent as a Ryker.

As Riya took her last few steps to reach her position at the head of the queue, she absentmindedly rattled off her coffee order to the barista and perused the assortment of cakes and sweet treats that were next to the till. She didn't notice the tall figure behind her watching intensely. Just as Riya was about to decide on the delicious cake she wanted to spoil herself with, after lunch, the barista handed her a steaming mug of coffee and she placed her hand around the handle and turned sharply in search of a table. "Whoa!" a deep voice said as Riya watched her coffee escape from her mug and splash over a broad and crisp shirt-covered chest.

"I am so sorry, I don't know what happened there. I am so clumsy they never should have trusted me with hot liquid, is there anything I can..." Riya froze mid-ramble and looked into the midnight-blue eyes that were looking down at her. She was stuck. She couldn't explain her gut reaction to this man but it was catastrophic, the electricity that was burning through her at only a simple touch was exciting and terrifying all at the same time.

"It's fine, don't worry about it, no harm done," the man smiled a gut-wrenchingly handsome smile and her heart fluttered — what was wrong with her! "The name's Nate Richards."

For a moment she just stood there not quite taking in the words that he had spoken. "Oh, ummm, Riya. Riya Ryker." As she said the words that came tumbling out of her mouth, she gave herself a sharp telling off in her mind. Here was a man — albeit a ridiculously handsome man — and she was falling all over herself and messing up a few small little words. This was not her, or at least it had never been. Until now.

"Riya." Nate drew out the name as he said it instantly liking the way it rolled smoothly off his tongue. He looked down at the red-faced beautiful woman standing before him and smirked. The minute he'd walked into this out-of-the-way coffee shop and seen her, he had noticed her. The way she was standing, with a mix of confidence and shyness, it was extremely intriguing and something he would like to see more of. "So, would you like to exchange insurance details, or would you settle for me taking you to dinner sometime?" He asked jokingly about the insurance but deadly serious about taking her to dinner. The shock at his words was evident from the small 'o' shape that her mouth had formed, and he

21

chuckled, nodding his head as if willing her to answer.

"That would be…" Just as Riya was about to answer his question, Nate heard the bell attached to the large glass door chime, signalling someone else had entered behind him.

"Hi. Sorry I'm late," the man who had come strolling through the door directed at Riya, and Nate took a step back. He had become so overwhelmed with the prospect of figuring this nervous, intriguing woman out that he hadn't even considered that she was already taken! The long silence that followed prompted the tall stranger to pipe up. "Sorry, did I interrupt something?" Nate raised an eyebrow at Riya whose cheeks turned a shade redder if that was even possible at this point.

"No, not at all, just a misunderstanding involving a coffee cup. I'll leave you guys too it," remarked Nate, perfectly ready, yet disappointed, to turn and walk away.

"Brother!" Riya heard herself announce as if to the whole world and she rolled her eyes at her own moronic-sounding outburst.

Nate pivoted on his feet. "Excuse me?"

"My brother… I mean this is my brother. Logan, this is Nate, my latest victim to be taken out by my coffee escapades." The two men shook hands in front of her and she watched, but even then, she could feel his gaze remain on her. She bravely raised her eyes to look at him directly in the eyes again and she saw the confident and humorous smirk that illuminated his face.

"Nice to meet you, Logan," Nate replied, still not taking his eyes off her.

"You too, I'm sure. Sorry to cut this short but I've got to be back at the office in less than an hour," Logan said sympathetically.

"Of course, of course. We should sit." Riya moved towards the seated area and Nate moved his arm allowing her to pass and as she did, she could hear him begin to order his to-go cup of coffee and sandwich meal deal over the counter. 'Well, there goes that,' she thought to herself sadly.

Riya listened to Logan begin to talk about the pitfalls he had encountered in the first part of his day. She felt guilty that she was only paying slight attention to him as most of her focus was still on the mysterious stranger she had just met, who apparently had the ability to command her attention even when he wasn't looking at her any more. Riya shook her head to try and wipe her thoughts clean and direct her energy at the conversation Logan was trying to have with her and then suddenly, a hand slyly placed a napkin in front of her. She felt his presence before she confirmed that it was truly him. She looked up and willed herself to avoid falling into the deep blues of his eyes. Nate winked and nodded down at the napkin in front of her and walked a few steps backward towards the door and with one more megawatt smile, he left. Ever so slowly she peeled her palm off the starchy fabric of the napkin and almost jumped up for joy when she saw his name and a phone number scrawled through the centre of it. After what seemed like hours, that was more like seconds, of trying to compose herself she looked back at Logan who was looking down at his menu quietly laughing and shaking his head.

Chapter Five

Logan sat down at the small round table opposite his sister and kept a broad smile on his face. Her scowl that conveyed just how embarrassed she was at the encounter he had just witnessed made the mischievous big brother in him leap for joy, "So...." he said with enough of a chuckle intermingled, so she knew exactly what he was hinting at.

"Shut up, Logan," Riya whispered dismissively as she picked up her menu and began to concentrate on the foods explained before her.

Logan sat in the unsteady metal wired chair and dusted his mouth off with his napkin. As places go it was decent, affordable, and allowed him to easily see his sister in between work. As he listened to Riya explain the horrendous board meeting that she had suffered through less than a couple of hours ago, he was forced to review his decision that had followed him around for the last ten years of his life. Both Riya and his older brother Thomas had opted to pursue careers that coincided with their father's software empire. He on the other hand had vowed to become his own person and create his own destiny. It was hard sometimes to feel almost like a corporate outsider as the rest of his blood relations spent their days together and focused on the same goals, but both his siblings and father were supportive of his move to focus on his architecture.

"What's new with you?" Riya asked Logan while taking her first stab into what looked like a deliciously sinful chocolate cake.

"Not much, you know, I'm pretty much just working around the clock at the moment." Logan felt a pang of sadness at the realisation that this was the first time he had lied to his sister, well not lied exactly but he had alluded to the truth. Something was new with him and he hoped that he would soon be able to bask in his joy with the rest of the family. Logan didn't often get involved quite as seriously as he was now, but this time was different, this time felt like it could be something epic. Problem was, it could all come crashing down around him at any moment.

Logan cleared his throat almost symbolically to also clear his mind. He then brought the napkin that was draped across his suit-covered leg and threw it across the empty plate in front of him. As always, the dainty way Riya had done this showed him how different the two were — she was born for etiquette and ladylike behaviour where as he was far from anything resembling a gentleman.

Chapter Six

As the knock on the large oak door sounded throughout his office Harry Ryker looked up over his glasses rim and watched as the large chunk of treated wood glided open. As the tall man with eyes the same as his and hair which was the spit of what his once was, came into focus, Harry couldn't help but smile. Every time he saw his children, he was filled with the same overwhelming feelings that fought with one another for dominance. Since his wife had passed more than ten years ago his children had been the reason that he got up in the mornings. They were his light in a pit of emptiness and he could not and would not forsake them for anything. Of course he had remarried, but it wasn't the same. Part of him thought that he had grown so accustomed to the loneliness of not having a partner in life that he jumped on the chance to marry the woman who actively sought him out, if only to spare his aching heart from more torment.

His second wife was a horrible person and he didn't mind saying it. She was cold, callous and money grabbing. However, five years ago when he had met her, he was lost, his children had moved out, his wife long gone, and he was alone in an empty shell of a home for the first time in twenty-five years. She had been beautiful and what to him seemed like, back then, confident, and self-assured which to a man of his power and wealth had been desirable traits in a mate.

Unfortunately, it had quickly become clear, after the ring was placed her finger, that these traits were simply the disguises of her biggest flaws — her selfishness and her maliciousness that fuelled her manipulative lifestyle. It was quite obvious to him that many were confused about why he would stay with such a woman for so long and he had often felt the need to abandon the ship that was their marriage, however, he couldn't. He saw the way the woman treated her children — children that were lively, funny and altogether adorable — and he knew that his real calling when it had come to this woman was to take care of, and show her children the kind of home and love that his own children had thrived on.

As Thomas stepped through into his father's office it was like taking a step back in time. When he had been a child he could remember visiting with his mother and the office had been identical to the one that he saw staring back at him. He often worried about his father and the way he seemed to lose himself in the past, but the man would never allow any feelings of sadness or anger at the loss of a loved one show to the children he had vowed to protect, or in the office where he was known as a 'shark'. "Hey, Dad, just came in to get your signature on the paperwork for the Hudson deal." Thomas set down the wad of paper that had the kind of details on that would make anyone else's head explode, but this was what he loved, the collaboration, the family, the lifestyle. He was a Ryker and he liked that he, from a very young age, had always felt part of something bigger than the sum of its parts.

"Yes, yes of course." His father motioned for the papers to be passed to him and re-adjusted his glasses that sat perched on his nose. The salt and pepper hair that covered his head now, somehow made him appear more masculine, and suave.

No wonder that his father saw more attention from the opposite sex than most men of half his age, yet he seemed to have no idea the effect he had on the female population. "You're still on for dinner tomorrow night, aren't you?" The question pulled Thomas from his thoughtful haze and made him focus on the issue at hand.

"Yeah, Dad, listen…" he said, half sigh, half trepidation even as the words escaped his mouth.

He felt his father's tension rise as if an invisible fist had gripped onto his father's body, "Don't even think about cancelling now — both of your siblings have confirmed, and I will not have another family dinner without my eldest son there." The tone in which Harry had portrayed this sentence had Thomas caught unawares. Not since he had started working at the company had he felt like a child berated, however, now it was clear that he was expected to be present and correct before dinner was served. To be fair, it wasn't his father he was angry at or his siblings in fact, he just couldn't stand his mother's memory being obliterated by her obnoxious self-centred replacement.

"Fine, I'll be there," the eldest Ryker sibling said, resigning himself, knowing that there was no way out this time and he was ging to have to grin and bear the next evening come hell or high water. His father had done everything for him and his family, so Thomas guessed this was the least he could do to repay him. Being the intuitive man that Harry Ryker was, he'd known the minute he'd brought Melinda home that Thomas had a problem with her and the way in which she behaved. He, for the most part, had accepted Thomas's loathing but as Thomas looked into Harry's eyes, he could tell that this was one of the few occasions that Harry Ryker was not about to be swayed by his son's feelings.

Harry's eyes softened as he watched the internal battle going on behind his son's eyes. "One night, that's all I'm asking, and I won't ask again." Harry watched as Thomas quickly nodded his head and a slight smirk formed on the corner of his mouth as if he felt embarrassed by his internal outburst. After a few minutes of silence, Harry cleared his throat and uttered his next set of heartfelt words. "I'm proud of you. Never forget that." With an almost sad smile, Thomas nodded and opened the large heavy door again and slowly walked out of the office. After closing the heavy panel, Thomas leant his forehead against it. Tomorrow couldn't come and go soon enough.

Chapter Seven

Lina watched her own leg bounce back and forth as if it were trying to levitate itself off her body and escape the tension that was coursing through the rest of her being. This was it. It might seem trivial to a lot of people, a job interview at a relatively small paper, but Lina felt like this was her turning point, her chance, her shot and something that no one could take away from her. Lina's plan was simple — nail the interview, get the job, learn her craft, and finally become independent enough to leave her past behind. As she wiped her freshly manicured hands down her tartan skirt, she didn't notice the older woman step out of the lift and lean over the reception desk to grab a clipboard. "Lina Simons?" the woman said as she searched the few people waiting in the lobby. Lina stood. "Um, yes, hi, I mean I'm..." She took a steadying breath and shook her head trying to shake away her nervousness. "I'm Lina Simons. Sorry, I am a little nervous." The older grey-haired woman gave her a smile and a pat on the side of her arm that automatically calmed at least part of her rapid nerves. "That's perfectly all right but there's no need to be! Come this way and we'll get started."

Sitting in the plush leather chair that was placed directly opposite the woman that would decide her future, Lina made sure to empty her mind of all other issues that may distract her from creating a great impression. "So, Lina, both Harry and Peter tell me you have a real passion for journalism and are very optimistic that this paper would be a great starting place for your career, but how about you tell me what writing means to you."

With one more steadying breath Lina made sure to speak directly into the eyes of the woman she hoped would become her boss. "Ever since I can remember I have used writing as my safe place. Whenever this world or my life have become too terrifying, I simply made my own world and a new life through words. As I grew older, those fictional stories I told myself became more and more factual and more about real life and real interpretations of the people and events around me." While Lina continued to speak, she was silently reading the woman's eyes to gauge exactly how she was doing. "The idea that one day I could write something that didn't exist before I thought about it and then the next have hundreds, even thousands of people reading it and considering my point of view is beyond motivating." By the end of Lina's last sentence, the woman, whose name was Sarah, as Lina had discovered by the plaque attached to the office door, slowly leant back on to the chair that looked like it was about to engulf her with comfort. She placed her hands in her lap and her lips began to form into a smile, quietly nodding as if she agreed with everything that Lina had just said.

"I think that you certainly have the passion that you need for a job like this, so how about you send me some of your work and if it is half as good as I think it might be, I'll give you a call and we'll get you scheduled to start as soon as possible," the professional woman suggested.

Lina stood as Sarah did. She took the outreached hand that was offered and shook it almost too excitedly. "Thank you so much!" As she walked quickly back down the corridor, she felt as if a huge weight had been lifted, she had a shot at this, she felt it. This was the first step, the first step towards the bigger picture becoming a reality.

Lina made her way to the nearby taxi rank and got in the back seat. She rattled off her intended address and leant back in the grey striped chair. Riffling through her bag at what felt like a hundred miles a minute she finally found what she was looking for. She opened the phone that must have somehow scurried its way right down to the bottom of her leather bag, pressed the call button and listened to the phone ring against her ear. "Hello?" enquired the voice on the other end of the phone.

Lina had never thought that a voice could be warm and comforting but this one was. "Harry? It's Lina." She could feel her own excitement in her voice that was now projecting itself through the phone.

"Lina! How did it go? I was going to call you, but I wasn't sure when you'd be finished." It warmed her heart to think that someone finally cared about what had happened during her days.

"Really well, I think. Sarah said the job's mine as long as my work is as good as my talk," Lina explained.

As Lina listened to Harry express his proudness of her, she finally allowed herself to relax. "So I guess I'll see you at home very shortly then?" Harry asked.

The question Harry posed was tricky, she couldn't tell him where she was going but couldn't lie to him either. "I'll be there in a bit Harry I just have to make a stop first," Lina eluded.

After saying their goodbyes, Lina dropped the phone into her lap and let her head fall back onto the head rest behind her. She smiled up at the probably un-hygienic roof of the taxi. This was it — her shot, her chance.

Chapter Eight

Over twenty-four hours had passed since the interview and Lina still felt like she was floating on a cloud. Not even the looming Ryker dinner could spoil her mood. All of them in one place at the same time was never a sign of good things to come, especially for her. They weren't un-kind or unpleasant in any kind of way they were just a reminder to Lina of what she wasn't or wasn't a part of. Thomas was the worst of them. He didn't speak down to her at all, in fact he rarely spared her more than a few words, and this highlighted everything that Lina had ever suspected of the resentment that had formed into a black cloud that hung above her head for all to see. From what Lina could tell from the way the house was still littered with images of Harry's first wife, who had died long before she had ever deigned to walk into the mausoleum styled house, and the way his children were towards her own mother, told her everything she needed to know. This family was still in a loyal bind to the woman that had obviously drawn loving feelings towards her like a magnet, and weren't likely to forget her existence for even a second, especially with the constant presence of a woman like her mother taunting them about the dissolution of a flawless memory.

The sound of her ringing phone was a calling card. Lina scurried around her bedroom to find where the culprit was situated and finally found it nestled under the many pillows that rested on her bed. Trying to cover up her rapid breaths which were a result of her frantic search, Lina answered the phone. "Hello?" she asked, trying to sound as if her mind hadn't counted down the seconds until this exact moment. The conversation that followed was all Lina could have hoped for, her luck had finally come in and she was to start her new career in a week's time. It seemed to her that her luck, that she assumed hadn't been formed properly when she was born, had finally rectified itself. The distraction that this revelation posed saved Lina from the usually present drop in her stomach when the doorbell chimed its happy tune signalling that at least one of the Rykers had arrived. She stood with reservation and made her way down the winding staircase to face her, what some would call, family.

As Lina reached the bottom step she came face to face with Riya, a woman who had, even Lina had to admit, a kind and somewhat welcoming persona. The woman smiled a beautiful, dimple-infused smile at Lina that could be considered genuine to the outside world. Riya didn't mean to be, but she was the most intimidating in Lina's opinion. Was it because sub-consciously they were both vying to be the number one daughter? Lina had no clue but all she knew was that currently she was standing in front of a beautiful, successful, and altogether cherished woman and envying her terribly. "Hi, Lina, do you know where Dad is?"

Even before Riya finished off the question the welcoming hug of Harry's voice appeared again. "There she is!" Harry bounded down the stairs and encased Riya in his big strong arms. Lina took note of the way he took a deep breath and closed his eyes as he welcomed Riya into his arms. What would it be like to have someone love you so much that every second they spent in your presence had to be mentally savoured whether the moment was big or small, influential, or ordinary? "We work together in the same building no less and I feel like I haven't seen you in weeks!" Harry said as she ended the embrace and he wrapped one arm around Riya's shoulders and spinning them around to head for the kitchen. Their voices and conversation left with them, leaving Lina to deal with the deafening silence.

Almost as if they had all been waiting to make a simultaneous entrance there was a light knock on the door and both Thomas and Logan came through the arched mahogany door. Thomas managed a tight 'hello' that she assumed was not directed at her before both retreated to their respective sides of the house. Why did it have to be so awkward? Lina thought to herself as she stashed herself away against the cold grey wallpaper that lined the passageway that ran down to the gardens. Thomas wasn't the one at fault, she knew as well as he did that it was the situation that had caused the ball of tension that seemed to engulf the pair whenever they were in the same room as each other.

With one last steadying breath she made her way down to the living room where everyone had congregated. Lina shyly smiled as she tried to shift her way to the back of an already crowded area. The only noticeable absence was her mother and she knew that Melinda was simply waiting for the right time to make her large and rather gaudy entrance. Riya smiled at her as she walked past and then returned to her conversation with Thomas. Harry gave her a squeeze on the shoulder as he poured himself a drink and gave a loud cough, signalling, he wanted everyone's attention. Lina took a seat on the cold stone raised fire hearth and looked as Harry stood, extending his long legs. "I am so happy to see all of you in the same place at last," Harry spoke happily and yet she could sense a sadness that pulsated out of his frame. At the same time Thomas looked down at his feet and scuffled as if he had become instantly embarrassed. "Initially this dinner was about seeing my family all in one place, however it has also become a celebration. Lina…" As Harry said her name, he offered her his large hand and gently pulled her to her feet. "As I was saying, Lina was given some amazing news today and was offered a brand-new job at…" As Harry beamed, Lina's muscles tensed, the tell-tale sound of clicking heels signified the arrival of one guest that Lina, just for a miniscule second, had been able to forget. While the rest of the room's occupants made her feel uncomfortable and sometimes out of place, Melinda had the power to turn her into metaphorical mush in the space of a look, and here she was strolling through the large oak door as if the whole room and scenario inside it hadn't existed until she had ordained to glance her eyes across it. Harry coughed and impatiently waved Melinda down into a vacant arm chair. The sign of obvious dismissal earned Harry a look that was completely devoid of loving emotion and more focused on sharp daggers that, in Melinda's mind, were probably hurtling towards Harry's face as he began to speak. "As I was saying, Lina has been given a job at the local daily newspaper run by Sarah Golding for Peter Torne." A chorus of congratulations echoed around the room and Lina managed a small, rather weak smile.

After a series of awkward hugs, the party shuffled towards the dining room. Lina stretched out her legs and hoisted herself out of the obligatory celebration. A shiver rushed over her as she felt a strong hand rest on the small of her back. "I know

I've said it already but congratulations. I'm proud of you." She then felt the unmistakeable chaste kiss on her cheek that she was only half expecting. With a pasted-on grin, much like the Cheshire cat's, plastered across her face, she subtly crept into the dining room.

Chapter Nine

The drum of her fingernails against the large oak table was the only sound that resonated in Melinda's ears. Melinda was indifferent to the large Ryker family at the best of times, but right now she had no time for anyone surrounding her. They talked and laughed like they were one big 'clique.' These people seemed to just fit together, to know what the others were thinking and feeling without so much as a word passed between them. Melinda found nothing more irritating than a group of people, especially this group of people, that were all about anything and anyone except for her.

Lately, Melinda had started thinking that it might be time to move on. Her gaze strayed to her husband and resentment echoed inside her. Harry had promised her everything when they had first met, she'd seen him sitting at the end of a bar twiddling his wedding ring with his head held low and a scotch sitting clamped in his other hand. Melinda had immediately seen a feather ripe for the plucking. "Trouble at home?" Melinda slyly asked as she slid both herself and her drink into the seat that, due to her movement, had moved even closer to the silver fox sitting next to her.

"You could say that," the salt-and-pepper-haired man said as he not so elegantly picked up his glass and downed the contents while simultaneously signalling the bar tender to refill the crystal glass in front of his nose. Melinda couldn't quite believe her luck as she noticed the platinum ring on his finger and his well-pressed Armani suit. Here was a man that could afford the best of the best and he was ripe for the taking.

"Need someone to talk to about it?" Melinda asked, giving a flick of her long blonde hair which not only showcased her shiny locks but also drew any man, within a five-mile radius, to other bodily assets that she possessed.

"It's the anniversary of my wife's death," the man said quietly, and she watched as he almost shrank into himself. As secretly as she could, Melinda smiled. Finally, her luck had changed, she had hit the jackpot. Within three months they had been married and it really hadn't taken much manipulation at all — a subtle hint at the possibility that she might be carrying his child and bam! She had reeled him in and scored herself the life of dreams. Or so she'd thought.

Looking back, Melinda couldn't decide if she'd do it all over again if she knew then what she knew now, the devotion to the dead wife and the utter closeness of the family that were currently chatting relentlessly around her. Harry had outgrown his use. Of course, being with him, meant being with his money, and that certainly was not something she was going to give up. Melinda had been through enough separations and divorces to know that she was entitled to something at least. Harry didn't care about her, didn't moon over her, didn't worship her and to be honest didn't seem to want to acknowledge that he had made her his wife in the first place. Melinda scanned the room and her eyes landed onto the two younger versions of their father at the end of the table. They could've been a possibility, an easy way to transition between money earners but unfortunately, along with the closeness of this hellish family, came a fierce loyalty, not to mention their own devotion to their deceased mother.

Melinda's son slept quietly upstairs, but her daughter was

sitting to the left of her. All this fuss, all these congratulatory toasts to a girl who had simply gone out and managed to get herself a job. Melinda was completely certain that it wouldn't be that hard, not as hard as repeatedly having to find a way for her family to live in luxury. With an irritated huff, Melinda stood and walked purposely from the room and headed straight into the kitchen, or more importantly the fridge, and grabbed her favourite bottle of wine. She poured herself a big glass and took a very large gulp. Deep down Melinda knew that this was it, she no longer had the option of going out and replacing the man she had grown bored with. Harry had been her last shot, she had known he was just as desperate for an escape from his own loneliness as she was desperate for someone to be her financial raft for the rest of her life. She was now stuck in this marriage of indifference for better or for worse.

A loud bellow of laughter came from the dining room and Melinda let out another sigh. They wouldn't miss her if she didn't re-enter the room so why bother? She picked up the bottle of wine, headed in the opposite direction and padded her way up the soft cushioned stairs. Melinda kicked off her expensive shoes and proceeded to remove her couture dress and change into her silk pyjamas. She slipped in between the bed sheets and sat upright clutching at her glass of wine like it was a lifeline, feeling one single tear slip down along her cheek, she angrily wiped it away and flicked off the bedside light. Alone and left in the dark, Melinda swallowed the remaining wine and sat unmoving, staring straight ahead into the darkness. Melinda's life could have been so much easier and far less mundane. As she sank further into her mattress, she heard the creak of her door. Surprise washed over her body. "Melinda, we need to talk."

Chapter Ten

He was in his house, and yet however illogical it was, he felt as if he were an intruder. The large door to his stranger-like wife's room moved heavily as Harry tiptoed in. Of course, that made no sense either. Harry had come to Melinda's room with the intention of waking her and demanding an explanation. A slight movement indicated to Harry that his wife wasn't as asleep as he had assumed. "Melinda, we need to talk," Harry quietly growled.

"Now this really is a surprise. If you're looking for a good time, I'm afraid you've come to the wrong woman. Married or not." Even as Melinda spoke to him in a rebellious and almost vacant tone, Harry felt a wave of sadness — fifteen years ago he had it all, a beautiful wife, three amazing children and a fulfilling career and now look at him. Stuck in a loveless and resentful marriage with a woman who no longer possessed any trait he either admired or respected.

A subtle scoff was all Harry offered to Melinda at her indecent entendre. "Here's the thing, Melinda, we are married, and at the moment I'm not going to do anything to change that fact. But some things are going to have to change." As he spoke the last few words Harry closed out the last few millimeters of light filtering from the hallway. He then lent the top of his shoulders on the wall surrounding the large formidable door and crossed his legs at the ankles.

Melinda quickly flicked on her bedside lamp and sat upright immediately as if preparing herself for a fight. "Look, Harry," Melinda started confrontationally.

Before she could continue Harry cut her off with a menacing look as he began to speak again. "No, you look! You've become too comfortable in this arrangement of ours. I go out and I work my arse off for my company and the money that pays for all of this." As he spoke, he stuck his left hand in the air and swirled his index finger around as if highlighting each penny that had gone into every item brought with his credit card that surrounded the different parts of the room. "So far, I have let you go on spending what you wish and relying on this family to support your neglectful mothering, but no more. This place and the people inside it mean everything to me and that includes your children. No matter the situation with us, I will ALWAYS be there for them, but your attitude needs to change."

Melinda swung her legs around so that she could stand up and face him on a more equal footing, "Fine! I get it. I'll cut down the spending. Now is that it because I don't feel like being berated like a child any more tonight." She raised her chin in a defiant symbolic move and was shocked to see what she could see within her husband's eyes. Rage.

Harry's tone was dangerously quiet and calm as he continued. "No, that is not it." Harry responded with a smirk, that even Melinda had to admit made his features even more handsome, and continued, "Your attitude needs to change. Your children can't stand you and mine are avoiding the house they should consider their home because of your indifference and hatred. I'm warning you, Melinda, continue to harm my family in any way and the money stops, the care stops, and I.

Will. Destroy. You." With his last chilling statement Harry cleared his rage-filled throat, stretched his back to its full length and left the room as silently as he had come in.

As the door closed behind him, Harry took a deep breath and closed his eyes. He heard the click of the door completely shutting behind him and the sound of a smashing glass ricocheted on the opposing side of the sturdy door. Good, Harry thought, his point had at least gotten through to the monster-like creature in the room behind him. Distant laughter brought a smile to his face. His family were the reason for his being.

Chapter Eleven

After Lina had made her way to bed, the Rykers were all that remained downstairs. Logan grabbed the many wine glasses that adorned the table and Riya picked up the last few plates that remained as they walked the remnants into the open-plan kitchen. Riya chuckled and rolled her eyes as Thomas stayed perched against the island flicking through something on his phone. "Would it kill you to help, big brother?" she said with a wink.

"Why would I do that when you two seem to have it all perfectly under control?" Thomas replied with a dazzling smile. "It's only fair, when you think about it. I've got a full day tomorrow, but you are the one with half a day off! Care to explain why that is?" Thomas asked suggestively as he knew full well that his sister was hiding something from him. Riya's cheeks turned bright red as she distracted herself by loading the empty dishwasher. There was no way in the world she was going to let Mr Over-protective know about her plans tomorrow. It wasn't like her to get so flustered and nervous around a member of the opposite sex but here she was taking half the day off work to prepare for her date with the oh-so-handsome Nate.

Riya decided to quickly change the subject, if only to stop her brothers probing into her life outside them. "What about you, Logan? What's new in your world?"

Her brother laughed as if he knew what she was trying to achieve by swerving the attention away from her own life. "Oh, you know, same old same old. I've got some plans in the works that could make the company a big name for itself." As her two brothers continued to talk, Riya made eye contact with Lina as she came down the stairs. Riya gave her a wide smile and tipped her head towards her brothers and rolled her eyes. Lina simply looked at her, quickly broke the eye contact and scurried into Rory's room. Riya let out a silent sigh. At the beginning there had been a part of her that resented Lina — she was the new baby and not only that she had taken her status as the only girl — but now all she felt was pity and a longing sense of sisterhood. It was a shame that Lina seemed to want to distance herself from all the members of her somewhat new family.

Chapter Twelve

As she tossed and turned for what felt like the millionth time, Lina felt a dreaded sense of unease. The early start that she was facing in the morning may have been the cause, but the nervous pit that lined her stomach was too distracting for Lina to assess. Suddenly sitting upright, Lina took in a few deep breaths and ran her fingers through her askew hair. The dinner with the Rykers had been tolerable. If she was completely honest with herself, it was more than tolerable. Without a doubt, Lina was now certain that herself and Rory weren't the main outliers of this family, it was Melinda herself. The boys had been polite, Riya had tried, and Harry had remained as adorable as ever. If Lina could have changed anything it was her own behavior — if only she could let herself be part of their family and accept the olive branches that they offered, she might be able to finally feel complete.

Lina twisted her body and draped her legs over the side of the mahogany bed frame and planted her bare feet into the shaggy carpet beneath her. Rubbing her eyes with the bottoms of her palms, Lina decided enough was enough. She certainly wasn't going to manage to fall into a sated slumber by trying so hard to do just that. As quietly as she could Lina opened her door and walked down the winding staircase. Ss a person Lina couldn't be still for any amount of time, she had to be doing something or else she felt useless and vacant of all purpose.

She let out a yawn and made her way into the large tiled washroom and grabbed the accompanying basket that was full of assorted garments. After loading the machine until it was completely full, Lina waited until she heard the unmistakable 'whoosh' of clothes being carried round the metal pan and headed for the kitchen.

Tomorrow was her day, her day to become her own person and the keeper of her own destiny. Lina stretched and picked up a cool glass from the elegant cupboard and filled it with the filtered water she had found in the fridge. Holding the clear-cut glass with both hands as if it were a delicate china cup, she took her first sip and savored it. The cool liquid that slipped down her throat refreshed her thoroughly. She subsequently let out a sigh. With a small 'clink' she set the glass down and perched herself on the small sofa that was in a hidden nook towards the back of the kitchen. Heavily, Lina's eyes began to rapidly blink as if willing themselves to stay open. Slowly and reluctantly Lina's body followed suit and began maneuvering itself into a more comfortable position and as the sleep that had finally managed to claim her invaded her senses, Lina realised that although her gut was twisting with nerves, she was extremely excited and looking forward to the upcoming new day.

Lina was awoken by a quick and sharp high-pitched sound. Blinking her eyes open she could see the pink sky signifying that the day was almost upon her. She let out a yawn and realised the sound that had pulled her from sleep was the washing machine in the room next door telling her the clothes she had endeavoured to clean were done. Lina padded her way half-heartedly towards the guilty machine that was to blame for her premature awakening. It occurred to Lina that the last time she had set foot in this room, her life had felt so hopeless and now, only a few days later, she had a new future to plan. Lina carried the basket up the shadowy staircase and rested it on the small display cabinet running along the other side of the banister. She began folding the pieces of clothing meticulously like they were about to be put in front of judge and jury, when she heard the subtle creak of a floorboard bending.

"What are you doing here?" Lina asked nonchalantly, both the tiredness and the task at hand, distracting her from the obvious glint in the other person's eyes. She didn't wait for a response, simply turned her back on the mystery early riser and continued with the task at hand. Everything went still.

Lina went rigid as a blast of a push threw her against the wall at the top of the looming stairs. A cartoon-like snap filled the sinister hallway. Pain radiated from her wrist and made its way, like a snake, up her arm and into her chest. Shock gripped her and Lina tried to overcome the fog clouding her mind, but it was too late. Her attacker moved and shouldered her awkwardly, catapulting her off balance and towards the steep incline of the covered marbled stairs. Her head contacted the stone floor and Lina felt nothing. Her mind drifted, her eyes closed and all she could think was, 'why?'

Chapter Thirteen

Logan turned over in his large bed to be confronted face to face with the warm glow of the sun, it seemed strange to other people, but sleeping with the curtains drawn had never occurred to him as in his mind, what greater alarm clock was there than nature itself. At least that's what he used to think. The joy that had held his hand for the last few weeks had suddenly morphed into a black hole threatening him from within. Rolling onto his back, Logan took a minute to stare absently up at the ceiling before the flood of things he needed to do invaded his tormented state. Everything had been good in his world, everything had been right and then a twist of hideous fate had intervened and ruined his chance at a fulfilled life.

With a glance at his clock, Logan heaved himself out of his bed and began his routine of early morning preparations for the day ahead. He had meetings set, designs to finish and a life to somehow get back on track. Without a doubt, Logan's world had been turned upside down and he no longer knew the reason for breathing, let alone thriving. Was he being punished? Did the universe want him miserable? It was of no matter. He'd stopped caring.

As Logan grabbed for his keys and stepped towards the door, his mobile rang. He checked the caller's name and forced a smile. He pressed the green illuminated phone and answered. "Hey, Dad, what's up?" As Logan listened to his father's voice he began to sound as if he were a million miles away.

Chapter Fourteen

Harry sat motionless and silent, his breathing had yet to return to normal. Every time he blinked, every time he stared at one spot for too long, he saw it, the crimson blood pooling around the lifeless body, the eerie stillness of everything as if the room itself was trying not to disturb the final resting place of a woman, a girl, who hadn't had the time to truly flourish.

As he had risen from bed that morning, with a dull ache resonating through his mind, thanks to the bottle of whiskey he had taken to bed as a companion for the evening, he stumbled his way into his en suite, not paying attention to much at all. The subtle smell of iron-like substance filled the foyer as Harry made his way towards the sink and poured himself a drink. Quickly downing the cocktail of water and ibuprofen, he stood and waited for the painkiller to wash through his system. He was acutely aware of a small beeping noise coming from the washroom. Harry sighed and headed for the noise. His wooden door creaked open and slowly started revealing the rest of the house. Everything stilled and the reality of what he was seeing seeped into the conscious part of Harry's mind. The beautiful girl he had come to see as almost his own daughter was lying still and spanned out on a cold impersonal floor, her head had blood surrounding it in an oddly ironic halo and the injury oozed tauntingly around her shrunken form. Even in this early stage, it was obvious that it had been the cause of the untimely death.

Later, sitting alone in the large house, he was waiting for the whirlwind that was his children to arrive and console him. Harry had luckily managed to keep Rory upstairs and preoccupied. The smaller child didn't need to see his whole world destroyed, he'd feel it soon enough. Logically Harry knew that he had done everything he should have, Rory was safe upstairs, Melinda was still in bed, his family had been informed and the police had been called. He couldn't, however, stop feeling guilty. Here he was sitting alone doing nothing while Lina lay dead and alone in the other room. Her mother was none the wiser and Harry knew he'd have to be the one to tell her before the police arrived. He swallowed the last of the whiskey at the bottom of his glass and raised himself out of his chair. It was the time to tell a mother that her first born was no longer alive.

As he approached Melinda's door he drew in a large breath and walked in, determined and fearful. The room in which you could practically see his money dripping off the walls was empty, an unmade bed lay in the centre of the room, the lights in the en suite were off. Melinda was gone.

Chapter Fifteen

The last few hours had been too surreal for Riya. She was perched on the side of the love seat with one arm around her father's shrunken form. Her step-sister was dead, her body still being examined in the laundry room and Nate, the man she had been messaging and calling since they first met in that small coffee shop only a few days ago, was sitting across from her with a police badge hanging from his belt and describing the next steps of the 'investigation.' This had to be a dream. When Riya had been a child and something bad had happened, her mother would tell her to close her eyes and wipe away the memory so she could carry on her day without being held back by a lasting pain. The last time she had tried this was the day she had been told that her mother would never be coming home again. Since then, she hadn't believed in its power but part of her was tempted to close her eyes and wipe away the mess that she was faced with today.

As her father stirred in her arms it drew her thoughts back to the present. The other detective sitting adjacent to Nate was informing the room that each person would have to be interviewed about anything they may have seen or known in the days leading into this catastrophic event. Immediately butterflies began circling in her stomach. Did they think it was one them? Did it look that way? This was her family, her life, comprehending that one of them could be capable of violently murdering a young girl who had, however strangely, become a part of their family, was something she was not sure she could ever do. As she looked up, tears brimming in her eyes, she realised Nate was looking straight at her. Although it had only been a few days they had talked more in those few hours than she had talked to anyone outside her family in that space of time for as long as she could remember. The other detective was still talking, but Riya couldn't hear the words flowing out of his mouth towards her ears. Nate's eyes were hypnotising her with concern and questions. How did they continue from here?

Nate looked away and so did she. What good was an attraction, a romance in the making now? She had a family to be there for, an investigation to be part of and a company to support. Both of her brothers were absent-mindedly staring at different inconsequential points in the room. Her father sat unmoving listening to the detective. She doubted, however, that he was taking any of the information in. It would no doubt take Harry a while to be in a fit state to work but their company had to be managed somehow. As a list of things to manage began forming in Riya's head, everybody's ears tuned in to the small sound of the door being opened ever so quietly and padding of feet that were obviously being tiptoed on for the quietest of movements.

Chapter Sixteen

"Melinda," Harry said as if sensing that the figure who had entered the house was that of the troublesome mother who lived under his roof.

Melinda moved towards the stairs and stopped as if sensing the presence of a large group of on lookers. "I'd thought you'd be at work already. I just popped out for some air," Melinda replied coolly. Harry stiffened at this obvious lie. He should be angrier but all he could do was muster up enough strength to lift himself out of his chair and motion for her to sit in his place. "What's all this?" Melinda obviously subtly alarmed at the site of two men adorned with police badges and a flashing light of a camera coming from the laundry room next door. "Surely you didn't think I was missing? I was simply out running an errand," Melinda said, and to anyone else it would have sounded like a brush off to a rather serious situation, but Harry knew better. A tenseness had etched itself into her figure. She made her way across the room to the large love seat and it was all she could do to stop her legs quivering with nervousness.

"It's Lina," Harry began, figuring it would look extremely strange if it was not him, her husband, to tell her the unfortunate truth.

"What about her?" Melinda said adopting a resentful tone.

"She's gone, she's…" As he tried to form the words a

lump of emotion rose to the back of his throat and Harry could swear, he felt as though he was drowning in sorrow. "She's…" Another shakily indrawn breath followed.

Thomas stood, moving for the first time since he'd entered the house less than an hour ago. "She's dead. She was killed."

The words seemed to echo around the parched room for what felt like hours. No one spoke. Harry couldn't hear a thing except from his own heart beating heavily. The 'matter of fact way' Thomas had put it both shocked and helped him. Thomas had done the thing he himself couldn't find the courage to do and yet the clinical blunt way he had done it was perhaps the first time Harry had been hit with what had happened.

Melinda sat breathing hard and slowly panting. 'She's dead, she was killed' played on repeat over and over again throughout her mind. "Where's Rory?" Melinda asked as she began picking at a non-existent piece of lint next to her on the chair. As Harry stared daggers at her for reacting in such a watered-down way he motioned upstairs, confirming her suspicions that the child had been kept away from the events of last night and the job of telling the boy his sister was dead was indeed down to her. Melinda sat, trying to conjure up more emotion, even if it were just for show, but nothing came of it. She felt guilty that she now had to go and tell her son that his sister was dead, she felt nervous as the two police men noted down her reaction to the news and she felt outnumbered as yet again every single Ryker was sitting surrounding her in their own judgemental way.

Suddenly, with her eyes darting from Ryker to Ryker, Melinda felt a swarm of panic chasing after her. "Excuse me," she managed to blurt out as she hastily rushed from the room and up the stairs. She slammed her bedroom door shut and rested her whole body against it as if blocking the whole world from entering ever again. The small sharp pants were becoming quicker and quicker with every second that passed. Melinda fell to her knees and clawed at the shaggy rug beneath her as she let the panic overtake her.

Chapter Seventeen

"Sir with your permission we'd like to start immediately on searching the premises for any possible evidence?" As Nate sat waiting for a response the milliseconds began to make his skin itch, so he tried again. "We could wait for a warrant but the quicker we find something, hopefully the quicker this… nightmare will be over for you." Why was it that sitting in front of this pool of victim's family was affecting him so much? He was always able to compartmentalise and turn off the necessary emotions to focus on completing another successful closing of a case. Of course, deep down Nate knew the reason this case was different, and it was all to do with the woman he could not stop looking at. When he'd seen her in that small coffee shop the other day, he'd known that he wanted something from her but the phone calls and texts since had thrown him for a loop. He had never experienced this much chemistry with someone.

Riya was funny, smart, and captivating. Now looking at her evoked every single emotion he had the ability to feel. Above all else, he was angry. Whoever had committed this crime had stopped any chance he had with her, from now on she was a suspect, her family were suspects and it could cost him his job if he ventured too close.

It was almost always someone close who committed this kind of crime and from what he had learnt so far, every one of the Rykers had access to the house even in the small hours. In order to find the answers to the death of this young woman Nate needed to do what he did best, he needed to ask difficult questions and when called for rustle some feathers — neither made his prospects at seeing more of Riya Ryker even remotely possible. The small whisper from the father of said woman pulled him from his thoughts. "Yes, of course, whatever you need."

Nate nodded and turned his attention to the rest of the room and asked, "The large area of woods behind the house, are they part of the property or are they public land?" Again no one spoke.

A while later a feminine voice pierced the silence. "The estate stretches back for about four acres and then it becomes public land, but I can't remember the last time any of us went very far out there at all." As Riya spoke she looked him directly in the eyes but quickly averted her gaze as she finished speaking. Nate cleared his throat to clear the fog in his mind and began ordering the forensics team to search the house and grounds.

Hours later, Riya watched as the ample amount of forensic equipment was loaded into many vehicles. Although she had carefully watched what the teams were doing throughout her childhood home, Riya had spent most of the last few hours making calls to the office, trying in some small way to take some burden off of her father so he had time to process. All the while trying to avoid the man who made her nervous with one simple look. As she watched the cars slowly drive away, she felt his presence before she saw him. "We're um… all cleared up now," Nate said somewhat anxiously.

"Thank you, if you need anything else just ask, myself or

my brothers would be happy to help," she said quietly.

Nate solemnly nodded and began to walk down the steps leading to the front door when he stopped and reversed his last movement. "Riya, look, I have had a great time talking to you for the last couple of days but this case... it changes things... we can't..."

Riya jumped in before she let the burning in the back of her eyes manifest into tears. "Nate, I get it. Your job is to tear this place and this family apart to get answers. You and I would be a complication for your job and more than likely completely against the rules so let's just forget it." Somehow, she managed a weak smile and Nate nodded and walked away.

Riya leant against the now closed door and lay her head back with a small thud. In the space of a few days, she'd managed to become so attached that now, she felt like mourning Nate as much as she was mourning Lina. As she closed her eyes and took a cleansing breath her phone vibrated in her pocket signalling a text had arrived.

Nate, I could never forget you...

Chapter Eighteen

Melinda sat staring at the brightly painted walls of her son's bedroom. Rory sat motionless staring at an imaginary object on the floor. As an only child Melinda had no idea about the bond between siblings. She had often wondered if she herself would have turned out any differently if she had been given a sibling to rely on and trust in.

"Rory, do you understand what your mother has told you?" Through the fog of thoughts Melinda hadn't heard Harry walk into the room. He had managed to silently squat down beside where Rory was sitting and fill his eyes with concern. "Rory?" Harry tried to gain the attention of the boy who was currently in a world of his own, a place where nobody could reach him.

In a move that was completely unexpected by everyone in the room, including herself, Melinda reached over and gently placed a hand on Rory's small and fragile-looking knee. Startled, Rory looked up and into her eyes. Confusion swam in the depths of his little irises and he was then conscious enough to direct his attention to his stepfather. "Lina…" came out as a breathless whisper from the suddenly timid little boy.

"Yes, Rory, Lina was hurt last night and she's… she died, buddy, I'm so sorry." As he reached the end of his final statement, Harry hung his head and Rory escaped yet again into the world where the pain couldn't hurt him.

Melinda stayed completely still, staring at the small bony knee she had clasped and not let go of since. How does a boy recover from something like this? It was a mystery to her. As soon as it was socially acceptable, Melinda decided that Rory would go back to his father for a few months, if not longer. She was not so naïve that she believed her mothering skills were up to dealing with a trauma like this one. Her ex-husband could untangle the mess that was waging a war in her son's head. Harry's sudden movement brought Melinda out of her own thoughts. He wiped at his eyes and shook his head. With one last look at Rory's slumped shoulders Harry quickly left the room.

Chapter Nineteen

The large whiteboard that covered the wall of the station was littered with pictures and notes which could only be described, at that time of night, as doodles. All the chaos surrounded the largest picture that rested in the centre of the board, a picture of Lina Simons' bludgeoned corpse. As a detective in the major crimes' division Nate had seen images like this one but he could never turn off the ever so slight feeling of sickness that followed the death of someone so young and in such a brutal way. Nate had seen worse crime scenes than the one before him, but he couldn't shake the feeling of a sinister evilness that surrounded this death. It could've have been an attempted home invasion gone awry, but it didn't feel that simple. That house, that family felt cracked, like something was tearing it apart from the inside out.

After clearing up the house and working the crime scene, Nate had spent most of the car journey home picturing the expression on Riya's face. In some ways he was angrier than he was concerned for the look of vulnerability on her face because she had dismissed him and the possibility of 'them' so quickly. Of course, he couldn't read minds but particularly for his part he had, for the first time in a long time, felt a real connection to this elusive and charming woman but obviously that sense of a future and belonging was not reciprocated on her end. What was he thinking sending such a message? She was out of bounds, completely untouchable and he still sent a message practically outlining in a bright neon sign how he felt about her. Should a person be able to feel this cast out to sea by a person he'd known less than a fortnight? Nate had no idea.

In any case, the issues he was currently debating were of no consequence to the task at hand. Riya was a Ryker and Nate had a very strong suspicion that at least one of them was involved in the murder of Lina Simons. Hers was a murder that reeked of family feud, of secrets that were being hidden by her own kin. The so far unsolved puzzle whirled through Nates brain. This was a problem he would answer. This would be a case he would solve.

Chapter Twenty

Thomas looked around the small dank room and inwardly shuddered. The small steel chair he was currently perched on, for that's all one could manage on a chair this size, made his back ache in a way that was becoming increasingly hard to ignore. 'Routine' they had said when he had received the call requesting this meeting, but Thomas felt anything but normal.

His stepsister was dead, his father was in mourning and he could not remove the image of Lina's stiff and lifeless body out of his mind. He had been the first one of the 'clan', as they had nicknamed themselves, to arrive after the fractured call from his father had come in and therefore it had been him that walked in to find his father staring at Lina's bludgeoned corpse. It had been like pulling teeth trying to get the strong man to step away from the frightful scene and sit down. Not since his mother's death had Thomas seen such desolation on his face. Thomas was more than a little annoyed at the care his father had shown Lina both in life and in death.

Thomas's myriad of thoughts, were interrupted by the subtle squeak of the cheap-looking door opening. The detective he recognised from the morning after the murder stepped into the room followed by another man around the same age, but by no means of the same height or brawn. "Good morning, Mr Ryker. Sorry for the early morning start but we thought we'd better hit the ground running given we've got a murder to solve," the shorter man began whilst Detective Inspector Richards cleared his throat and sat confidently down on one of the two metal, slightly more comfortable looking, chairs. Although the other man was continuously explaining why Thomas was needed, Richards was the one who seemed to hold all the power in the room. His never-ending gaze made Thomas feel as if he were under a microscope and that all his innermost thoughts were being read without him saying so much as a word. "How about we start with where you were at five a.m. Thursday morning?" the smaller detective asked as he flipped the cover off his notepad and poised himself to begin writing.

"At that time, Detective, I would have been asleep at home. As most people would be," Thomas added, trying to add some humour into his tone of voice.

"Alone, sir?" the man prompted.

Irritably Thomas replied, "Yes. Alone."

Nate sat silently watching for any sign of nervousness or secretive behaviour. Something was wrong but he wasn't sure what and to what extent. As his partner Sam, or Detective Constable Turner as he was known in rooms such as this one, finished talking, Nate leant forward and placed his elbows on the slightly cool surface of the table. "What was your relationship to Lina Simons?" At the rather blunt question, holding none of the formal pleasantries that his partner had layered on rather thickly, Thomas Ryker became momentarily startled but quickly re-established the wall of poised emotionless indifference that he had tried to walk in with earlier.

"I suppose she was my stepsister," Thomas replied almost too nonchalantly, which made the hairs on the back of Nate's neck stand up to attention.

"You suppose? Why's that, given that she WAS your step-sister and has been for a number of years?" Nate replied as he casually leaned back into his chair and crossed his arms over his chest.

"Yes. Fine she was my stepsister legally. Her mother is *married* to my father but since her arrival I have not been living at home so my interactions with her have been limited. Does that answer the question more to your liking, Detective?" Thomas replied, becoming increasingly more annoyed with the conversation. He wasn't sure why but every time anyone questioned his family relationships his guard went up.

"It seems I've annoyed you, Mr Ryker. That wasn't my intention, however, it does rather nicely bring me to my next question, although I feel like I already know the answer." Nate paused and lifted one dark eyebrow, almost daring Thomas to oppose him in some way. "How did you feel about Miss Simons?"

Thomas kept his eyes locked on Richards', despite the desperate need to pull away and pretend he was anywhere but there. Without realising, he began answering before his brain could tell him to stop. "Why don't you tell me how I felt about her? Given you seem to think you know everything that's going on inside my head."

Nate inwardly smiled. It was one of his guilty pleasures to break his suspects mentally when they believed themselves to be better or smarter than him. He knew after this short conversation that Thomas Ryker was indeed a suspect, could even be his prime suspect given the man's obvious attitude towards the deceased. "Well, firstly, Thomas — may I call you Thomas?" Nate continued not waiting for a response, "It would be obvious to anyone with half a brain that you did not like your stepsister and that's fine. People have their opinions and sometimes have no reasons for said opinions, but the anger is alarming, and I would say altogether very telling." And with one last shrewd smirk Nate leaned back waiting for the response that could tell him at least something pertinent to the case.

"OK, Nathan. May I call you Nathan?" Thomas began with a dangerous tone of voice. "I admit my feelings about Lina were not pleasant ones. My childhood was idyllic, I had a father and mother who loved me and my siblings more than anything and then my mother died. We spent a long time getting over the shock, but we remained a loving family that nobody could come between. But then Melinda came along. With Melinda came one, almost adult, child who followed suit of her mother. My father's... my family's money was spent on anything either of them wanted and was never questioned. My father was still grief stricken even after five years of being without his wife and he was tempted by a two-bit, gold-digging tart, which was one thing but then he brings his wife's daughter into the family house, the house that my mother designed, and treated her as if she were his flesh and blood. They both took the place of a woman who gave her everything to create a wonderful family and home and didn't even regret the fact. So yes, Detective, I disliked Lina and was angry at the girl for stealing my father's heart. Are you happy?" Thomas finished with a deep sigh as his slowly realised what he had just disclosed.

"So, is it safe to say that Lina was an obstacle you wanted removed?" Nate glowered at Thomas, he could feel Sam next to him diligently scribbling down notes, taking everything in.

"After what you yourself have just admitted, and the emotion I saw from your father the day of the murder, Lina had 'wormed' her way into what you considered yours and you would like her to simply give up her hold on the man that will define your future in the world, both financially and reputationally."

"She wasn't blood!" Thomas seethed towards the detective. "She had done nothing other than bat her eyelashes at a broken man and she was his daughter. He listened to her, wanted to set her up with a career outside the family business and support her financially for her whole future. All the while he was beaming with pride for her, yet when his own son decided to stick it out and BE there for the family firm — having to work for every penny without any help, he just expected me to be fine with it." By this point, Thomas was breathing heavily and trying but failing to regain his composure.

"So, what I think you're saying here is that you'd lived your whole life almost waiting to be your father's number one child, to have him look at you like you'd conquered the world. Then here comes some young girl, a girl insistent on spending all the money you were counting on being yours, who just took all that love and praise right out of your grasp." Nate saw the recognition of feelings in the opposite man's eyes and continued with one last chilling statement. "Why wouldn't you be happy for the girl standing between you and all that you wanted, to be lying on a cold floor covered in blood with no breath in her lungs?" And with that, Nate could feel the next statement coming out of the other man's lips before he'd even began speaking.

With cold and unfeeling eyes, Thomas straightened and

stared directly into the leading man's eyes. "Unless you wish to charge me 'Detective'," he said venomously, "I'm done. Any more information you would like, you can get from my lawyer." Thomas stood and confidently strode towards the closed door, swinging it wide open as he stormed out leaving the door swinging into the outside wall with a dangerous-sounding crash.

Nate watched as Thomas Ryker quickly marched his way out of the station. He chuckled and turned to Sam. "I think somebody may have a slight chip on his 'rich kid' shoulder."

Chapter Twenty-One

Thomas slammed the door to his sleek black Range Rover and gripped the leather covering on the steering wheel until his knuckles appeared to look almost transparent. He hadn't meant to lose himself like that in front of those relative strangers. In Thomas's book, emotions were something you dealt with privately on your own and failing that, only with your nearest and dearest. However, it seemed he had royally messed things up by airing his dirty laundry to the people who were probably trying to decide whether any of the family, especially him, after his outburst, were capable of murdering their stepsister.

Harder than was necessary, he quickly leant his head and neck back until it bumped against the head rest. It was there and, in that position, that Thomas remained for several minutes just staring at the grey interior that lined the roof of the large, supposedly intimidating car.

There would be questions, he'd put the wheels in motion, he'd made the threat and he in no way believed Detective Nathan Richards would simply back off and leave him be. He could now almost guarantee he was on top of their suspect list. What had he done?

Chapter Twenty-Two

Riya turned over in her comfier-than-normal bed. Last night she had come back to her cottage for the first time since Lina's death. She had either been by her father's side or working out of his home office to keep 'The Ryker group' ticking along whilst the family tried to heal. As she stretched her arms above her head, she let out a large sigh. As she twisted her legs out from beneath her duvet, she mentally prepared for the day ahead. The police had already told her father that Lina's body could not be released until the post-mortem had been completed, but Nate had assured her that by the end of the week they'd be able to bury her and give her soul some sort of peace.

She worked through her morning by sitting at her rustic wooden table and her mind began to wonder. How would her family progress from here? How was it possible she was now sitting, inside her comfy cottage at the edge of the city, surrounded by all her homely possessions, and picking out flowers to decorate her stepsister's coffin? Riya did not have the answers to these questions which annoyed her to no end. She needed help! With a frustrated groan Riya put her delicate hands into her long dark hair as she leant her elbows on the vintage wood. That was how her morning continued until she heard a rather sharp knock on her small front door.

As Nate's face appeared behind the slowly opening

barrier, her heart rate doubled. How had she managed to miss a man she barely had enough time to get to know? Riya had no clue but that didn't stop her opening the door as quickly as possible once she realised who her unexpected visitor was. Whilst taking in his large handsome presence, Riya was startled to see another man standing behind him. Both were wearing dress shirts, ties and looking sombre.

"Good morning, Miss Ryker, we were wondering if you had a few minutes to answer a few questions for us?" Nate kept his face focused on a spot on the wall behind her as he tried to remain completely impartial to the woman who had somehow inserted herself into his mind.

Riya struggled to find her voice to answer but eventually managed to squeak a response in an almost breathless tone. "Yes. Yes, of course, come on in."

Nate motioned for Sam to go before him as they both walked silently behind Riya. Her house suited her, he thought, it was small but not tiny, there were family pictures on almost every single wall they passed and the eaves that were visible, running down the walls and across the ceilings gave the home a very 'warm' vibe. As Riya moved into a cosy lounge Nate and Sam sat on a large chenille grey sofa where she had motioned them to whilst she herself had settled into a patchwork armchair that sat perfectly to the side of them.

"I'm surprised I hadn't had a call from you before now if I'm honest," Riya stated and then noticed the slight widening of Nate's eyes and realised what he thought she was referring to. She quickly continued, "My brother said he was specifically asked to come down to the police station to talk to you."

Nate visibly relaxed. It wasn't that he was scared that Sam

may report him for having an inappropriate relationship with a person of interest, but it would complicate things. Sam answered her quickly. "Yes, well, we like to keep our questioning out of a person's place of work and the station was the only other option for your brother at that time of day, but we called ahead to your father and he told us you were here." Which seemed to satisfy Riya's interest in the difference in scenarios.

Nate leant forward indicating to Sam that he would take over from here. "Miss Ryker…"

"Call me Riya, please!" Riya almost shouted before realising how she'd just cut the man off and shrunk back into her chair.

"That's very kind of you," Nate continued, trying to remain as aloof as possible. "Can you tell us what your relationship was like with Lina Simons?" Although he tried to ignore it, Nate was desperately hoping that her response was even slightly more human than her older brothers had been.

Riya began with a sad smile lifting her lips. "Lina has…or had been my stepsister for about five years, after my father got married to Melinda who, as you know, is Lina's mother." She realised both men were waiting for her to continue her explanation with a wary and expectant look. From what Thomas had said about his own version of this meeting, she suspected that they were waiting for something sinister to come out of her mouth. "She was quiet, but a nice girl overall. Lina never really stayed in any kind of spotlight, she just seemed to hide away a lot."

"So, you didn't spend much time with her then?" Nate said, almost desperate for some insight into Lina's life. So far nobody's perception of the young girl was the same as another's.

"No, not really. When Lina first came along, I was still studying at university and was only really home for Christmas and Easter. After I'd graduated, I lived at home for less than a year before moving out on my own," Riya explained cringing inwardly, she understood that her life, to some people, seemed fairy-tale like and money-enriched to the point of excess. So much so they believed that she had been handed everything on a silver platter.

Nate nodded slightly. "Was there any particular reason you came home for less than a year? Seems like a relatively short amount of time to then move out on your own." Trying and failing to not sound sceptical at the facts before him. Did every one of the Ryker's dislike the Simons girl so much that they either left their home or harbour uncontrollable anger towards those of a different blood line?

Riya blushed and looked down to the shaggy white rug that took the severity out of the cold, lightly shining Harwood floors. "Yes, I did leave fairly quickly but not for the reasons you are suggesting," she said, raising one of her eyebrows to feign confidence. "I have been lucky enough to have a father that is overly generous. He can't help but feel the need to wrap every single one of his children, Lina and Rory included, in bubble wrap, which is how I managed to get such a high paying job with my father's company and was able to afford to move out within such a short time. Once you go away to study and live on your own for over three years you get used to your own space."

Sam nodded as he once again continued to write notes. Nate wasn't sure what was so pertinent about Riya's statement that warranted note taking, but Sam was a genius at reading body language and tone of voice. "And was there any tension between you and Miss Simons?" Even Sam stopped writing to spare him a quick glance of surprise at his monotone and bluntly put question. Usually in questionings such as these Nate had a reputation of being a friendly giant whom people couldn't help but spill their secrets to, but apparently in that moment that role was not his.

Riya stumbled over her words as she took in Nate's rigid frame, and the way his jaw had tensed the minute they had locked eyes at the door. "Not on my side, I don't think. To begin with it was weird to have another woman in the house and even weirder to not be the youngest 'child' any more but I got used to it." She even managed a small smile at the end of the sentence, despite Nate's harsh gaze.

"Is there anybody you know of that had something against Lina? Maybe had issue with her place in your family?" Nate could hear the acidic tone that his voice had taken on. He hadn't meant to close down completely but the minute she'd answered the door looking all soft and warm in her plaid pyjama bottoms and faded grey T-shirt, he hadn't been able to think about her in the way he needed, as a suspect. Nate knew he had angered her the minute her eyes flared.

"My family is kind and decent and I *cannot* believe any of them are capable of this kind of... crime!" She took a long calming breath and continued, refusing to believe that Nate could turn so easily and so coldly as if there were no feeling behind his eyes at all. "Lina was a sweet girl and, from the small amount she liked to give away, she had big dreams. I don't know what her social life was like and that's my own fault for not putting enough effort in and although I know in my head that I cannot know for sure what people are capable of, my heart refuses to believe that my family could even think about hurting someone whom they had lived with."

"And where were you on Thursday night, Miss Ryker,

around five a.m.?" Nate asked in an irritated tone.

Riya straightened her back and looked him in the eye. "I was already at work. You can ask night security — they let me in about four thirty and there are cameras all over the office building that will show I didn't leave until I received my father's phone call the following morning around nine a.m."

"Four thirty is an unusual time to start work, is it not?" Nate asked sarcastically.

"I haven't been sleeping. I've had… some… things on my mind," Riya replied, raising an eyebrow, almost daring Nate to ask more.

"I think that's all for today. Thank you, Miss Ryker. We will be sure to check your alibi." Nate stood up and kept his eyes on some coving to avoid looking into Riya's startled eyes. She stood up and wiped off some imaginary lint from her clothes and led the way back to the front door. It felt as if they had been in this awkward cycle for hours whereas in fact it had only been about ten minutes.

"We'll be in touch if we need any more information, Miss Ryker. Thank you so much for your help," Sam replied, trying to smooth over any remining tension as he passed by Riya quickly while she stood leaning on the door. Nate followed suit but stopped as he caught a whiff of her subtle perfume. Her eyes caught his and the whole world seemed to stop spinning. Her bright eyes pleading with him for something and he cursed the universe for putting them in such an awful situation. Nate had to will his hand to stop from reaching up and tucking the small lock of hair, that had escaped her messy bun, behind her ear. Nate cleared his throat quietly, which caused Riya to look at the ground, and moved away from the house and back to his car.

Chapter Twenty-Three

As he opened the door to the dark Volvo XC40 and slid himself into the surprisingly comfy leather seat, Nate twisted himself sideways to wait for Sam's interpretations. The man himself failed to notice that Nate had joined him in the car as he sat and furiously wrote into his notebook. As detectives they had been trained in interviewing, efficiency and reading people but Sam was on another level. Although Sam sometimes struggled with connecting all the evidence together into a plausible story, he was a brilliant mastermind at reading between the lines of a person's dialogue.

Tired of waiting Nate began, "So..." watching as Sam reluctantly pulled himself away from his notes.

"She seemed nice," Sam said casually. A little too casually in Nate's opinion.

"OK, you thought she was *nice,* anything else of note from the piles of paper you've written on in the last fifteen minutes?" Nate dryly replied, shooting daggers at the similar-aged man.

"Wow. I thought you were trying on a new routine in there, but I can see now you're just going for a different personality for all walks of life," Sam said with a chuckle caught at the back of his throat. "Well, when I said nice, I meant it. After we'd met her brother, I wasn't sure what to expect but the difference is startling. Usually, you can find some sort of correlation between the attitudes of two people raised as closely as these two were but there was nothing!" Sam began getting excited as he always did with mind puzzles such as these. "It either says she's an incredibly good actress, which, given the blush that stained her cheeks every time you looked at her, is highly unlikely, or that her brother is a highly aggressive man who has several issues that have gone unattended for numerous years, causing him to break the patterns of behavior he was taught as a boy."

Nate considered what Sam had deduced and waited. Generally, there was more to Sam's revelations and Nate decided, as he usually did, to wait out the storm. Second after second passed and Nate couldn't stand it any more. "Well?"

Sam coughed clumsily and hoped that his notebook would protect him from his colleague's anger. This woman had gotten to Nate, that was evident from the way he stiffened every time she was mentioned and by the way that, when he thought no one was looking, he stared at the picture of her that was lining the large board in the station with an odd expression taped across his face. "Well, when talking about who she thought would hurt Lina, she said her 'heart couldn't believe that a member of her family could hurt someone that they had lived with'. Note the language." Sam finished on a smirk but noticed Nate's inpatient expression and decided to take pity. "She believed that they were incapable of hurting anyone in the family, not that they were incapable of hurting anyone — her language was very specific."

"And what does that mean in terms of this case?" Nate asked, feeling like an idiot.

"It means that there could be something in the past that makes Riya Ryker believe that one of her own IS capable of hurting someone that isn't part of what they deem the 'family'," Sam replied coolly.

Nate considered the statement for a while, wishing, once again, that Riya wasn't in the middle of everything he was trying to unravel. He was left with only one choice. This family had secrets, secrets that needed to be unearthed in order for this case to be solved. "It's time to start digging into the Ryker family more thoroughly."

Chapter Twenty-Four

Melinda stood, as her suede, four-inch heels sank into the earth. Her hands were clasped fiercely in front of her and her eyes remained glued to the large oak tree lurking in the distance. It's strength and worldly wisdom kept her own strength from crumbling. Without looking, Melinda could feel the coffin being lowered into the dark pit carved into the ground. All the details from the flowers to the guest list were unknown to her, she had organized nothing, invited no one and had not decided on anything but the truth still remained. This was her only daughter's funeral. Her husband, in name only, stood to her left with his hand on her son's small shoulder as the child failed to truly understand what was going on. All the boy knew was that he had been forced to wear the contraption adults called suits and that he hadn't seen his sister in a whole week.

The family never strayed from the almost military formation they had landed in as they lined one side of the burial site. The minister carried on with his service as Harry stood firm, but his hand struggled to keep his grip gentle as it rested on Rory's shoulder. No one seemed to truly be present at today's ceremony, they all looked as if they were a million miles away. Harry hadn't slept, hadn't really eaten, and had not said more than two words to anybody since Lina's body had been found. A whole week had passed since the last breath had passed through Lina's lips and Harry wasn't sure the reality had yet sunken in. Riya had been a godsend, she'd done both her own job and his for the last week and organized the whole funeral which had turned out to be the best way to give Lina a proper goodbye. Logan was struggling in ways Harry wasn't sure how to comprehend and Thomas had become silent — he'd seen the police and then nothing, no words, no emotion, just a stoic show of a man. Throughout it all Harry couldn't help but feel like a failure. Twice tragedy had come calling at his door and both times he had left his children to guide themselves through it while he withered inside.

In the distance Harry saw a small movement. Two men, both wearing long dark trench coats, stood in the distance. He couldn't see their faces, but he knew exactly who they were, the height, the stature and the confidence emanating from the larger man told Harry exactly who was standing watching and waiting for one of them to show themselves up. Detective Nathan Richards.

Chapter Twenty-Five

Riya continued to flitter around the large reception room that was nestled within her father's house. Some may find it graceless to host the wake in the house where the murder took place, especially since there was still plastic yellow tape covering the door to the wash room, but this way Rory had some sense of normalcy and her father, once he'd had enough, could retreat upstairs and have the privacy she knew he craved in times of distress. As she smiled slightly to a couple who she knew she really should know the names of, Riya surreptitiously spied her family members also doing what they considered their 'duty'.

As she made sure that the buffet was still relatively full for those guests who had yet to make their way down the table of tasty dishes, her mind wandered to Nate. He'd come to the funeral to stare at her, at her family and then simply got into his car, along with his partner, and left. No words of sympathy, no professionalism, he simply came to ruin the day of mourning to do what? Simply to put them all on edge, to show that they were always watching. Surely there was no way simply staring at them for half an hour had furthered their case whatsoever!

As the dregs of the guest list slowly filtered out over a few hours, and as her brothers drank whiskey after whiskey and headed off to bed, it occurred to Riya that this was the first time since Logan had left home that the Ryker 'clan' had all been under the same roof. In any other circumstances she would have been thrilled by the fact, but not this one. A death had brought them together. That had to mean some sort of bad luck or omen.

As she finished loading the large almost commercial sized dishwasher, she vaguely heard her phone sound from the room next door. Wishing that she had the heart to just ignore the message and slouch off to bed, Riya made her way into the lounge, yet another room she'd have to clean after she'd unloaded the dishwasher and successfully had her cup of tea in the morning. Grabbing the phone, Riya almost shook as she saw the name of the person texting her at that time of night. In reality it was only nine o'clock but the day had taken all the energy out of her. It was him, the man she was trying to tell herself not to think about. Nate was a heartbreak she had to avoid.

Nate, Hi

Riya struggled to tell her fingers to move across the screen of her phone. Even after the initial struggle was over, she was still at a loss for what to say, he was the one who had said they couldn't talk like this any more, even though she had assumed as much the minute he had walked in and announced himself as lead detective, and yet here he was offering an olive branch. An olive branch she wasn't sure, after today's events, she wanted to take. Curiosity getting the better of her, Riya decided to play it out and see what, if anything, the man wanted.

Riya, Hi…

Waiting with bated breath as she watched the three dots moving, she anxiously readied herself for Nate to finish typing. The message staring back at her was terrifying.

Nate, Come outside.

Chapter Twenty-Six

Standing as he leant against the door of his car, Nate had no idea what he was doing there. Yes, it had been confirmed that she had an alibi, but what about the rest of her family? He'd watched her intently at the funeral as she held herself and everybody else together. Usually at a victim's funeral Nate and Sam would have gone over and offered their condolences. It was a great way to see the people at the heart of an investigation with their shields down, but this time it had been different, he couldn't have gone over to them even if he had wanted to. He'd been stuck at the sight of her. Riya Ryker was a strong, beautiful woman who made his heart beat faster whenever he thought about her. If he was watching someone else go through the irrational chain of events that had led him to be standing outside this house, he'd had laughed and called the person a fool.

Nate hardly had any time to wallow in his own ridiculousness because the large door, to the shockingly regal house, opened slowly to reveal the woman of the hour. He'd forgotten what it was like to stand in front her with nobody else around to help them avoid the inevitable. Riya made her way down the hard-stone steps leading to the front door. She was still wearing the black sheath dress, she had changed out her black leather pumps for what appeared to be some sort of slipper-boot hybrids. She looked formal and comfy in one very elegant package as she sauntered across the road to where he was standing. "Hi," Nate managed to choke out.

Riya straightened her slightly hunched back and looked him dead in the eye. The vulnerability he saw reflected killed him. "You said that before," she stated quietly.

Nate knew that his behaviour the other day at her house, and again today at the funeral, must've hurt her, but seeing it was a whole lot worse than knowing it. He continued, trying to see the fire light in her eyes, as it had the first time he'd met her. "I know. Just at a loss for what to say, if I'm honest." He gave a slight smirk "I just knew I had to…"

"You had to what, Nate?" Riya replied coolly.

It was now or never, he thought as he watched her slowly begin to shut down. "I had to see you." Nate watched in hope as Riya's expression softened. "I had to apologise for the other day, I was rude and angry about the situation that we're in." As she began to open her mouth Nate pressed on. "And I'm sorry for today. I wanted to come to you… I mean, I wanted to offer my condolences to you all, but I couldn't bear to see the sadness in your eyes knowing I couldn't do anything about it." As he said those last words, he stepped away from the car, so he was directly in front of her and gently used his hand to drag the shiny waves of her hair off her shoulder and behind her ear.

"Nate…" Riya said in a whispered plea.

"I just wanted you to know that… hell, I don't even know. All I know is that I couldn't bear the thought of you angry at me, thinking that you meant nothing to me." Nate was well aware that he was sounding desperate and yet his hand remained cradling her cheek.

"We hardly know each other," Riya muttered unconvincingly.

"Tell me that it's only me, then, that I'm the only one who feels this connection and I'll go and carry on with the case as if nothing happened. But I don't think you feel nothing. I don't think that I can feel this kind of need without you feeling something for me in return." Nate was whispering now as his face leant closer and closer towards her own.

"But Lina, the case, it's all too..." Nate stopped her by covering her mouth with his own. What was meant as a small gesture turned into something more. With a groan Nate moved his other hand to mirror the one that was still tangled in her hair. As their tongues mated, Nate spun her around and backed her up against the side of his car. Riya's hands moved to curl around his shoulders, and he wanted to yell in triumph to feel her finally touching him. He pressed his body against hers and heard a small moan that vibrated against his lips, he had no idea how much time had passed but Nate couldn't seem to get enough. Smiling, he pulled back slightly by kissing her a few more times lightly across the lips until their faces were completely separate, but bodies were still plastered against each other's.

Both breathing hard, Nate rested his forehead against hers and gave her one of his trademark grins and in return was offered her own version that brightened up her face. "I'd better go," Nate rasped as he moved the back of his hand down her left cheek.

"Yeah, OK," Riya said frustratedly, knowing that they couldn't continue, as her eyes bore down into his. Nate gave her one last chaste kiss on her lips and then placed one on the top of her head and set her away from him.

Riya slowly moved around him to head back into the house when he stopped her by reaching out and grabbing her wrist. "Tomorrow I'll be coming here and talking to the whole family — there's been some new evidence found from the post-mortem and…"

Riya stopped him with a hand to the middle of his chest. "Thank you for telling me," Riya said while offering a small smile and then, taking them both by surprise, she reached up and brushed her lips against his cheek. With one last look, she turned and headed back up the steps and through the door. Finding himself, once again, leaning against his car door, Nate let out a sigh and a shake of his head then slid into the driving seat and sped away.

Chapter Twenty-Seven

Logan watched as the brake lights faded into the distance. The amber liquid that filled his small glass burnt its way down his throat. He'd lain in bed hoping that the scotch-filled slumber would allow him to get some rest without a combination of memories and dreams haunting him. He'd watched the rest of his family almost fall apart at the graveside and he'd had enough. In the space of half an hour he'd watched the coffin hit the bottom of the hollowed-out pit and he'd found the reserve of whiskey that would be his companion for the evening.

Tears and sadness had been the themes of today, but he couldn't understand why the rest of the guests had been showing that level of emotion. His world had gone dark and yet nobody bothered to realise. In his twenty-eight years on this planet, he had been exactly where everybody needed him to be, supported whoever needed a shoulder and this was how he was repaid. The death itself may not have been the reason for his foul outlook but at this point he would have used it to gain some sort compassion at least. The waitress that he had sought out for some companionship had done the trick for a short while, the thrill of the chase and the release that finally came when he had convinced her to follow him into the garden had excited him on some level but his heart hadn't been in it and he'd made sure the woman had known too. She had offered her phone number and he had simply zipped up his fly and walked past her.

What had he become?

Chapter Twenty-Eight

The call came in early the next morning. Both detectives were on their way to speak to them all. Harry's first order of business was to make sure that they all were indeed accounted for. His sons were easy to locate, they were sitting around the kitchen island looking rather sorry for themselves and he could understand why, the combination of both their aromas was similar to that of a run-down pub in the early eighties. Riya, usually one to breeze in and out of rooms, shuffled her way to the kettle without saying a word. Everybody who needed to be there was there. All except one.

As if he'd conjured up the image of a beast, his wife walked in. The usually well-put-together façade of a woman was no longer recognisable, she was make-up-less, pyjama-covered and her face was not displaying any of what he considered her 'masks'. Interestingly, instead of throwing some disguised insults at both himself and his children, Melinda saw the kitchen full of people and almost fell over herself in an effort to escape.

Without disrupting the unusually quiet breakfast that his children were pushing around their plates, Harry slipped into the corridor in search of Melinda. He didn't have to look very far as he found her leaning against the wall just meters away from the entrance to the kitchen clutching her hands to her chest. "Melinda," Harry said softly, more softly than he had for the last four years of marriage. As such, Melinda looked at him, startled. "The detectives are coming over to talk to us about Lina. Can you be in the lounge in about twenty minutes?"

Melinda momentarily flicked her eyes to his, only to look back down at the floor in the next second. "I'm sure you can handle it." Melinda tried to make herself sound more confident than she obviously felt and then pushed past him trying to make her way back to her room and her personal make-shift bar.

Harry grabbed her arm, not enough to cause harm, but enough to make her realise how serious he was about be. "No." Stepping forward so he was as close as he could bear, he said, "You were her mother, they want to see all of us but most of all YOU. They haven't managed to get you to speak to them since Lina died, so you will be in that room with the rest of us. Is that understood?" Harry asked the question with as much of a menacing tone of voice as he could muster.

"Fine!" Melinda replied with a spark of the usual poison that laced her voice. She marched past him and headed to the lounge to lie in wait.

Chapter Twenty-Nine

Riya was a nervous wreck. Hearing the car pull up on the long, stoned driveway only intensified her anxiety, not knowing how she was going to be able to remain calm and nonchalant in front of the man who had set her world on fire and then caused her to lose any chance at getting anything resembling a good night's sleep the night before. Leg bouncing, toes tapping, Riya could hear the murmuring of her father inviting Nate and his partner, the partner who was perfectly lovely but whom she couldn't even remember the name of, inside to the commune of Rykers that awaited them.

Harry led the men into the centre of his home not really knowing what awaited him. "Detective Richards, Detective Turner, I believe you know everybody in the room." Harry stated moving over towards the chair that he had obviously been allocated. "We are all here, as per your request. I've left Rory upstairs, I don't think he needs to hear any more about the details of his sister's death." Well aware that he was beginning to ramble at the detective, Harry quickly stopped talking and waited for the news that called for a gathering such as the one before him.

"No, no, of course, I think it'd be best that your stepson was unaware of certain information that has come to light." Nate remained calm and ended his confirmation with a small smile. This was not an interview or an interrogation, despite

Riya being the only one of them with an alibi, this was a necessary meeting to relay some facts that had come out after the post-mortem report. Nate could have told the family immediately after the pathologist had found the evidence but, despite the chance that one of them was a murderer, the family had deserved to grieve in peace at the funeral. "As you are aware, Lina's post-mortem report was completed three days ago." Nate became acutely aware of Riya bracing her hand on her father's arm almost if she were trying to protect him from whatever heartbreak was around the corner. "The pathologist has determined that Lina was killed by massive blunt force trauma to her head which caused her skull to fracture, which led to severe bleeding." And then he waited for the inevitable questions.

Unable to stay on his 'best behaviour', Thomas rose from his end of the large sofa and cleared his throat arrogantly. "So... what you're telling us that she died exactly the way we all assumed she did?" Thomas had no idea where his anger came from, but the man just seemed to easily bring it out of him.

"Thomas!" Harry scathed at his son in a half shout and half whisper.

"No, Mr Ryker, although it was a given that Miss Simons had died from some sort of head trauma, it was not clear to what extent." Nate was seething. This man was a bully, used to getting his own way and making those of the population whom he deemed 'below' him feel like sub-humans. He would not hijack today, he would not make this news worse for those in this room that were actually grieving. "There were numerous contusions and abrasions all over Lina's body and our pathologist believes this is the result of falling down a large set of stairs. One of her wrists also seems to have been broken and the position of the break would seem to suggest that it happened as a result of a struggle."

"I'm sorry, Detective, but I don't understand. My daughter was found in the washroom not at the bottom of the stairs," the woman who had managed to avoid both Nate and his partner for over week spoke with a seductive tone. Many things about this annoyed him, her daughter had just died, her husband was in the room and the woman he wanted was listening. Add to that she was almost old enough to be his mother and her whole attitude repulsed him.

"Lina had a small fight before falling and it would appear, she was moved and then the evidence subsequently cleaned away," Nate said and flickered his eyes at Riya who was looking horrified at what this meant. It meant whoever had done this had thought it appropriate to try and deflect suspicion off anyone who had access to all areas of the house, which indicated it was more than likely that someone in this room was the person to have committed this act of violence. She glanced at him and then reached out to lay her hand against her father's in a show of support.

"So, what happens now?" Riya's father asked.

"With your permission, sir, we would like to do a forensic work up of the whole house rather than just the crime scene. It may hold vital information to catching your stepdaughter's killer." Whilst he was still speaking, Thomas had given one last sarcastic laugh and sauntered out of the room as Nate watched Harry slowly nod his head to the detective's request. Lina's mother simply swallowed a large gulp of the clear liquid in her glass, a liquid that Nate would bet good money had not been water.

Chapter Thirty

Men wearing neon overalls covered the house, it felt as if they had become a museum exhibit in their own home. Large lights were being moved from room to room as Harry stood in the midst of all the chaos. Flashing lights of cameras causing his eyes to keep readjusting were coming from every room. Because he had been a willing participant in today's forensic investigation the uniformed officers involved were being incredibly respectful of the house and all that it housed, this could have been the fact that he had allowed today's antics or, more likely, it was because their boss, Detective Inspector Richards, was standing by watching everything with his razor-sharp vision. Harry thought this was strange, this man owed them nothing and in the interest of finding Lina's murderer Harry would have thought it be imperative to scour the house no matter the carnage, and yet here he was acting as if he was trying to gain some sort of approval.

"Boss!" came a bellow from the landing at the top of the twisting staircase. "We've got something." And with that the detective began jogging up the stairs two at a time. All Harry could do was keep listening as the men murmured about samples and spatter.

"Right, we need to get the blood matched to Miss Simon's and then we'll have found the set of stairs where the crime took place." Hearing this, Harry's heart began to pound. It was one thing to be told that his stepdaughter had fallen down the stairs to her death, it was another to know that they had found evidence, blood, on a particular step that showed she had been put through an unthinkable amount of pain. "Mr Ryker?" The detective's voice filtered through his thoughts.

"Yes, Detective? Sorry, I was in a world of my own for a minute there," Harry offered.

"That's quite all right, sir. We were looking at the top of the main stairs here and there's a small indentation on the wall next to the banister. Easy to miss given the dark colour of the wall but I was wondering if you have happened to notice it before?" Detective Richards asked whilst giving Harry enough room to pass him. Harry slowly, through bated breath, began climbing up the murder weapon. Arriving at the wall, he reached out, attempting to touch where the yellow marker had been placed but the detective grabbed his arm. "I'm sorry, sir, but if it is evidence, we can't have anyone contaminating it."

"Of course, of course, I don't know what I was thinking," Harry began nervously. His life had become surreal. "I don't believe this was here before, but again I can't be sure. I raised three rambunctious kids in this house, anything could have happened," Harry tried to offer with a smile.

"Mr Ryker, is there anywhere that you, your wife and stepson could stay while we finish here? It would be easier on you, given how far into the house the crime scene spans," The detective asked with a hand to his shoulder.

"Yes, of course. Will we be able to still have access, or do we need to pack for indefinite stay away?" Well aware that he was once again beginning to sound anxious.

"You can of course have access," the detective began as he also reached into his pocket where he pulled out a business card, a business card Harry had already been given but had also misplaced within hours of receiving it. "Give me a call if you need access and I'll make sure you have some privacy with as few people as necessary getting in your way," Richards said. Harry thanked the man and made his way further into the upstairs portion of the house. Behind him he could hear the arrival of the other, shorter, detective.

Chapter Thirty-One

Nate watched as the patriarch of the Rykers sadly walked towards the bedrooms. The man looked as if he had broken into millions of pieces, yet his frame and the way he held himself made Nate believe the man had once been the back bone of the family whose lives were currently falling apart. He hated this case. He knew he needed to be harder, to be the irritable detective who didn't take no for an answer until he found the correct one, but something was stopping him. This wasn't a family that had been ruled out of being the perpetrators, they were the family who were all prime suspects but all he could see was the connection each of these people had to Riya. Ridiculous, he knew, given that they had no future, even after the mind-altering kiss.

Sam sidled up next to him. It took some time for Nate to pull himself out of his thoughts and focus on the task at hand. "Found anything?" his partner asked.

"A few things..." Nate spent the next half an hour taking Sam through each marking, each blood spatter and each fingerprint that showed the progression of Lina's murder. It was now clear that Lina had suffered a small fight at the top of the main staircase which she had then been pushed down. The hair fibers that had been found pressed into the wallpaper at the top of the stairs proved she had been forced into the wall as her wrist had become trapped behind her until it had snapped. As he finished his explanation of the findings to Sam, he decided what was next on the agenda. So that he wouldn't allow his sentimental side to talk himself out of it, he made his intentions clear. "Once the family are out of the house, I want the whole house turned upside down, every drawer opened, every cupboard emptied and every hiding place discovered."

Sam looked skeptical. "Don't we need a warrant for that, boss?" Sam asked in a slight whisper.

Grinning, Nate replied, "Don't need one. We were given permission by the owner to do what we needed to do."

Chapter Thirty-Two

Melinda woke with a start. Something was very wrong. Her usually comfortable mattress felt as it had been replaced with rocks and her pillow, that she had carefully molded to her head's specifications, felt as if was lead-lined. The sound of metal scraping against metal made Melinda's already fragile head throb against her skull. "Mrs Ryker. Someone wants to see you." A booming voice spoke, which made Melinda sit up right far too quickly for the way she was feeling. Her mattress felt different because it was different. It was simply a blue gym mat on top of a large piece of stone and her pillow was no thicker than a two-pound coin.

Suddenly, it dawned on Melinda that she was in a police cell. The night before was a haze. After being told by her ever-resentful husband that they needed to move away for a while, Melinda had become belligerent. Harry, the man who knew she wanted no part to play in the happy family farce, had told her quite plainly that himself and Rory were moving in with Logan and she could either go with them or find somewhere else to temporarily stay, so that's what she did. Within the hour she had checked into The Lodge hotel and spa, which happened to be the most expensive luxury hotel within fifty miles and had been perched on a bar stool in the bar holding a gin and tonic. She vaguely recalled leaving the hotel after being refused service, and then finding herself in some seedy bar in a less than wholesome part of town. She could see herself in some sort of shouting match, but after that, nothing.

A large burly beast of a man stepped through the grey painted metal door, which even in her state Melinda thought ridiculous, and moved his arm, gesturing for her to follow him. Without looking in a mirror, Melinda could feel the mascara that had crusted far beneath her eyes and the fuzziness of her head. Knowing that asking for time to freshen up would be futile, Melinda stood up and pointlessly tried to smooth out the wrinkles in her knee-length silk skirt. She shook her head to the side, held her head high and followed the man into the dank hallway outside.

It did not take long for Melinda and her 'jailer' to reach the intended destination. It was a small room with a table in the centre, one chair sat on the far side whilst two chairs sat opposite. There was a small camera in one corner of the ceiling with a red blinking light that called to anyone who walked into the dirty little room. As Melinda took her seat the large reflective glass looming in front of her glinted in the dim room. Her last thought before the two detectives arrived, was of how old and tired she looked.

Nate shouldered his way into the room and held the door for Sam. "Ah, the illustrious Mrs Ryker," he began in a comical tone. "We've spent an awful amount of time trying to get you to talk to us and all it took was a few bottles of gin and a dive bar." Ending his statement with a Cheshire cat grin, Nate waited for the poised woman, who may not have shed so much as a tear for her deceased daughter, to answer.

"I've been busy making arrangements, Detective. What is it exactly you wanted to discuss?" Melinda replied, laying on her best sultry gaze.

"Well, there's the small matter of your only daughter's death, and so far, you have managed to avoid answering any of our questions," Nate answered, already losing patience with the woman.

Melinda, not seeming to get the point, continued, "As I said, Detective, I've been rather busy, but I'm here now so ask away." She finished with a bat of the eyelashes.

"Where were you when your daughter's death occurred last Thursday? As I understand when your husband tried to tell you about his discovery of her body you were not in the house and your bed had not been slept in. I'd be interested to know what would take you out of the house where your children were at five a.m. in the morning." Both himself and Sam waited, so much so his colleague had stopped his incessant note taking.

"Not all women prefer to stay monogamous in their marriage, Detective." Believing she had explained as much as was needed, Melinda leant back in her chair.

"So, you're saying you were with another man at the time of your daughter's death?" Sam interjected skeptically, leaning forward with his elbows braced around his small notepad. Melinda nodded slyly and tilted her head as if trying to meet Sam's eyes. "We'll need his name then, if you please."

"Ah, see, that I can't do, Detectives, he's a very private man and I wouldn't want to hurt my husband any more than was necessary," Melinda offered.

Nate and Sam looked at each other, it having dawned on both of them that Melinda was lying about something at the very least, if not everything. "Mrs Ryker, if we don't receive a name, we won't be able to confirm your alibi and without an alibi you will be considered a prime suspect in this murder."

Her eyes widened as Nate stopped speaking and so he continued. "Your daughter is dead. There is nothing that should be more important to you than finding her some sort of justice. Give us a name and you can be out of here within ten minutes."

Pursing her lips, Melinda readied herself for the impending fight. "I don't believe my private life is any of your business, Detective."

"It is when it interferes with my murder investigation," Nate coldly replied, clearing his throat. "Without a name I will assume that all of what you just told me was a lie and therefore, I will also assume you are lying to cover up something worse than adultery which may in fact be murder. This would then mean I'd have to read you your rights and subsequently charge you. Does that sound like something you'd particularly enjoy, Mrs Ryker?" His tone of voice indicated that he was not a man she wanted to mess with.

Melinda seemed to consider her options then lowered her head in resignation. "Fine," she whispered, "I was at a bar, I can't remember anything more than that." For the first time, since she had breezed into his investigation, Melinda looked as if she wanted to disappear, to be anything but the centre of attention.

"What time did you leave this 'bar'?" Not wanting to give her an inch of sympathy for fear she may use it against them, Nate removed all emotion from his voice.

"I…" Rapidly blinking her eyes Melinda tried to hide the quiver in her voice, "I passed out in one of the booths. The owner must have left me to sleep it off. It was light when I woke up." Melinda shivered, recoiling further into herself.

"We'll need the name of this bar," Sam began as Melinda

and Nate seemed to be locked in a battle-of-wills staring contest.

The words broke through the haze and Melinda rattled off the name of the bar and the street it was located on and made a move to stand up. Nate held up his hand to steady her movement. "We have more questions for you. Sit." Finishing with a sharp nod down towards the chair, Melinda seemed to get the message.

Rolling her eyes, Melinda planted herself back into a sitting position she had rehearsed time and time again. Trying to maintain her dignity and composure after the last twelve hours was tricky and Nate was remotely impressed with this woman's gumption. The façade faltered as Nate asked, "What was yours and your daughter's relationship like?"

In a higher pitch than usual, Melinda tried to remain calm. "It was like any other mother-daughter relationship. She was my world, my best friend." Her sniffling as she finished the statement could have been considered moving if not for Melinda's eyes darting from detective to detective in order to gauge their levels of sympathy at her imaginary plight. Recovering quickly with the dawning lack of belief coming from across the table, Melinda continued. "Of course, we had our issues and it was hard raising her alone but she was my daughter and I cared very deeply about her."

"Not exactly as emotionally distraught as most mothers in this situation usually are, don't you think, Sam?" Teasingly ignoring the shocked look on Melinda's face, Nate turned to his partner.

"I'd say she's the calmest mother of a murder victim we've ever seen." Sam then looked Melinda up and down. "Quite remarkable, really."

"Is she hiding all the emotion on the inside, do you think?" Nate pursed his lips, leant forward, and returned Melinda's shocked stare. "Or do you think that this woman is as heartless as the rest of her family seems to believe?"

Bingo! He'd hit a nerve if the rise of fury slowly filling her eyes was anything to go by. "If you knew anything about that family, Detective, you'd understand what the last few years of my life have really been like. You'd understand that *my daughter* was nothing more than a desperate girl trying to claw her way inside the bosom of the beast that is the Ryker family." Her vacant gaze made Nate believe Melinda was mentally not in the room any longer. It was interesting to see how the woman became someone else with the flip of a metaphorical switch. "I tried to give her love," Melinda said in a breathless whisper, "I tried to find something in her that I adored but nothing came. She was born, she grew up and every day I was either furious or completely bored with her. Since the moment I found out about her I couldn't stand the thought of her. She ruined any chance I had, don't you understand! The girl broke my future and I STILL worked to provide for her but that wasn't enough. I was her mother and she was my daughter but that is where my connection to her ends." Her eyes glazed over as she stared vacantly through both men who were watching the woman unravel. Nate motioned to Sam and the other detective ran out of the room.

A short time later, Melinda was still physically in the room but mentally missing as Sam returned with a small pearly white plastic cup filled with water. The setting down of the unstable cup seemed break Melinda's trance as she looked back up at the waiting men in front of her. "What did you mean that Lina 'broke your future', Mrs Ryker?" This time he chose to adopt a more caring tone. Melinda was on the verge of giving them all the information they needed.

Continuously whispering, Melinda crossed her arms and lent the entangled limbs on the cool surface of the table. "You don't know what it's like to find yourself shackled at nineteen to a baby that needs you, needs you for things you have never understood. I was all alone, just me. My head kept telling me that she was the reason I couldn't make anything of myself and after a while it became clear that was the case. After I'd started believing it, everything felt a little better. If I channeled the anger to where it belonged everything seemed a little clearer." Tears were running down her face now Melinda looked ghostly. "She broke my life before it had a chance to start."

"We checked records and you never listed the name of Lina's father." For curiosity and the case's sake Nate felt the need to find out more. Lina's beginning felt like it was tied to her end.

"I don't know who it was." She was looking more tired by the second. "Just another one of my 'clients', as my stepfather called them" Melinda explained with an ironic smile.

"So, you were…" Sam chimed in.

"Yes. I was a pro… I was paid, or more importantly my stepfather was paid, for my… services. Services that came to an end when he kicked me out for daring to become pregnant." Another smile caused Nate's gut to churn, he felt bad for her and there was always something to be said about how a person was molded into the person they had become. Melinda had lost her home, albeit a horrific home, because of her pregnancy. He could see where her mind had jumped from that rejection to blaming the child, but he couldn't understand it. As a child of a 'broken' home Nate thought himself lucky, both parents had loved him, done everything for him. Even when his father had moved back to America, they had remained a family who cared about one another, with Nate travelling to stay with his father during every school holiday and spending a long time on the phone with his mother whilst he was there. Although he saw broken-down family relationships almost on a daily basis, Nate was never not taken by surprise by the severity of the harm done by bad thoughts and past mistakes.

A knock on the large mirrored window broke him out of his trip down memory lane. He immediately understood. "That'll be all for today, Mrs Ryker. I believe we are letting you off the charge of drunk and disorderly with a caution." Melinda didn't even acknowledge he had spoken. "Your husband is outside waiting to take you home. We'll be in touch." As they stood, she stood almost on impulse and followed the uniformed officer out into the reception area.

"Well, that was enlightening," Sam said, looking slightly shocked at the change in person they had witnessed over the last hour.

"Do me a favour and make sure the tapes are sent down to Ruby," he said, referring to the police stations resident psychologist. "I want to know what she thinks about our Mrs Ryker." Sam nodded and hurried off to complete the order. Nate leant his head back against the wall and looked blankly into the magnolia ceiling.

Chapter Thirty-Three

Sitting in his navy-blue Jaguar F-Pace, Harry turned off the engine and silence filled the leather-lined interior. Melinda stayed half curled and half cowering in the passenger seat beside him. Her bag was covering her scuffed Louboutin shoes haphazardly and her hands remained clasped, clutching the handkerchief he had handed her as they'd stepped out of the police station. "I don't want to be here," came a small voice that was unrecognizably, his wife's.

"You need to shower then get some sleep and after last night I'm not sure going back to the hotel is a good idea." Both of them were still staring straight ahead, not giving their spouse any reassurance.

"Oh, and now you care what I do?" Melinda venomously replied.

"Like it or not, you are still my wife," Harry said, taking on a dangerous hushed tone. "Picking you up after your arrest is not something I want to see a repeat of. Is that understood?" Harry's hands appeared to be turning almost snow white as he gripped the steering wheel. Melinda let out a small singular laugh. "I won't have this family made a fool of. You will stay here and be grateful that my son has opened up his home to us." They sat staring at each other for what felt like minutes until Melinda angrily grabbed her bag, slipped out of the car, and slammed the door as hard as she could.

Harry watched as Melinda stormed her way into Logan's house. He'd received the call early this morning that Melinda had been arrested late last night for drunk and disorderly behaviour. He was surprised to learn that his reaction to this was a simple role of the eyes. Never in his life had he imagined that he would not be shocked to have to go and retrieve his wife after she'd spent the night in a cell. It was enlightening and freeing, as it gave him the out he had been looking for. After the investigation into Lina's death died down, he would be getting out of this marriage.

Chapter Thirty-Four

As she ended the phone call Riya couldn't help the smile that had crept its way onto her features. It was wrong, they shouldn't be doing it, but she couldn't seem to stop. Two days had passed since the funeral, so two days had passed since she'd last seen Nate — seen, yes, but not spoken to. For the last two nights she had spent the better part of her night speaking about everything and anything with the very man who could be risking his career for her, for them. It both warmed her heart and terrified her all in one.

Why couldn't they have met months ago? At least then they could've been clearer on where they stood when death had come calling.

Changing into her comfortable grey jogging bottoms and well-worn white vest top, Riya threw her hair into a messy bun and compulsively brushed her teeth. As she was climbing into bed, ready to feel the sweet relief of sleep, there was a loud knock on her door. Startled, she jumped up and quickly grabbed her favourite black 'zip-up' hoodie and headed for the door that was making far too much noise in her opinion. As she swung the front door to her homely cottage open, she was startled to find Logan bracing both of his hands on the door frame outside.

"Logan?" Riya asked worriedly. Logan didn't do this, didn't turn up in the middle of the night breathing heavily. As

Logan looked up Riya's heart broke. Her strong big brother, the rock of her life, was standing in her doorway, tie askew, five o'clock shadow covering the lower part of his face, and he was sobbing.

Chapter Thirty-Five

Walking into her lounge, cradling a steaming hot mug of tea, Riya could feel the tension in her brother's shoulders whilst also being able to smell the alcohol that imbibed him. The usually silently strong man was now a ghost of his former self, the eyes that were usually kind and caring were now misted over in fear. "Here," Riya said as she handed the mug to Logan. He looked up and quietly thanked his sister, knowing full well he would have to explain to her why he was sitting cold and unfeeling at the end of her comfy sofa. Logan knew it was inevitable that she would find out but for the life of him couldn't bring himself to crush the loyalty he saw reflected in her eyes.

Shuddering as if a chill had come over him, Logan shocked himself as he felt tears tumble down his cheeks. Riya muttered a curse and wrapped her arms around his large shoulders as he began to sob. He hung his head in shame as he struggled to compose himself. Riya sat up and moved onto her knees so she could rest her chin on top of his head. With no concept of time, they sat embraced and Logan allowed himself to fall apart as his sister tried to sooth him with hushed sounds.

As the sound of weeping subsided Logan gradually began to relax. "Talk to me, Logan," Riya began as she slowly stroked the top of his head.

Riya shifted as if to move away, but Logan's arm

tightened around her in a silent plea. "I messed up," Logan stammered with a large whimper.

"What do you mean you messed up?" Riya asked, becoming more nervous by the second.

"Lina," Logan rasped and her whole body froze.

"Logan…" Praying that what he was about to say was not what she thought it might be.

Riya's reaction startled him. "I didn't hurt her!" Logan stood, knocking her slightly off balance from her kneeling position.

Softly, so as not to anger him further, she spoke. "Then what?" Riya asked as Logan began pacing in front of her.

"I…" He stopped mid-room, looked her in the eye, stared for a few seconds and then looked down at the ground. "I loved her."

"You mean the way a brother loves his sis…" Riya started.

"No," Logan growled and then watched as recognition registered in his sister's eyes. "I *loved* her," Logan repeated as quietly as he could.

Riya spent the next minute sat deadly still. Shocked and confused, she needed to know more. "Did she know?"

Nodding his head, Logan replied, "Yes, we were together for about six months."

Riya's eyes widened. "Six months." She was not sure how to feel about this latest information. "And how did the two of you…" Riya made her hands mingle together as if to wordlessly explain her point.

"I went over one day to grab some things out of the loft, she offered me a drink and then…" reminiscing, Logan began smiling.

"OK! Not sure I need to know all the details." Riya had

suddenly realised that this was her brother and some things were better left unsaid. "But if you loved her and she loved you I don't see how you've done anything wrong." Ever the optimist, Riya smiled.

Once again, Logan's somber expression returned. He half sat, and half fell into the armchair resting in the corner. Silently clapping his hands together and resting his lips behind them. Eyes closed, he whispered, "I asked her to marry me."

"Logan! Why didn't you tell us? You know we would have been delighted for you both. Thomas would have come around and you know Dad would have..." Logan interrupted Riya mid-ramble.

"She said no," he replied stiffly.

"But..." Riya rose to question.

"Turns out I may have loved her, but she didn't necessarily love me," Logan said roughly.

"I really am trying to understand, Logan, but you're not making much sense," Riya softly spoke.

"The night before she..." Logan gulped in a large breath of air, "died. After we'd all finished having dinner, she met me in the garden. I kissed her and told her I had a surprise for her." He gave a singular loud laugh and his eyes sharpened. "I should have known something was wrong, ever since that stupid interview she'd stopped smiling, her eyes had stopped following me around rooms and I had to fight to get even a minute of her time," he finished scathingly.

"Logan," Riya snapped, eager and somewhat anxious for him to get to the point.

"I pulled out the ring." As he mentioned the diamond, he reached into one of his hidden pockets and made eyes at the large, rather gauche, in Riya's opinion, diamond. "I even got down on one knee." Logan chuckled as if he found the fact overly hilarious. "I told her I loved her and that I wanted to spend my life with her and do you know what she did?" It was with this statement that Riya realised just how drunk her brother was.

"No, Logan, I don't," Riya replied, not sure whether it was best to talk about when Logan was unable to maintain one emotion or another.

"She laughed!" Logan said as if it was a punch line to a rather dull joke. Speaking more somberly now, he continued, "The woman I loved laughed and said she didn't need me, my money or a marriage any more."

"I don't understand..." Riya asked, knowing that the young girl had hurt her brother more than anyone else ever had.

"Neither did I." Logan cursed. "I asked her what she meant, and she said that I had looked like a safe bet. My money would have kept her comfortable, especially when my father died, and she could have spent her life ignoring any kind of responsibility."

"Lina wasn't like that, Logan," Riya implored.

"Wasn't she?" Logan exploded throwing his arms out to the side. "Did any of us really know her? We all believed she was a hard-done-by girl, ignored by her mother but charming once she came out of her shell. Whilst all along she was just a carbon copy of the woman who ruined us! She used whoever could keep her 'happy' and when someone else, or in my case something else, took her fancy, people and their feelings were cast aside into the gutter."

Standing and then kneeling in front of her fragile brother, Riya softly coaxed, "Logan, you did nothing wrong."

"The detective asked me about my relationship with Lina and I said nothing. I said she was my stepsister and that I didn't know of any reason why someone may have killed her," Logan confided.

"But you didn't hurt her," Riya stated, alarmed at the unreadable look in her brother's eye. "You didn't, did you?" As soon as she'd spoken, Riya regretted it and tried to apologise, but the damage had already been done. Logan's eyes turned from hurt too cold in an instant.

"No. I did not," Logan stated stiffly.

"Logan…" Riya tried but he silenced her with a wave of the hand.

"What do I do?" Logan asked as if no longer sitting in a comfortable lounge but sitting across from a business foe.

Chapter Thirty-Six

Leg bouncing, eyes glued to the petite blonde desk sergeant, Logan sat in the midst of the chaos that was the reception area of the police station. "Are you sure this is the right thing to do?" he asked his sister quietly.

"The more up front you are the better it'll be in the long run." Riya finished by trying to place her hand on his.

Recoiling his hand away from her grip, Logan was skeptical if the police really needed to know and would be far more comfortable at home, especially given it seemed his sister believed him to be guilty of murder. "Fine, let's get this over with then."

As if on cue, the detective who he believed was called something like Richmond or Richards walked through double metal doors which were half covered by the reception desk. Logan, sitting hidden by the large mahogany barrier, watched as the man spotted his sister and with a large grin started walking quickly towards her. "Riy…" His voice faltered as he spotted Logan. "Miss Ryker, Mr Ryker, what can I do for you today?"

Chapter Thirty-Seven

Nate watched as the slightly older man walked past him towards the way out. The man obviously cared deeply for Lina Simons but the fact he had neglected to disclose that information in their first interview was worrying. Logan had said that his sister had convinced him to speak out as soon as she had found out, but there had been a tightness in his voice whenever he spoke Riya's name. Could the man be upset with his sister for forcing his hand to fess up? Or was it just that both Ryker sons became automatically irritable when questioned by someone in law enforcement? Nate had no clue, but pieces of the puzzle were starting to come together, and the image of Lina Simons was changing with each piece being laid into place.

Nate followed the man until they once again reached his sister. "Thank you for coming forward, Mr Ryker." He offered a curt nod towards the man in recognition. Logan rolled his eyes and turned towards the automatic doors.

"Logan…" Riya started after her brother.

"I'll find my own way home," The other man replied without turning around. He lifted his hand giving her a dismissive wave and disappeared into the street.

"Want to talk about it?" Nate asked and watched as Riya jumped at the voice pulling her out of her hurt haze.

Sighing, Riya turned to face Nate with a small smile. "He

thinks I believe he murdered Lina."

"And do you?" Nate asked softly.

"No!" Riya replied, the spark coming back into her eyes. "I said something that I shouldn't have but no, I don't think Logan did it." The tears in her eyes made his heart break. He touched her shoulder and guided her towards the private meeting room that sat inside the reception area and straight onto one of the upholstered chairs.

"I'm sure he knows you didn't mean it," Nat said, trying to comfort her but not really knowing how.

"Logan is a brilliant man and more loyal than anyone I've ever met. My whole life it's been me and him against the world and I repaid him by accusing him of murder. I'm not sure there's any coming back from that," Riya stated by wiping the palm of her hand across her forehead, more tears forming on her eyelashes.

'Interesting,' Nate thought. No mention of Thomas in that statement. Nate made a mental note to ask her about that once she'd calmed down.

Throwing his arm around her shoulder, Nate leant his head against hers whilst she cried. The sobbing subsided and she placed her hand on his knee in thanks. What was meant as an innocent show of appreciation made the electricity in the room multiply. Heads still together, eyes meeting until everything froze.

Nate watched with unrestrainable lust as Riya's eyes flickered towards his lips and stared like she was mesmerized. Nate's free hand found its way towards her face and slowly turned the porcelain cheek, so she was now directly in front of his eyes. Riya's eyes gradually closed shut and she leant forward and Nate, not one to disappoint, took charge by pulling her forward until their lips met. What started out as a slow exploration was gaining in force and passion as Riya and Nate both raised their bodies so they could become as close as their seats would allow. Riya moved her hands, they cradled Nate's face as his moved to her rear, trying to pull her even closer. A moan echoed around the room and Nate wasn't sure which one of them it had come from.

The jostling of the doorknob ripped them apart, both heavily breathing. Riya touched her hand to her lips as if it would remove all evidence of the illicit kiss. The desk-sergeant walked in half a second later, took one look at the slightly frazzled pair and tried to make a quick exit. "Sergeant?" Nate asked, annoyed at the interruption.

"Sorry, sir, but Sam just called." Knowing that his partner and the desk sergeant were a little more than friends, Nate chose to ignore the lack of professional ranking applied to her statement. "He said that Ruby was ready to talk to you up in her office," she finished.

"Thanks. Tell him I'll be there in five," Nate said, giving the uncomfortable woman a reason to leave the room where things had just become a little bit too steamy.

The desk sergeant quickly disappeared around the door and once again Riya and Nate found themselves alone. Riya looked down into her lap and Nate cleared his throat. "I'd better go," Riya said as she rose from the chair.

"Riya, can I ask you something?" Nate asked hoping she wouldn't take offence with his poor timing.

"Of course," Riya replied, a bit too formally for Nate's liking.

"When you said it's always been you and Logan against the world," Nate began and, after seeing her small nod in recognition, continued, "you didn't mention Thomas. I guess I just wondered if there was a reason for that?"

Riya took a while to respond, probably because she'd never considered it herself. "I love Thomas, I do, but he's always been…" she struggled to find the words, "closed off. He's my brother and there is a great bond there, but he never lets me or Logan in, almost like he's afraid of what we might find," Riya finished. After a slight pause she shrugged her shoulders as if shaking off the feelings of unease the relationship she, and Logan for that matter, had with Thomas sometimes brought.

"Sorry. Just curious. I had an interesting conversation with your brother and wanted to see if it was just me he's taken against," Nate suggested.

Riya interjected, "I don't think he has taken against me or Logan, I just think he's never really allowed himself to be happy."

Nate nodded. "Thanks for that and for bringing Logan in."

"I thought it best," Riya added demurely.

"I'll show you out," Nate said, smiling down at her. Everything about this woman had captivated him from the moment he had met her. Never once considering himself to be a man capable of commitment, Nate realised that in a space of a fortnight, everything had changed, he was starting to see a completely different future for himself. Ridiculous, he knew, but there was something about her that made his whole outlook change.

As they reached the doors leading to the outside world, Nate felt Riya stiffen like she was bracing herself for something. Riya span quickly on her heal and worriedly looked into his eyes. Trying to stop the panic rising throughout his body, Nate bent his head lightly and said, "I'll call you tonight. Same time?"

"Nate, we can't do this any more." Riya tried to sound self-assured but fell short. "This is only going to hurt you and your career if we carry on." When Nate began to argue Riya quickly carried on. "I can't be the reason that you lose your job. I won't be." Determination coursed through Nate's veins until she asked the one question, he didn't know how to answer. "Can you promise me that nothing bad will happen to *you* if we carry on?"

Nate closed his eyes in recognition and felt her brush past him to leave.

Chapter Thirty-Eight

Nate stormed through the station until he reached Ruby's office. Sam was already perched on the corner of the fragile-looking desk as Ruby milled around tidying up odds and ends. Riya had walked out, just left him and now he had to try his hardest to understand the ins and outs of a person's mind. "The girlfriend says hello," Nate snidely remarked to make his presence known. At the reference Sam's face went a bright shade of pink and his head dropped as if to study the blank notebook in front of him. Nate murmured an apology for his less than stellar mood and Ruby motioned for them to sit on the comfy chairs surrounding her office.

"So, boys, I've had a look at your tape of Melinda Ryker, and I've got to say it's impressive," Ruby said. She was a woman in her sixties and had laugh lines to prove it but everything else about the station's psychologist was a contradiction to her age. She dressed in clothes that women twenty years her junior would be afraid to try on, her makeup and hair highlights consisted of many different shades of bright colours and her views on life were so liberal that they often made Nate blush. The woman was a breath of fresh air to a building that saw too much despair and she was a brilliant psychologist, any case she contributed to was helped exponentially and her insights into suspects that Nate had sometimes brought in, had saved him months of investigation.

In Nate's eyes this woman was worth her weight in gold, and then some!

"First of all, you were right, Melinda Ryker has some severe mental health issues that have contributed to her current attitude," Ruby explained.

"Anything suggesting that she is a plausible murder suspect?" Nate asked, knowing that Ruby had the ability to know if a person's health impeded their ability to cause harm, which unfortunately, was not often the case.

"From what I've seen so far, Melinda is more than capable of committing a crime like this one. She has also convinced herself of her hatred for her daughter which means she would hurt her if the right circumstances arose," Ruby stated and then reached for her oval-shaped glasses with a purple rim to read her notes more clearly.

"So, she is more than likely our murderer?" Nate suggested, fully understanding it would take more than this brilliant woman's say so to close this case.

"Well... Melinda is a damaged soul. I believe this started with a severe case of prenatal depression followed by a similar postnatal depression which was intensified by her living situation or lack thereof. Her depression went untreated after Lina's birth and so manifested itself. Melinda's only way of coping through Lina's first years was to place the blame on someone close, that being Lina, and after that it became second nature. As Melinda's depression relapsed her hatred towards her daughter grew. Her stepfather had installed a worthlessness to her and made her believe that she was only worth something if a sexual favour were involved," Ruby explained.

Nate and Sam sat trying their very best to share Ruby's enthusiasm but were just as content to gain the useful information she was depicting. "That's great, Ruby. Is there a connection between Melinda's sexual ideals and Lina's?" Nate asked, referring to his recent conversation with Logan Ryker.

"There could be. Because she was taught that her best use was to sell her body, Melinda began her pattern of giving away her body for money and security in a more biblical sense. This would have been a lot harder with a small child in tow, thus increasing her resentment towards Lina, but she did it successfully. Lina may not have known but her morals were defined by her mother's and even if she didn't want to, she would have subconsciously started to adopt some of her mother's tendencies," Ruby said, nodding. "It would not be surprising if Lina began a path similar to her mother's."

"That's brilliant, Ruby. Thank you so much." Nate rose and Sam took the hint and began shuffling his own papers in an attempt to follow his superior. Both men headed for the door, minds full.

Ruby stopped them just before the door. "One more thing, from the small trembles in Melinda's hands and her darting eyes I think it's safe to say she's an addict, given the situation it's likely related to alcohol. She was arrested, held, and interviewed over the course of about ten hours where she wasn't given anything remotely alcoholic and she began going into withdrawal. She's highly dependent and if something were to stop her drinking in a time of desperation, she could become enraged and extremely unpredictable."

Chapter Thirty-Nine

Logan stormed through the door to his new-build. The slamming of the door echoed around the large open-plan room, and it was at that point that Logan noticed his father sitting in the large brown leather chesterfield that pointed towards the wood burner that sat in the centre of the room. After hearing the loud noise Harry turned his eyes towards his son and seeing his wounded face silently asked what was wrong with a slight tilt of his head.

Logan said nothing and moved to the set of large staggered glass shelves that acted as a makeshift bar. Grabbing two crystal tumblers he poured two healthy servings of Macallan single malt scotch, handed one to his father and slouched into the identical chair opposite. There they sat, in complete quiet watching the flames dance and crackle until Logan stretched his legs and moved his arms so he was leaning against his own knees. This seemed to break the unspoken vow of silence between the two men who looked so much alike. "Dad?" Logan asked.

Harry didn't really respond but made a non-committal sound and waited for Logan to continue.

"What was it about Melinda that captivated you for those first few months?" Logan asked, trying to sound casual.

Harry, taken aback by the odd question, seemed to ponder for a minute. "I guess she was so sure about everything when

I was still looking for something to make sense."

"What changed? How did you go from feeling like that, to this?" Logan asked by waving his hand towards the ceiling showing the distance between husband and wife and the chasm that was growing by the day.

"She got what she wanted," Harry said bitterly.

"But…" Logan tried to find some other explanation, if only to make himself feel better about his own situation.

"Logan, I've tried to see it from every perspective but there's no denying It. Melinda wanted an easy life and I gave it to her. That's all she ever saw in me," Harry explained.

Logan knew his father was right, but something was bothering him. "But why does she think like that? There must've been a reason why she felt the need to use you like that."

"Oh, no doubt about it. There is something that changed Melinda's life and her outlook. Problem was she's never felt the need to open up, to explore her feelings, so the problems between us grew bigger and bigger until they were unfixable," Harry finished.

Sensing his father had finished speaking about the subject of his marriage, Logan swallowed the last of his drink and refilled both of their glasses. "Your sister called me," Harry stated as Logan's hands shook whilst holding the bottle of expensive liquor. "She didn't mean it, son," Harry continued in an oddly soft voice.

Nodding, Logan replied, "I know, but that doesn't mean it didn't hurt to hear." Realising that Riya had spoken about the events leading up to his trip to the police station, Logan wasn't sure to what extent his sister had re-laid his outburst to his father. "She say anything else?" Logan asked into his glass.

"No," Harry replied. "But there's more, isn't there?" Harry said drinking from his own glass but leaving his heavy gaze on his son.

Logan stopped mid sip. With his statement to the police, he knew everything would eventually come out. He had to tell his father but that didn't mean it was going to be easy. The man had loved Lina almost as much as he loved Riya, he'd protected her, cared for her and sacrificed for her, and now his son was about to tell him that he had come in under the radar unbeknown to anyone, least of all the other occupants of the house. "Yeah. There's more," Logan conceded, well aware they were speaking in almost monosyllables.

"You can tell me anything, you know that," Harry said. Logan then began to tell his father everything.

Chapter Forty

Walking down the cobbled street Riya heard her phone ring once again. Knowing full well who the person on the other end of the call was Riya chose to ignore the loud high-pitched noise, not for her sake but for his. Nate wasn't thinking, wasn't considering what she could end up doing to his career. After all the phone calls and texts, before and after Lina's death, Riya knew how much Nate's work meant to him, it had become not only his home but also his family after both of his parents had died. She would not take that away from him. She was trained in corporate law but even she knew that an inappropriate relationship with a person of interest could cause serious problems, especially in a high-profile case such as this one. Nate could be sanctioned, demoted or worse depending on the situation, which was something she could not be a part of.

Reaching the sleek black door brought Riya out of her ever-present thoughts of Nate. What she had said that morning bothered her. Riya had never considered her closeness to one brother over the other but after the thought had been put in her brain it had started to eat away at her until she had to do something about her internal guilt. Somehow, she'd found herself travelling towards Thomas's hidden-away house anxious to see if there was any kind of distance between the two of them. Before she managed to talk herself out of it, Riya rapped confidently on the smooth door.

Minutes later her eldest brother casually opened the door. "Hey, kiddo!" Thomas greeted. A smile appeared across his handsome face and Riya felt that there was something different about him and chastised herself for doubting the strength of their connection. Thomas moved to let her in and Riya, not for the first time, cursed the man's décor. Minimalistic, no character and no individuality, Thomas's house felt more like a mausoleum rather than a place for relaxation and comfort.

Riya heard a deep chuckle behind her. "You never could hide what you're thinking," Thomas said and chuckled as he leant against the first wall in the large kitchen come office.

"What do you mean?" Riya asked, trying to find some part of the room that showed some sort of human emotion.

"Your dislike of my house," Thomas said with a raised eyebrow.

"I don't dislike your house!" Riya shot back, afraid to upset him.

"Riya, you know I spend the majority of my time at work. This place," he motioned to the house, "is just somewhere where I eat, sleep and occasionally drink. Speaking of which…" Riya watched as Logan sauntered over to the kitchen's attached breakfast bar and grabbed an unopened bottle of wine. Offering her a questioning gaze, Thomas went in search of the corkscrew.

Hours later, Riya was relaxing on Thomas's large 'L' shaped sofa when she felt something nudge her shoulder. She tried to bat away the annoying perpetrator, "Riya!" they whispered, but Riya was just too comfortable to consider answering. It happened again, but this time too loud to ignore. "Riya!"

"What!" Riya snapped, only half opening her eyes.

A chuckle followed her outrage. "You fell asleep. Kiddo. I told you there was not a chance in hell you could out drink me," Thomas half whispered, half chuckled. Riya groaned in response and slowly sat up, feeling the numbness in her hands and a fuzziness in her head. The huge mirror taking up most of the wall in front of her let her know that the surprisingly comfy couch had left an imprint straight across her left cheek.

"I've got to go home," Riya groaned.

"No, you don't," Thomas chuckled. "Now what kind of big brother would Ii be if I sent you home alone in this condition?" He leant back next to her and patted her feet that were still curled up in the dark blue cashmere blanket. Suddenly, Thomas stood up, swaying as if he were a tree in the wind.

"Obviously I'm not the only one who had one glass too many!" Riya said, laughing as if it were the best joke she'd ever heard.

"Come on!" Thomas barked trying to help a still giggling Riya up and into the spare room. "You need to sleep this off," Thomas finished, slightly pushing her towards the stairs.

"Yes, brother dear!" Riya said with a dramatic bow as she headed upstairs to pass out but not before grabbing her phone off the small table that sat next to the bottom step.

"Scram!" Thomas joked, feeling lighter than he had in years.

After the disastrous interview with the detectives, and then subsequently the overwhelming anger he'd felt when he saw them the day after the funeral, Thomas had realised his anger was not healthy. It also was on the verge of taking over and then God knows who he'd end up hurting. The healing scabs on his knuckles and the bruises on his ribs proved that nothing good came of becoming riled up. The man he had ended up in the ring with the night after his interview had fared far worse than he had from what Thomas was hearing but he'd live, luckily. He'd make sure the man was taken care of financially if he needed to but as far as Thomas was concerned, that man, that fight, had been his last.

The doctor he spoke to earlier had made him an appointment for the following week. She'd made the appointment, but he'd made the step of reaching out to find her and, apparently according to Dr Fiona Parish, that was the hardest step on the road to healing. If Thomas had been told a year ago that he would willingly have sought out the help of a therapist, he would have laughed, and yet here he was anxious to get his life fixed.

Thomas smiled as he heard the door to his spare bedroom close. Tonight had meant more to him than Riya would ever understand. For so long he had felt alone, desolate, and angry, but one night with his sister had given him hope. Riya had come to him, she'd sought him out to help her get through some issue she was debating internally. For what seemed like forever he had been fighting his impulse to share with his siblings, they'd been close but not really bonded and all he wanted was to have the kinds of relationships with them that they had with each other. That night he felt like he had made a start.

Chapter Forty-One

Stumbling into the minimal bedroom, Riya, trying not to fumble, awkwardly took off her necklace that had hung round her neck every day since her sixteenth birthday. It was a small pendant, no bigger than a five pence piece, that bore the mark of St Christopher on one side and her and her mother's initials engraved on the other. It had been for her sixteenth but her father had made a point to tell her that it had been her mother who had decided what her gift was going to be many years before. Gracefully placing the chain delicately on the bed side table, Riya hoped that her mother would have been happy watching tonight's events. Granted, she probably would have rolled her eyes at the drunkenness but, she would have loved seeing the once buttoned-up eldest son let himself laugh and joke with his sister about everything and anything.

A ringing pierced through Riya's trip down memory lane. In her drunken state she didn't think twice about picking it up to answer. "Hello!" she sang down the phone.

"Riya? Are you OK? I've been trying to call you all night!" Nate's angry tone came through from the other end of the blaring phone.

"I'm fine, Nate, why wouldn't I be?" Riya replied while giggling then throwing herself onto the large bed in the centre of the room.

"You sound funny," Nate bluntly replied.

"Do I now?" Riya teased.

Nate chuckled, losing his harsh tone of only moments before. "You've been drinking."

"Of course, I've been drinking! I'm sad and happy, what else was there to do!" Riya said rolling onto her stomach and kicking her legs behind her like she was a character in an eighties chick-flick.

"Happy and sad? Don't you think those two feelings contradict each other?" Nate said, eager to see what she may disclose with her walls down.

Riya sighed into the phone. "I'm sad because you don't understand and I'm sad because we can't carry on whatever this is," Riya finished with a groan.

"I understand, Riya, I just don't think I want to," Nate replied with a laugh.

"You are a very confusing man, you know," Riya replied sleepily.

"I know I am and you, Riya Ryker, are just as confusing," Nate argued humorously.

"Well, that's not very nice! I really was starting to like you, but now I'm not so sure," Riya hiccupped.

"Where are you, Riya?" Nate asked, suddenly more serious now.

Riya considered her words very carefully. "I'm nowhere special."

"Ah, so you're at home and drinking alone!" Nate teased.

"No, I am not alone!" Riya answered too quickly. "I just so happen to be staying at my brother's tonight," she finished and heard a sigh of relief coming through the phone but was too drunk to understand its meaning.

"That's good," Nate affirmed. "So you and Logan made

up?" he asked in a more relaxed tone.

"No." Riya sighed but hoped her sadness over the fact didn't find its way into her voice. "I'm with Thomas."

Bristling at the name, Nate tried to say something that made him sound more upbeat than he was feeling. "Sounds like you two had a pretty good night."

Smiling wide, Riya couldn't hide her excitement. "We definitely enjoyed ourselves, that's for sure. I may not think the same thing in the morning though."

"Riya... about what you said..." Nate began.

Quickly interrupting him, Riya said, "I meant every word, Nate."

"But if we both feel it, and I'm the one risking something, surely it should be my decision?" Nate implored.

"Just forget about me, Nate," Riya finished, and quickly ended the call with a press of a button. The alcohol was getting the better of her and Riya felt herself slowly slip into a deep tormented sleep.

Chapter Forty-Two

The next day Sam came into the station with a burst of energy. He quickly paced his way in front of Nate. "They've got something at the house, boss." The slightly out of breath statement gave Nate something to think about, other than his emptier than normal life. Removing his coat from the back of his worn chair, Nate silently followed Sam through the station towards his car.

Unlike Nate, Sam had chosen a slightly smaller model of car to work in and Nate felt like he needed to be concertinaed in order to fit into its low and dinky seats. Groaning, Nate struggled to buckle his seat belt, feeling irritated with himself for breaking his policy of always driving himself. "What did they say when they called?" Nate asked Sam, hoping talking about work would distract him from the feeling of being crushed within a tin can.

"They didn't say. Just said they had something we'd definitely want to see," Sam said. Typical, Nate thought — it wasn't like they were trying to solve a murder or anything. The forensic team had started at the top of the stairs and worked their way down to try and follow the path of the murder. It had been Nate's idea, and it had been a good one. They now had a specific timetable of events and injuries that had led to the fatal fall causing Lina's death. When this case went to court, they would need as much detail as possible to make themselves and the investigation appear plausible. Interestingly, for the last thirty-six hours they'd been working on the upstairs of the mansion-like house.

After Nate's decision to stop worrying more about the Rykers' feelings, he had given the go-ahead for his forensics team to rip the house apart. Any trace of something out of place, any unexplainable mark, Nate wanted to know. The car slowed to a stop and Nate looked out the slightly smudged window. This place had housed a family, but all that Nate saw was the perfect place to become lonely. The house, the family all appeared to be perfect but there was a sinister feeling that came with both that he simply could not ignore.

Running up the stairs, Nate was passed by numerous people, all covered in stark white protective clothing. The smell of chemicals burned through his nose and Nate realised the number of yellow markers had at least tripled in the last two days. Sam continued on behind as Nate followed the path laid out by the small triangular cones. "All right boss?" the chipper overall-covered man in charge said. It always amazed Nate how happy the boys in white were to ransack another person's home, but the gleam in the man's eyes told him that his expertise had, once again, paid off.

"What've you got for me?" Nate asked brusquely.

"Not in the mood again today, I see!" the man whose name he should know joked. "I've found some clothes you might want to take a look at."

The man led Nate and Sam over to the transparent evidence bag. Out of nowhere a pair of dusty blue rubber gloves dangled in front of his chest. Grabbing the starchy material Nate sharply blew into them and slipped them on. Opening the red sealed bag Nate pulled out a long dark blue shirt with white buttons running down the centre. Despite the large looming dark red blood staining most of it, the stench of the room reached Nate's senses first. The overwhelming smell of Chanel permeated the space, suffocating all who entered. He recognised the smell because Melinda had somehow imprinted it on every surface in the station and yet the amount in this one room was enough to cover everyone in the suspect pool, until they were soaked. "Where did you find it?" Nate asked, once again focused on the bloodied shirt.

"Once we moved the bed, we found a loose floorboard. This was the first thing we pulled out, followed by some photos and cash," the man now crouching down in front of a removed floorboard said.

"And do we know that it's definitely Lina's blood?" Nate asked, flicking through the assortment of photos that were now individually wrapped as evidence.

The man spoke confidently whilst shaking his head. "Not for sure but we have confirmed it is of the same blood type as Miss Simon's. We'll have a definitive answer for you by the end of the day."

"That's great, thanks. Do you mind if I hold on to these?" Nate asked, waving the pile of plastic-covered pictures.

"No problem. I'll give you a call if anything else comes to light," the man said nodding and then turning his back on both detectives as if dismissing them.

Heading towards the door with Sam in tow, Nate had to begin formulating a plan. Sam thanked each person for their work as they passed them. Such a friendly man and Nate often wondered if this life, this career, was the best choice for someone with such a generous persona. For someone with such a great brain and heart Sam could have achieved anything he'd set his mind to. Was there something Nate was missing? Was there something about his partner he did not know? Most of the detectives he had met had joined the force for very particular reasons, he himself had joined after his university roommate had been stabbed to death during a robbery gone wrong, but Sam was a mystery. What had brought this happy-go-lucky man to this dark but rewarding profession?

The car came into sight and Sam was still trying to see over Nate's large shoulder to find out what had captured his boss so intensely about the old pictures that had been discovered. "What do you think?" Sam asked, trying to tempt Nate to speak his so-far silent thoughts.

"Have a look," Nate said and handed the pictures to Sam.

"It's just some random men..." Sam said cautiously, not understanding the relevance to these pictures.

"The men are doing day-to-day tasks. They don't know the pictures are being taken," Nate explained. "This one's name is Charles Brooks, he's an investment banker worth over ten million." Pointing at the next picture Nate continued, "This one's Malcolm Thomson, he comes from old money and a lot of it. Every single one of these men is worth millions and Melinda seems to have been doing surveillance on them. Testing the waters, so to speak!"

"I'm sorry but..." Sam struggled sometimes to understand the connections his boss could see so well.

"If Lina were to find these, what do you think she would have done? She'd made a life here, her stepfather had welcomed her with open arms, she'd found herself a man, thoroughly connected with the Rykers, to take care of her financially. She was set. If her mother, the woman she already had some major issues with, told her they were moving on, I'm not sure that would've gone down very well at all," Nate finished, walking around to the passenger side of the car.

"And the shirt? Surely that's the final nail in the coffin?" Sam asked as he settled himself into the driving seat.

"I'm not so sure. Something about it seemed off, sloppy almost," Nate said thoughtfully. "I guess we'll just have to have another chat with Melinda Ryker."

"Now?" Sam asked.

Chapter Forty-Three

The knock on the door came at about eight p.m. that evening, interrupting the fraught dinner without conversation. Harry and Logan sat on one side of the chrome table while Melinda and Rory sat opposite as they all poked at their food with little to no interest. Logan stood, wiped his hands against his thighs. Opening the door, his eyes widened slightly at the sight of Detective Inspector Richards and Detective Constable Turner somberly standing before him, the flashing lights of the police cars behind them illuminating their bowed heads.

"Good evening, Mr Ryker, sorry for interrupting your evening. Is your stepmother home?" Detective Richards asked.

Hearing the mention of her name, Melinda stood and shouldered her way past her husband and stepson, who were both standing, forming a blockade across the front door. "Detective!" Melinda sang, absent-mindedly smoothing down her always pristine hair. "What can I do for you?" she asked gleefully, almost as if she had forgotten her breakdown in front of the two men days before.

Nate stood forward, reached into his back pocket and pulled out a pair of handcuffs. "Melinda Ryker, you are under arrest for the murder for Lina Simons. You do not have to say anything…" He continued reading her rights, trying to ignore the shocked expression of the two grown men still hovering by the door and the tears falling down the face of the sweet boy who was currently clinging to the leg of his stepfather. "Anything you do say may be given in evidence," Nate finished and nothing happened, Melinda stood staring dumbstruck and frozen until Nate intervened. "Ma'am, please turn around." Slowly, Melinda turned around, still holding her confused gaze.

The metallic crunch of the handcuffs closing around Melinda's trembling wrists was the only sound that echoed around the group of people convened at this particular door. Nate gave a gentle nudge to the woman shaking in front of him. He guided her towards the nearest marked police car and was just about to place his hand on her head as she ducked into the back seat when a squeal vibrated around him. "No!" was all that Nate heard before a small being rushed around the outside of his leg and clawed his way down to the hard concrete below.

Rory was on the floor wailing, trying to maintain his grip, now on his mother's feet. Not wanting to scare the child, Nate silently pleaded with Harry to try and console the boy. Harry got the message and started towards the scene unfolding before him. Talking softly, Harry tried to coax his stepson away from his mother but Rory kept kicking out his feet, avoiding anyone's touch.

The whole time Harry Ryker remained crouched on his knees, talking to his obviously very upset stepson. Nate kept his eyes on Melinda. The woman didn't flinch, didn't appear moved and kept her eyes staring straight ahead at all times. "Mummy!" Rory screeched at the top of his lungs.

Upon hearing the piercing cry Melinda's eyes turned icy. With no emotion, no empathy, Melinda looked down at her last remaining child. "Rory!" she said sharply, looking him dead in the eye and stiffly yanking her feet away from his tiny hands. With the sudden movement Rory fell, hands first, towards the rugged ground. He landed but didn't cry, simply rolled himself into a small ball and gently laid his forehead against the rough stone.

Placing Melinda in the back seat of the beat-up police car, whilst simultaneously stepping over the small lifeform, Nate nodded at the driver to take her away. Heading towards Harry who now stood talking with his son in hushed tones, Nate cleared his throat. When both men looked up, they scurried towards the man who seemed to have some answers about the strange turn of events happening around them. "Detective?" asked Harry.

"We've found some bloodied clothes underneath your wife's floorboards that seem to suggest your wife was the one who both pushed Lina down the stairs and moved her body," Nate explained.

"Jesus!" Logan hissed, turning around, and pinching the bridge of his nose.

"What happens now?" Harry asked in a daze.

"We'll be in touch, Mr Ryker," Nate simply stated and walked away.

Chapter Forty-Four

"What do we do now?" Logan whispered hysterically. It was now well into the night, but he couldn't think about sleeping right now.

"Calm down, Logan," Harry firmly said. Rory had finally stopped weeping and was now curled up under a large blanket on Logan's hidden sofa, which was under the eaves of the stairs. There was no way Harry wanted the job of trying to calm him to sleep again if he woke from Logan's panic. Harry had hardly been able to stop the spinning carousels of questions in his own head, he wasn't sure he had the capability to deal with Logan's melt-down as well.

"Your wife was just arrested for killing your stepdaughter. I'm not sure either of us should be calm right now," Logan said cynically.

"Panicking about it is not going to fix anything, is it!" Harry said, screaming.

Logan, seemingly taken aback by his father's rudeness, threw himself down onto his chair to watch the flames dance once again. Everything was crumbling and the Rykers would never be the same again. Harry growled into the darkness of the room and stormed his way up the stairs. Logan was surprised, this wasn't a man he recognised. His father, for the most part, had always been calm and collected, never really raising his voice, and yet he'd just turned into a stranger.

Logan wandered over to the kitchen countertop and held his phone in both hands. Looking down at the machine cradled in his palms, Logan was once again tempted to call his sister. Riya would have known how to calm down his spinning head and she would have known how to handle their father. Logan rested his head on the phone, he knew she hadn't meant to accuse him of murder and he had forgiven her for that. Now he was just embarrassed by his temper tantrum at the police station and could still see the hurt in her eyes. The detective would have taken care of her, much to his annoyance. Surely it was violating all kinds of professional ethics to be emotionally involved with a suspect? After watching the man who had just wreaked havoc on his family kiss his sister on the day of Lina's funeral, he'd wondered if it had just been a fluke, a left-over bit of desire from their coffee shop meeting but now, after seeing them react so keenly to one another at the station, he wasn't so sure.

Logan couldn't help but feel he was losing his sister and avoiding her many phone calls and visits of apology was his way of preparing. He was happy for her, but God knew he was terrified of a life, not being her highest priority.

Chapter Forty-Five

"The time is 8.25 p.m. Ms Melinda Ryker has been charged with murdering a Miss Lina Simons. Present in the room is Detective Inspector Nathan Richards, Detective Constable Sam Turner and Mrs Ryker's legal representation." As Nate waited for Melinda's lawyer to state her name for the record, he mentally prepared himself for the fight ahead. After the last interview, Nate knew better than to believe this would be a simple hunt for the truth.

With the legalities out of the way Nate took his stance, leaning back in his chair. "Here we are again, Mrs Ryker," he said with a lopsided smile.

"So we are, Detective," Melinda replied coolly, her mask securely in place. Without saying a word Nate began laying picture after picture down on the cool surface of the table. Melinda's eyes followed his movements and caught on each picture. "I know what this looks like," Melinda said quickly.

"It looks like you've been having a bit of fun lately," Nate said patronizingly.

At the tone of his voice Melinda bristled. "Can't a girl have some fun once in a while?"

Nate smiled. "I have no problem with you having fun, Mrs Ryker but these pictures look like part of a blackmail scheme. Am I wrong?" In response, Melinda raised a single eyebrow. "Did you find out that Lina was the one doing this? Is that what made you snap?" Nate asked, waiting to watch her response.

A high pitch laugh followed. "Lina couldn't pull this off!" Melinda said, still chuckling as if the idea was ridiculous.

"Really? Because there's only yours and her fingerprints on them," Nate calmly said. Melinda rose in her seat to respond but a calming hand around her wrist stopped her. She leant back. Her lawyer whispered into her ear, at which point Melinda's face shut down of emotion and her lips thinned. Melinda wasn't going to say anything more on this subject, but Nate had all he needed. Melinda was good, but not that good, she couldn't have pulled out that level of surprise if it weren't genuine. There was more that could sink Melinda yet.

Without warning, Nate pulled the large plastic bag, which had been resting against his seat, and slapped it down loudly against the table, the contents of the bag purposefully hidden from view. "Recognise this?" Nate asked.

"It is a shirt," Melinda snapped. The lawyer leant forward and whispered something in Melinda's ear and a blank sheet covered her face almost instantly.

"No need to be irritable, Mrs Ryker, it was merely a question. A question, I might add, that you didn't answer," Nate replied cleverly. "Have you seen this shirt before?"

"No, I can't say that I recognise it, Detective. Should I have?" Melinda answered, much to the dismay of her lawyer, Nate suspected.

"It was found under your bed, has your hairs all over it," Nate explained with no further insight.

Melinda femininely laughed. "I have many clothes, Detective, I can't be expected to remember them all," she replied, flipping her hair gracefully over one shoulder.

"This piece of clothing is different," Nate said with a look that promised humor. "This piece of clothing is covered in your daughter's blood," Nate added by quickly flipping the bag over to show the large red stain marring the otherwise perfect material.

Melinda pursed her lips as her eyes flared. Nate was looking for either surprise or recognition but was not rewarded with either. In his mind, mothers who look at their child's blood should be wailing, should be in shock or inconsolable, Melinda was neither, she was just silently passive. "I beg your pardon, Detective, but what is it that you are trying to say? That shirt has nothing to do with me," Melinda said scornfully, folding her arms across her chest and leaning back into her seat.

"It has everything to do with you, ma'am, it is covered in both yours and your daughter's DNA." Sam chimed in for the first time, "This piece of evidence was found underneath your bed."

Melinda's complexion changed almost instantly to ghostly white. "But I didn't... I haven't ever seen it before," Melinda stammered, trying to grasp at what was happening.

"Explain the DNA then," Nate gruffly asked.

"I suppose... it must've..." Melinda panickily grappled for the right answer.

"I would warn you, Detective, my advice to my client at this time is to not answer any more of your questions, however leading they may be," the lawyer added, throwing a pointed stare at Melinda, who was still gawking down at the bloodied shirt.

"That's fine. Makes it more interesting that way," Nate said with a knowing smirk. He wasn't sure that Melinda had the capability to remain quiet for very long at all. "Tell me what the fight was about."

Melinda looked startled. "Which fight?" she asked.

Sam stirred in his chair. "Interesting you say 'which' fight instead of 'what' fight — sounds like it was common for you and your daughter to violently fight."

"Did this one get out of control, Melinda?" Dropping all formality Nate pressed on. "Had Lina crossed the final line? Had your daughter taken away a bit too much of the attention and made you snap?" He finished,

"We understand why you did it, Melinda, after everything you've gone through. Get it off your chest and tell us how it felt," Sam pushed.

Still Melinda remained silent, but Nate could see herself physically stopping the words from tumbling out of her mouth. "Blood, DNA, motive, opportunity and history of a rocky relationship with the victim. Added together, Melinda, it does not look good. If you have anything to tell us now is the time to do it," Nate finished, taking a casual stance in his chair.

For minutes they waited. Nate began tapping the tip of his pen against the table. It was a small sound but in a silent, constricting room it bounced off the walls and vibrated in everybody's ears. Still staring at Melinda, Nate could see her breath become quicker and shorter the quicker he tapped.

She snapped. "Stop it!" Melinda screamed. "Just stop! Leave me alone. I can't be here. I have to leave!" she repeated over and over again whilst grappling for the door.

"Melinda," Nate warmly said, "why don't you sit down and tell us what happened, it will make you feel better." Gently throwing his arm around her shoulders to guide her back to her seat, Nate gradually calmed her down again.

"I swear to you, Detective, I did not do this," Melinda whispered.

149

Chapter Forty-Six

"What do you think?" Nate asked, leaning against the now closed door of the interview room.

Sam let out a frustrated sigh. "I honestly don't know. My head is telling me that if we press for this, CPS will gladly take it and win. All the evidence fits."

"But?" Nate pressed.

Sam looked at the door behind them with a conflicted look. "It doesn't feel right."

Nate nodded. He understood because he felt the same way. Melinda was not a good mother, that was clear and her feelings for her child were not even remotely normal. He wouldn't put it past her to murder her child, but the way Lina died did not relate to Melinda. It was too physical, Melinda was a woman who enjoyed throwing abusive insults at her targets, not throw punches at them. Poison, he could see, neglect definitely, but a shove from the top of the stairs? Nate wasn't so sure. "You're right, it doesn't, but I'm not sure we can ignore this kind of evidence," Nate finally said.

"So, what DO we do?" Sam asked, confused.

Nate could feel the wheels turning in his head. "We keep her here, send in Ruby to evaluate her fully and we keep investigating. As far as the outside world knows, Melinda Ryker is our prime suspect but we cannot rule any of the others out."

Sam smiled as, for the third time since stepping out of the interview room, Nate checked his phone. "Waiting on someone, boss?" he asked coyly.

"What?" Nate replied, not really paying any more attention to his partner.

Sam decided to push his luck. "Does this have anything to do with the reason behind your foul mood for the last couple of days? Perhaps something to do with the beautiful Miss Ryker?"

The growl from his superior told him he'd made a tactical error in questioning his fascination of the intriguing woman. "Leave it alone, Detective Constable," Nate spat and stormed away.

Chapter Forty-Seven

Harry slammed the phone down on the granite table. The man had the gall to try and pull a stunt like this with Melinda arrested less than twenty-four hours ago — it was ridiculous! Dominic Shaw was a difficult man. Harry had come across him a few times in business over the years, but the last few years had put a strain on an already inactive relationship. Dominic was Rory's father and apparently wanted his son home. With news of the arrest circulating the local news and in many social circles that himself and Dominic both belonged to, Dominic was losing his patience with the agreed custody agreement.

The boy was HIS family as well and any interruption to his already emotional schedule could do harm. Harry knew, even before he'd finished the call, he was going to fight this. Rory would remain with him until the summer holidays were over in four weeks' time. Petty behaviour, he knew, but Harry had no control over many things in his life right now. This he could control. This he could fight.

Logan chose that moment to walk down the thin metal stairs. Father and son stood metres apart, caught in a look that wouldn't end. "Look, son, I'm sorry for overreacting," Harry said softly.

Logan nodded but averted his eyes to the floor. He cleared his throat, mumbled a quick "its fine," and walked swiftly out of the door. The door slammed behind him and Harry swore he felt the room vibrate. It wasn't the first time he and his son had disagreed, nor would it be the last but this time was different, Harry was the one who had acted out of anger and hatred, he had taken out all of his frustration on his child, his boy, who had opened up his home to him and a woman he despised.

Harry had decided late the night before that he needed to pull his act together. Starting with actually running the company he had started so many years ago. Stepping through the large glass doors which were like the golden gates to his own empire, Harry let out a breath of relief. Strangely, it felt as if he were home after a long absence, when in truth it had been just under a fortnight and his house was his home not his work. His brogues made sharp clicking sounds as he walked across the pristine floor and made his way over the platoon of lifts lining the main wall. "Good morning, sir!" the cheerful voice of Maggie, the receptionist, hollered with a bright smile.

"Morning, Maggie," Harry said in reply but not nearly as cheerfully. The ring of an arriving lift caught Harry's attention and he quickened his walk to catch his ride up to the family of offices that held court on the top floor. The cliché music that played within the metal tin can juxtaposed everything Harry had been feeling for the last twelve days and grated on his nerves to no end.

Obviously, the office gossip train had not broken down with his absence as Riya was already waiting for him as the metal doors opened. Riya's worried expression was the first thing that struck Harry. "I'm fine, honey!" he implored. The last thing he wanted was Riya upset about his way of coping with death or lack of it in his case.

Riya looked at him skeptically. "You may think you're fine, but I know better," she said with a look of superiority and

153

both hands on her hips. Harry laughed at the sight of her. This was a pose she had not adopted since she was in her teens and he relished the memories that came with her all-knowing look. "I don't know why you're laughing, I am allowed to worry and am fully capable of holding down the fort if you need more time!" Riya finished as she became quieter and quieter so not to embarrass him.

Harry warmly placed his arm around her shoulders and began walking them in the direction of her office. "You, my love, are all I worry about, so it seems we're even."

Dramatically rolling her eyes, Riya snuggled into his side as they continued to chat about inconsequential things. A door closed and both of them looked up to see Logan walking towards them. Both gave him a nervous smile but he simply put his head down and gave them a wide birth and he sauntered over to the lifts from where they had just come. Looking at each other in confusion, they headed to the door which Logan had just come out of.

As he always was, at that time, Thomas sat already ensconced in work. He looked up and chuckled. "Uh oh, this looks like trouble!" he said jokingly.

"Logan was here early today," Harry said as he sat comfortably in the chair opposite.

"Yeah, he called in to see if I wanted a session at the gym later," Thomas replied casually. "Why are you both so interested?"

Both going to answer, Riya managed to speak first. "He's mad at me," she stated both firmly and sadly. The slight nod and knowing eyes from Thomas were not lost on her and she quietly excused herself and went back to work. As she left, business continued just like usual and both Thomas and Harry settled into the day's chaos.

Chapter Forty-Eight

The walls were suffocating her. The small window, that would give her a view of the outside world, was placed above where the wall met the ceiling as some sort of twisted joke. She was suffocating. Everything felt hot, her neck burned, and clothes itched. Melinda's breathing was becoming faster by the second. She ripped at the top of her station-issued sweatshirt and dragged her nails roughly over the fragile skin lining her neck. The more she scratched the more difficult it was to breath.

Darting her eyes around the small cell, Melinda rushed from side to side, forgetting where she was or why she was there. Her breathing became more ragged and loud as if the air itself was refusing to let her live. By that time tears were streaming down her bare face and most of her skin was red raw from aggressive clawing.

Gripping her hair and gritting her teeth, Melinda began viciously breathing through her open lips. The large metal door stood formidably in front of her, daring her. She ran the few steps towards him and placed her hands against the cool steel. Nobody came, nobody could feel the pain she was feeling, nobody cared. Melinda began slapping her hands forcibly on the door over and over again, still no one cared. Hands now red and throbbing out heat in a show of pain, Melinda pulled her neck back as far as she could and sharply brought her face to the door with a large gasp. Melinda had no idea how long she stood there, attacking the door with her delicate head. Blood poured into both her eyes and her mouth until the taste of metal filled every one of her senses. Melinda vaguely heard a series of deep bellows but was unaware and uncaring while the pain let her feel something real. Her weapon of choice suddenly disappeared and a band of arms like steel wrapped around her waist while strong hands steadied her own. That was all Melinda remembered because almost instantly everything faded away and her world went dark.

Chapter Forty-Nine

Four days, closing in on four nights and the phone had rung at the same time every night. Twice. What was between them was fast and fierce — the idea of losing him completely terrified her which was why when the phone made its piercing tone, she shuddered in joy but never answered. Why couldn't he understand she was doing this for him? It was hurting her to hurt him, but it was for the best!

Waiting, not bothering to pay attention to the mindless drivel that was playing on the screen in front of her, Riya considered her current situation. At this point there was no use in denying that she was in lust with the persistent detective. It sounded so trivial, so carnal to say she was simply 'in lust' with the man but it was far too soon to say what she truly felt, it made her feel stupid just thinking about it. Rain poured down and ran down her windows by the litre, still no call. Maybe he had given up on her. It's what she had told him to do but the reality was far worse than she had imagined. Curling herself into a ball at the end of her sofa, Riya laid her head on the padded arm rest and closed her eyes, not sleeping just enduring the pain within.

Thunder rolled over the sky and an occasional flash of lightening lit up the room around her. At first, she didn't notice the loud banging against her door as it mixed perfectly with the storm outside, but it came more relentlessly than even the weather. Riya made her way to the door, not knowing who would be mad enough to be out in this kind of weather, it never occurred to her to check through the small peephole for who was disturbing her silent suffering. After opening the door Riya couldn't speak. Nate stood with both hands on the door frame, his head leaning forward, and his eyes were heavy. "Nate?" Riya managed to ask huskily.

"I can't do it," was all that Nate said before standing upright and stalking towards her. His hands covered the sides of her face and brought her lips to meet his. Nate was dripping wet from the rain, but Riya didn't care — he was here! Nate's lips wouldn't relent as they branded her to him. His tongue invaded her mouth, making her gasp. Moving his hands from her face down to her hips, he pressed against her and moved her, so she was pressed between the wall and the man tormenting her. On their own accord her hands went to the buttons on his shirt and began opening them roughly. Nate moved his hands off her body for only a second as he ripped his shirt off his shoulders and grabbed the bottom of hers, pulling it quickly over the top of her head. Riya's breathing had become erratic as she reached for his neck making him take her lips again. His hands made their way up her now bare stomach and painfully took their time teasing her bra-covered breasts. Trying to diffuse her never-ending heat for this man, Riya fumbled with his belt. Learning she couldn't do this in her current state without looking, she reluctantly pulled their mouths apart to tackle the buckle.

Nate took the opportunity to move his lips over the slope of her neck, taking extra time to nibble on her ear lobe, making her moan from the back of her throat. He heard the sound of his belt and buckle landing on the hardwood floor and almost shouted in relief. Nate pulled off the tight leggings and underwear she was currently wearing and growled in satisfaction when she was finally naked in front of him. Riya was in no mood to wait and grabbed his boxers which came off quickly in their heightened state of arousal. She wound her arms around his neck, and he took the lead.

Covering her behind with his large hands, Nate guided her legs up and around his hips. The loud moan from them both, paired with the rain pattering on the roof were only thing either of them could think about. Nate teased her with his fingers as she scraped her nails across his back. When he swiftly entered her, the feel of him was enough to make her cry out. Never in her life had she felt this alive with pleasure and it was all because of this man. As he started moving their eyes locked and the frantic dance continued. She couldn't get enough of him, couldn't touch him enough! Gasping loudly as the pace continued to quicken, Nate buried his face into her shoulder, making inconsequential sounds every time they moved as one. Riya was now frantic and grabbing onto Nate as if he were her lifeline. Nate, obviously just holding onto his control, pinned her arms up and over her head as he moved them towards their peaks. Riya knew what was coming as the pleasure started burning faster and hotter. Her eyes shut in ecstasy and light burst behind her eyelids. She was vaguely aware of Nate coming to his own release and gently releasing her hands so they could rest against his shoulders.

For minutes afterwards they stood entangled and breathing heavily. Riya stroked her hands into his thick hair as he roamed her body freely. Nate leant back so he could rest his forehead against hers. His eyes made her heart expand, such hope and undeniable lust. She gave him a wide grin and stroked his cheek.

"Hi," Nate whispered with his own large smile.

Riya giggled and lowered her legs, she slipped her hand into his and led him upstairs. "Hi yourself," Riya whispered as she pulled him into her bedroom. Whatever might come their way they could deal with tomorrow. Tonight, he was all hers.

Chapter Fifty

Darkness surrounded her, her eyelids wouldn't lift, and it felt like someone had weighed her body down with rocks. There was something locked around both her wrists and ankles but without being able to see, Melinda had no idea what the restraints were and who had put them there. A pounding head was the only thing she was able to feel. "Melinda," whispered something through the darkness but Melinda made the decision to ignore it. Whatever it was it didn't sound like it could be any kind of cure for her currently throbbing head. "Melinda." The voice persisted and Melinda mentally swore. "I know you can hear me. Why not try and open your eyes?" Soft as the voice was, it in no way tempted her out of her stupor.

The feel of a hand gently grasping her own startled Melinda, working almost like a jump start to her eyes which opened with a piercing pain. Moving her pupils to see who her companion was, Melinda was surprised to find an older lady looking sympathetically at her. The woman had grey hair except for the neon green stripe that made up her fringe and she smelled of Patchouli so much, it made Melinda's nose wrinkle up in protest. "There you go!" the stranger said optimistically. Melinda tried to raise her head to gain some sort of idea of where she was and why she felt as if there were road works going on within her skull. "No, no, no, dear, that won't do you any good. You have quite the head injury from what I hear." At those words Melinda wanted to scream. She could do whatever she wanted to do no matter what this out-of-date hippie said. She tried sitting up fully this time and had to let out a small yelp. The stranger laid a gentle hand on her shoulder and helped her back into her previous position.

Apparently, her eyes gave her thoughts away and the stranger chuckled. "No, don't look at me like that, dear, I'm only here to help!" The stranger nodded while daring to pat her hand as if she were a child. "In any case, I can see you have questions, yes?" Melinda managed a sound of acknowledgement but couldn't seem to control the use of her mouth and tongue. "You are in the hospital after you repeatedly rammed your head against a rather large door." The stranger continued after a pause of amusement, "A tip, dear, if you want a fight, next time chose an opponent that is not made of solid metal." Another tap on the hand and Melinda had had enough.

"Who are you?" Melinda managed to choke out angrily.

"Oh! Where are my manners? My name is Ruby and I'm a psychologist," Ruby stated proudly.

That got Melinda's attention! Sitting up despite the pain, Melinda prepared for the fight ahead. "Well, I don't need you, so you can just get on your way," she said, waving her hand dismissively.

"Yes, Melinda, you do need me," Ruby said, taking on a more serious tone. This woman was so sure of herself and the need for her existence and it irked Melinda that anyone had that kind of self-esteem. Of course, she wouldn't tell the quirky therapist that, she'd only want to over-analyse it.

"You know nothing about what I need, and I definitely

don't need someone like you telling me why I am the way I am," Melinda, trying to sound more put together than she felt, said.

Looking Melinda dead in the eye, Ruby smirked at the woman's denial. "Melinda, like it or not, you DO need me. You're charged with murdering your own daughter and this morning you took it upon yourself to try and bash your own skull in. Whether you like it or not, Melinda, I am your last hope. You either talk to me and let me do what I do best…"

"Or?" Melinda interrupted, hoping the annoying woman would get to the point.

"*Or,* you prove to the judge, who will be presiding over this case, that you aren't showing willing and seeking the help you so obviously need and landing yourself the maximum sentence that first degree murder comes with," Ruby said, not wanting to give Melinda an inch. Almost instantly Ruby felt the fear finally dawn on Melinda and when the other woman looked up, Ruby's hunch was confirmed, Melinda's walls were coming down. Time to start work.

Chapter Fifty-One

Riya had no idea what the time was, and she didn't care. All she cared about was that Nate's large frame was cradling her against his chest from behind whilst their hands and fingers entwined out in front of them. There was no rush, no impending deadlines, just the weekend with Nate to look forward to. Feeling Nate place a kiss on the curve of her neck made Riya smile. It wasn't often that she just existed, but in this moment with this man she was more than happy to pretend that the world outside didn't exist.

Unfortunately, it did. "What happens now?" Riya asked quietly.

Shifting his body slightly so she was able to feel his arousal, he gave a husky laugh. "I might have a few ideas."

Giggling loudly when he tickled the skin of her hips, Riya screeched, "Nate! I'm serious!"

After another kiss, Nate lifted himself ever so slightly so he could see into her eyes. "I'm finished pretending that I don't want this."

Completely confused about how anything between them could be long-lasting, especially at the moment, Riya wasn't sure she was functioning correctly. "But…"

"Here's how I see it," Nate interrupted as he turned her so they were face to face. "Neither of us is going to be able to pretend that this didn't happen, so the best way forward is to lay low until the investigation is finished with and then see where things go," he said, finishing with a kiss to her lips, which lasted longer than either them had intended.

Pulling away by pushing her head back further into her pillow, Riya played with his hair as she spoke sincerely. "I just don't want you to be hurt."

"As long as I've got you, nothing is going to hurt me." Nate hung his head suddenly and scrunched his eyes up. "Too corny?" Nate asked with half a grin and half a grimace.

Laughing again, Riya smoothed her hands over his head and nodded sarcastically. "Definitely."

Kissing her into silence, Nate joined the laughter. "You, Riya Ryker, are going to be the death of me!"

Returning his look with one filled of humour, Riya replied, "I can guarantee it'd be a good way to go!" And with her last teasing statement the whole process started again.

Hours later, both exhausted into a deep sleep, Riya was startled awake by an obnoxious knock on the door. Never in her life had she had so many visitors in the space of just a few weeks, times were definitely changing. At the second knock, Riya sighed and slipped out of bed. She'd already donned Nate's large shirt, as if it were already second nature, but when her feet touched the cold wooden floor, she rushed to pull a pair of her old and comfy bed socks over her frozen feet. Looking back, she smiled when she saw Nate still sound asleep with his arm outstretched towards her vacant pillow.

Hurrying through the house, Riya didn't even stop to consider what she looked like. Once again forgetting to check who was calling at her door so early in the morning, she swung the door wide open and welcomed her unknown guest with her most dazzling smile. When Riya realised who was in front of her the smile faltered, she was in shock but not necessarily in a bad way. "Logan!" Riya gleefully announced.

Logan stood on his sister's doorstep. God, he'd missed her. When anything of note happened in his life, she was the one he wanted to talk to. "Hi," Logan nervously greeted her. Riya moved to the side to let him in and he gladly accepted the invitation. Walking into her homely little cottage made him feel more at peace than he had since Lina died. He automatically went straight into the kitchen and sat at one of the stools in preparation. "Tea?" Riya asked as he watched her reach for the kettle.

"Yeah, that'd be good, thanks," Logan replied stiffly.

"Look, Logan, I'm sorry. I shouldn't've said what I did. I was confused and taken back by the whole you and Lina thing, I should've just trust..." Riya rambled

"No. I'm sorry, I shouldn't have reacted that way. I think I'm just a bit lost after losing Lina that I felt I needed to be angry at someone. That someone should not have been you," Logan said honestly. He was rewarded when Riya ran around the breakfast bar to envelop him in a hug. "I've missed you."

"I've missed you too!" Riya replied almost in tears. The emotional reunion was interrupted by the whistling of the kettle sitting on the hob. Pouring drinks out for them, Riya was vibrating with energy which was unusual given her lack of love for mornings.

"You're very happy this morning?" Logan asked skeptically teasing.

Riya dumped both tea bags into the bin behind her. "I can't be glad to be on speaking terms with my brother again?" his sister asked, keeping her face hidden.

"Of course, you can but on any other day you'd have

punched me for waking you up at the un-holy hour of eight o'clock," Logan finished with a wink.

Ignoring him completely, Riya put the milk away in the fridge. "Have you noticed a difference in Thomas recently?"

Laughing at her diversion tactic, Logan said, "I guess. He came to me the other day and asked if I wanted to go to the gym. I can't remember the last time he did that. Why do you ask?"

"I showed up at his house the other day and he was different. Happier, freer. We had a good night, although my head didn't feel that way the next day. We've gone to lunch twice since then, I think something's changed for the better," Riya explained.

Logan was clasping his mug in both hands, nodding. "Maybe we should do dinner or something just the three of us? Could be a good way to put the last few weeks behind us."

Riya began nodding and was about to respond with enthusiasm when Logan's eyes darted to the dark hallway behind the kitchen. The shuffling footsteps caught him by surprise. Raising his eyebrows at her blush, he asked, "Have you got company, little sister?"

Riya's eyes were quickly darting between her brother and the still-hidden person behind the shadows. "Ummm... yes. Logan, you know Na... Detective Richards." Hearing his name, the man himself stepped out from the darkness, he walked towards Riya and placed a kiss on her forehead. Obviously, Riya had stolen his shirt as the man was walking around in only his jeans whilst looking far too intently at his sister.

"Yes, I do. Good to see you, Detective," Logan responded tersely.

"You too," Nate replied casually, not as tense as either Ryker in the room.

Logan stood and adjusted his jacket and cleared his throat. "Thanks for the tea. I think I'd better head off, I've got some work to do." Riya began to argue but he stopped her by gently hugging her and kissing the top of her head. "Give me a call later and we'll do lunch on Monday?" he asked, successfully smoothing over her unease.

"Absolutely! I'll call Thomas and see if he wants to join?" Riya asked questioningly.

"Sounds like a plan." Logan walked towards the door but shook his head when Riya started to follow. "I'll see myself out, you enjoy yourself!" Logan said, hoping she wouldn't be ashamed by being caught with a man in her bed. It wasn't her issue. What he was feeling was completely down to his own prejudices and worries. Logan gave her one last hug and made his exit.

Riya turned on her heel to face the man currently resting his hip on her kitchen's work bench. She smiled as he grabbed her half-finished cup of tea and took a long sip. As casually as she could, Riya asked, "Are you working today?" hoping the answer was no.

Placing the mug back down on the counter Nate walked over to her and put both his hands on each of her hips and shook his head. "Nope. I'm all yours until Monday. If that suits you?" he asked jokingly.

Smiling, lifting herself up to meet his lips, she murmured, "That definitely suits me."

Chapter Fifty-Two

The weekend had come and gone. Never in his whole career had Nate been irritated by his obligation to show up to work. After the best weekend of his life he was pleasantly exhausted. Riya was everything he had thought she would be. Their chemistry both in and out of bed was electric. The time he had spent simply talking with her had excited him more than any other conversation had managed, and after experiencing the bliss that came from being with her, he was now adamant he wouldn't be letting her go.

Nate had managed to leave his phone in the glove compartment of his car all weekend. He had no idea what awaited him as he returned. Walking through the automatic doors the hustle and bustle of reception was at its peak. Nodding a polite hello to the desk sergeant, Nate made his way through to his desk. He'd only just managed to place his coat haphazardly over the back of his chair when Sam came rushing towards him. "What's the rush, Sam?" Nate asked.

"Have you heard?" Sam asked, struggling to keep the latest developments to himself.

"Heard what?" Nate replied distractedly whilst trying to log onto the computer system.

"Melinda Ryker is in the hospital. Apparent suicide attempt." Even before Sam finished, Nate was rising to put his coat back over his shoulders preparing to deal with the colossal mess that was his murder case.

The drive to the hospital was a short one, both men considering the reasons behind Melinda's self-conflicted violence. Flashing their IDs at the nurses' station on the large sterile waiting room, the men walked swiftly through the hospital's corridors. Depressingly, in their line of work they quickly became very familiar with the hospital's layout, so much so the regular staff even knew them by name.

The cream door with a small window within its frame was all that separated the two men from the unstable woman whom they had left in a cell. Taking a deep breath, Nate pressed down on the cheap handle and shouldered his way into the room. Seeing Melinda lying in a nylon-covered bed took both men by surprise, the normally polished and put together Melinda was lain against the small cot of a bed with her face turned towards the small square window to her left. The hands that were usually manicured meticulously were chipped and rugged as her fragile-looking wrist remained cuffed with ugly yellow restraints with trademark gauzy, brown leather buckles.

Ruby stood as Nate and Sam entered the room. Both men nodded in her direction as a polite greeting then focused on the shell of a woman in front of them. Sam remained with his back glued to the wall, but Nate moved into a chair that was directly opposite the aging psychologist and right in front of Melinda's face. "Hello, Melinda," uttered Nate softly. Melinda's eyes didn't even flicker in recognition of the greeting. He looked at Ruby for advice and her nod of encouragement told him to keep trying. "Melinda, we will help you as much as we can — you just have to talk to us. Help us to make sure that something like this, or worse, doesn't happen again."

Melinda rolled her head to stare lifelessly at the ceiling. "I didn't do this, Detective, I did not push my daughter down the stairs, but you won't believe me. What is the point of pretending that we like each other? You made your mind up about me a long time ago. There's no point trying to plead my case with you."

Nate awkwardly pulled his jersey fabric chair closer to Melinda's side and continued. "Why don't you try and convince me of who you really are, Melinda?" Nate asked softly.

Melinda didn't move her head but rotated her eyes to look at him. "What is the point?" Melinda asked, taking on a flat tone. "You are a detective, you are not in the same league of men that I am accustomed to dealing with. You are worth nothing compared to the men that I have stood beside and, therefore, I have no interest in conversing or convincing you. I can guarantee that by the time a trial rolls around I will have been able to work my magic on whichever judge is passing judgement and I will make sure to leave you jobless in the process." Finishing on raised eyebrows, Melinda stayed still as Nate's face morphed into shock and surprise.

With his eyes darkening and voice lowering, Nate decided it was time to do away with pleasantries and sympathy. "Your case is solid with or without a confession. Even if you could find the intended judge, I doubt his sights are set so low as to look at the future ex-wife of one of this country's most respected businessmen. You're a career gold-digger that is closer to dotage than you'd like to admit. After this scandal, You. Are. Done," he said, punctuating his last words to really get his message across to the high and mighty likely murderer.

Melinda used bent elbows to lift her head and shoulders to meet the detective's harsh eyes. "You have no idea the power a woman like me has. Watch yourself, Detective, or you could be in bed like this very soon," she finished in a deadly cold voice.

"Threatening a police officer," Nate said, drawing in a breath through his already clenched teeth, "that won't look good on your record. Here I was thinking you wanted to stay out of jail, Melinda!" Nate joked sarcastically.

The fierce woman who had confronted him only moments before vanished in an instant. The tigress was replaced with a wide, tear-brimmed-eyed ghost. "Nate..." Ruby started, standing from her seat, and reaching for the siderail of the bed.

With an overemphasized shrug of his shoulders, Nate gave her a questioning look. "What was it, Melinda, a power play? Gain some sympathy so we entertain your innocence?"

"A word outside, Detective!" Ruby almost yelled. Moving Sam out of the way with a mere glance, she opened the door briskly and glared across the room at Nate waiting for him to obey her command.

Marching out behind the currently raging psychologist, Nate waited for her to begin her tirade with stiff arms on his hips. "Of all the men on this police force, I honestly thought you had two brain cells to rub together, but obviously I was wrong!"

"Ruby! The woman is a murderer at worst and gold-digging narcissist at best. If I need to make her cry to get justice for a twenty-one-year-old girl I do not need your permission," raged Nate, annoyed. He was fully aware that he had let this woman and her attitude towards the middle class get the better of him.

"There's something else behind Melinda's attitude and you know it. Give me some time and I will hopefully get some answers for you, but I will not get anywhere, if every time I take a step forwards, you take me two steps back," Ruby implored. "I cannot guarantee that she really is your murderer but we both know that she has to have something to do with why her daughter died."

Ruby's speech gave Nate time to get a firm grip on his temper. Pinching the top of his nose, he hung his head. "I know. I'm sorry. Did her outburst towards the door the other day teach us anything?" Nate asked with only a hint of hope.

Ruby sighed and leaned against the wall beside him. "She can't remember it, Nate. It's like she blacked out and became someone else, found a person inside of her that was capable of that kind of self-harm and let them take over." Nodding her head as if agreeing with herself, she continued, "She is a severely damaged soul. Numerous different people are within her and they are all scrambled into one sick hybrid that she's terrified of. I can't see any sort of judge that is going to even consider trying her in this kind of state."

"Shit!" Nate slapped his hands back against the wall. Running his hands through his hair, Nate looked back at Ruby. "Keep trying with her. Whether she's guilty or not there is something going on and that woman is at the centre of it."

Abruptly saying goodbye to Ruby, Nate stormed through the hospital to make his escape. Sam diligently followed him and watched as the mental war battled on inside his skull. The car felt claustrophobic as they drove through the familiar streets and Nate practically leapt out of the vehicle as soon as he had pulled on the handbrake. Sam tried, but failed to gain his attention as he flew into the dank station toilets. Nate placed both his hands on the off-white sink and looked at himself in the cloudy mirror. Living in the knowledge that he'd just verbally attacked a woman who was at her lowest and hadn't felt bad about it until minutes after. Every time he thought he'd solved a piece of this puzzle a wind came along and blew all the pieces away.

Nate splashed some tepid water over his face, shook himself dry, pulled himself together then confidently walked out into the station. Get through today, he told himself, and he could figure out a proper plan of action tomorrow. Tonight, he would relax, cook, and enjoy the company of the beautiful woman who meant far too much to him. This case was belittling and demeaning, always one step ahead of him, but he wouldn't let it win, he had too much waiting for him after it was finished!

Chapter Fifty-Three

Leather shoes echoing against the pavement, the mellow and humid air making him thankful for his linen shirt as Thomas hailed a taxi. Muttering his intended destination to his driver, Thomas sat back on the worn polyester seat and looked on through the window at the city he had grown to consider his own. As it blurred past him, Thomas chuckled to himself, two sessions in two days and he already felt lighter. Thomas had spent the first ninety-minute appointment discussing his particular information and his upbringing but today, for the first time since it happened, Thomas had opened up about his mother's death. As the eldest child, Thomas had always suspected that he recalled the most about the tragic events of that fateful day.

Simply speaking to the stranger had helped him. He could breathe again. Thomas was under no illusion that he still had a long way to go but his darkness was shared now, it was not only in his own hands, which for some reason helped. Quicker than he thought possible, the cab pulled up slowly to the curb outside the restaurant. Paying the driver swiftly, Thomas stepped out of the vehicle and buttoned his jacket.

In no time at all Thomas spotted the two people that were his companions for the evening. "Thomas!" squealed Riya enthusiastically as she danced over to him with her arms opened wide. Taking her hug happily, Thomas gave her a muffled hello and moved onto his brother. Logan looked somewhat surprised by his elder brother's hug rather than the usual friendly handshake but quickly recovered and returned the embrace.

"It's good to see you," whispered Logan solemnly into his ear. Thomas replied by slapping his hands onto his brothers back in agreement. Once the men had sat themselves down, the three siblings lined the circular table and began perusing the menu. Once the formalities of ordering had been taken care of, they began the ancient ritual of teasing and reminiscing.

About halfway through their main course Riya placed her knife and fork down gently. "Do you think Dad's OK?" she asked wistfully.

Both brothers, understanding that their delicious food would have to wait until their sister's mind had been eased, put their own cutlery on the table more robustly than Riya had. "He's just grieving, Riya. Give him time," replied Thomas quietly.

Riya aimed her eyes up towards the ceiling in a moment of thought. Deciding against allowing her brothers to continue with their meal, Riya took a deep breath indicating she was less than thrilled with her eldest brother's trivial response. Looking at each other with knowing eyes, both brothers faced their sister head on.

"Riya, he doesn't cope with death well. Least of all deaths that he blames himself for," Logan said knowingly.

Riya looked wide eyed at the men next to her, not really understanding why their tone had suddenly dropped. "But it wasn't his fault. Lina dying it should upset him, yes, but surely…"

Interrupting his sister before she got too excited

explaining away their father's outbursts of late, Thomas interrupted. "You were too young when Mum died. You won't remember the way Dad was for the first few months after the accident... it wasn't good," he finished sadly.

"I wasn't that young, Thomas!" Riya replied in half a whisper and half a shout.

Thomas and Logan looked at each other in agreement but Thomas was the only one to speak. "You were six, Riya. You were their surprise, their unexpected angel. Dad made sure you were in bed before he lost control." Even before Thomas had finished, Logan had picked up his tumbler full of whiskey and downed the double amber shot.

Riya let out a half-hearted laugh. "You are not seriously suggesting that Dad..." Taking note of both her brothers' serious stares, Riya cut her statement short. Looking from one brother to another, Riya wanted answers. "Thomas?" she questioned and when she received no response, she began on the other man who had apparently been holding out on her. "Logan?"

Logan gave his sister a heartfelt stare and decided to tell her the whole truth. She needed to hear it and they needed to say it. "It's important that you know it only happened twice and since then..."

"Please just spit it out, Logan, you're making me nervous," Riya interrupted.

"When Mum died, after the shock had worn off, Dad started to drink. He wasn't himself, he was distant, he was cold, he was nasty." Riya rose to interrupt him again, but he beat her to it. "To everyone but YOU. You were the spit of her, he could lose himself in your six-year-old world and not face real life. But then you'd be at school, be watching some cartoon or you'd go to bed and the happy-go-lucky father disappeared," Logan finished with just a hint of cynicism.

Thomas watched as Riya took a large gulp of nothing. Reaching out, he took her hand in his and took over the burden of telling Riya the truth from his brother. "It only happened twice and since then he has been physically and mentally making up for it to us and to himself." At Riya's singular nod, Thomas decided to continue. "He lost it. Drinking clouded his head and he lashed out. He'd had a rough day and needed someone to take it out on. The first time it was a few slaps each but the second time nothing could have stopped him." The tears forming on the edge of her eyelashes made Thomas stop. He squeezed her hand firmly and looked at her to make sure she was truly understanding what they were trying to explain to her.

"He beat you?" Riya rasped out in shock.

"No lasting damage, Riya. He made sure to cut down the drinking, got help and never laid his hands on us, or you, again. He was struggling and didn't know how to handle it properly, that's all," Logan stated, understanding now that his sister needed comforting more than he needed to wallow in self-pity.

By the time they'd finished, Riya was physically shaking. Her tears had nothing to do with her own pain but the thought of her brothers' pain. They'd been grieving their mother, a mother they remembered a far lot more clearly than she did, and their father had beaten them both in some twisted way of dealing with his own heartbreak. Sitting there wondering how all three men, who had been her whole life for the best part of twenty years, had kept this secret from her, Riya felt Thomas move his elegant chair closer to hers and then cradle her in his arms while she wept.

Thomas felt the shudders run through Riya's body and mentally cursed himself and Logan for doing this to her in such a public place. They had destroyed her perfect image of their father forever and Thomas wasn't sure she could forgive their father as quickly as they had. In the corner of his eye, he could see Logan wave down a waiter for the bill, effectively ending their dinner in a more somber way than he would have liked.

As she watched her brothers both drive away in taxis, Riya jumped into her own car with her mind still racing. Digging for her phone in her seemingly larger than normal bag, Riya couldn't stop the events of tonight from circling around her brain over and over again. With a press of a few buttons Riya could hear the dialing tone which mysteriously calmed her racing pulse and waited. Within a few rings she heard a voice that put a smile on her tear-streaked face. "Finished with dinner already?" Nate asked her warmly through the phone.

Taking a deep breath in order to hide the wobble in her voice, Riya replied, "Yeah, turned out to be a bit too soon for a fun night out."

"Riya, what's wrong?" Nate asked, immediately worried.

Sniffling down the phone knowing that she'd given her impending breakdown away, Riya decided she had to see him, if only to make herself feel a little bit better. "I found something out at dinner. I can't tell you, they made me promise, but..." she stumbled finding the words, believing she sounded ridiculous.

A soothing reply floated through her currently shaking phone. "Riya, whatever it is, honey, you can ask," uttered Nate strongly.

"Can I see you tonight?" Riya whispered down the phone, terrified of his rejection.

"I'll be at yours in ten," was all Nate said and immediately the clouds in Riya's head began to shift.

Chapter Fifty-Four

Nate watched the lights of Riya's small compact drive up next to his already parked car. The engine turned off and he watched in fascination as her high-heeled covered feet stepped out one by one. The woman slowly making her way towards him was the epitome of class, she was beautiful, sleek, and funny. Not in a million years had he imagined ever being so lucky as to find a woman like Riya Ryker and now that he had her, he wasn't going to let her go. They had obstacles to overcome but he was already working on solving them, the first of which was to find out who had put such a desolate expression on her face.

With the weakest of smiles, Riya stepped past him with the keys outstretched in her hands. Opening the door, he followed her into the darkness of the house. Nate watched as Riya moved around her kitchen. She hadn't said a word, but still her face remained misted over with sadness and it was killing him. When the woman in question grabbed her kitchen worktop with her dainty hands and looked to the sky in an effort to calm herself, Nate had had enough.

Walking over to her, Nate didn't ask permission but turned her into his arms. The small act of affection was all it took, the damn broke and the tears flowed. All Nate could do was stand there and whisper words of calming comfort while he felt each shudder to his very core. Slowly, he moved them into her small lounge and sat, for what felt like hours, just holding her. After the crying subsided, he lifted his head from hers and lifted her chin between his fingers. Now looking her in the eyes, Nate wanted answers. "Riya, tell me who upset you." His voice was still warm, but he could feel his anger bubbling beneath the surface.

"I promised them I wouldn't tell," replied Riya, hiccupping.

Tilting his head in silent disbelief that she wouldn't eventually tell him, Nate asked, "Why not?"

Releasing another long breath, this time through her nose, Riya paused. A promise made to her brothers was important, but this man had dropped everything to be by her side the minute she'd asked. Did he deserve to be left completely in the dark?

"Riya?" prompted Nate hopefully.

"I promise it has nothing to do with Lina." Watching Nate's shoulders drop in relief, she knew she'd said the right thing. "Something happened after my mum died that was just..." Riya couldn't continue as the flashbacks of Thomas and Logan's hurt faces popped into her head.

Deciding that she was too worked up to go into any more detail, Nate chose to change the subject. "Tell me about her."

Sitting up from her position against his chest Riya asked, "Who? My mum?" Wiping her eyes.

"Yeah, tell me about her," Nate said, nodding his head encouragingly.

"I can't really remember much about her. I see her smiling sometimes and doing things like reading to me in bed, but other than that everything I know I learnt off Logan or Thomas," muttered Riya sadly, slouching down into the sofa.

Keeping his hand stroking her hair, Nate was wary not to

ask anything too loud, trying not to disturb the peace that had now settled over her. "Not your father?" he asked, taking note of the way she had just stiffened at the mention of Harry Ryker. Nate thought it interesting that her body's response was to tense at the reference of the man she, up until then, appeared to adore but kept his musings to himself.

"No," stated Riya firmly. Shaking her head to clear the fog from her mind, she sat up straight, gave him the best smile she could manage and asked, "Fancy a drink?"

Chapter Fifty-Five

Something was wrong. Thomas had come to see him for some reports but barely looked him in the eye and Riya, who usually was in work come hell or high water, had called in sick and ignored both of his worried phone calls. Thomas returned with a now complete set of reports and tried to make a speedy exit until Harry intervened. "Thomas."

Stopping, Thomas froze but didn't turn around. Afraid that his expression would give him away, he twisted his head slightly to acknowledge his father's words. Thomas waited for the question he wasn't sure how to answer. "What's going on?" said Harry forcefully.

Accepting his fate, Thomas spun to face his father and tilted his head ever so slightly to the left. "I had dinner with Logan and Riya last night." Truthfully telling his father only part of the story.

"Ah, so your sister is in bed with another hangover?" chuckled Harry seemingly forgetting his worries from only moments before. Unfortunately, Thomas's lack of humour made him look at his son questioningly.

"No, Dad, Riya's not hungover," Thomas stated quietly. "She knows, Dad." Harry's look of stunned silence told Thomas that his father understood exactly what his sister now knew.

Glaring at his son, knowing the can of worms that had

been spilled to his only daughter. "How?" Harry managed to growl across his desk.

"She asked, Dad, so we told her. You couldn't expect us to lie for you," stated Thomas ruthlessly. For the first time, Harry realised exactly how daring his son could be. The boy who used to cower every time he'd heard a shout, was now a man that bent the knee to no one, not even his own father.

"It was a private issue!" roared Harry aggressively. The smell of the spirited alcohol, ever present in his breath, was not lost on his eldest son. Harry stepped around his large desk and moved towards his son menacingly.

"A private issue, Father, that neither I, nor Logan were willing to keep from Riya any longer," Thomas said quietly but firmly. The look on his father's face would have scared him fifteen years ago but no more. Revealing this secret would set him and his brother free and the three siblings could begin to put the past behind them and move towards the future.

Harry lowered his eyelids, so he was glowering at his son. "A secret that was not your business to share!" he shouted.

"Not my business?" Thomas asked incredulously. "Hiding three broken ribs from anyone that could take us away from you is not my business?" yelled Thomas hurtfully. Facing his father and watching the last decade and a half disappear, Thomas saw the change in his persona even before Harry began towards him with his teeth bared. In the blink of an eye Harry raised his fist and brought it down against Thomas's jaw forcefully. The younger man, who had not done anything to defend himself, now brought his own fingers up and touched his bleeding lip to examine the blood. Ruefully smiling towards his heavily breathing father, Thomas evilly smiled and rubbed his hands together.

It seemed to take Harry a while to truly understand what he had done. Eyes changing from hatred to concern, Harry reached his open palm out towards his child's face to console him, however Thomas slapped it away as he gave one last look of defiance and sauntered out of the room. For a long time, Harry simply stood and vacantly looked through the still open door. Hanging his head in shame, he sat frustratedly back in his office chair. With nothing else to do other than relive his foolish actions, both today and in the past, Harry violently opened the top drawer of his desk and removed the large bottle of vodka from its hiding place.

Chapter Fifty-Six

Fingers flying across her keyboard, Riya focused solely on clearing her work in a timely fashion, hoping that the faster she typed the more she could ease the anxiety resting in the pit of her stomach. All morning she had been jumping at every small sound and shadow, fearing that it might be her father. It wasn't that she was afraid of him per se just that she had no idea how she would be able to stand the sight of the man who had beat his children. Riya considered the looks on the two men's faces as they had divulged the shameful secret that had been buried within fake pleasantries. Despite the forgiving words both men had spoken she could feel the pain behind their words, physically the boys may have healed but mentally the men had suffered every day of their lives.

A tapping on her office door stopped the incessant click of her keys. Looking up, Riya sighed in relief as her brother made his way across the carpeted floor. The relief only lasted a second as Thomas lifted his head to speak. With a gasp, Riya ran around to lift Thomas's chin. Examining the split and swelling lip, Riya no longer felt the need to cry, all she could feel was the burning anger of betrayal and loyalty. "It's fine, Riya," said Thomas as he flinched his way out of her tender grip.

"It is not fine!" retorted Riya, leaning back against the edge of her delicate desk. "What happened?"

"I told him that you know," mumbled Thomas guiltily.

Shocked by his statement, Riya's eyes went wide and she was at a loss as to what to say. "And that was his response?" Waving her hands in the direction of his face. Thomas nodded sadly. "He can't do this," Riya harshly whispered and stepped around her brother in an effort to confront her father. Knowing his sister too well to doubt her intentions, Thomas's hand whipped out and caught Riya by the wrist.

"No, Riya," he growled.

Resisting the urge to stamp her feet like a child in the midst of a tantrum, Riya glared at her brother. "I don't understand!" she shouted in pain.

"It's done, Riya. He has no power over us and this," pointing towards his lip, Thomas continued, "proved it. He hit me and I didn't flinch, showed no fear."

This only seemed to intensify Riya's anger. "You shouldn't have to prove it to him! He should never have laid his hands on you!" On the verge of screaming, Riya placed her open palm against her forehead and began pacing the room. Every image she had from her childhood falling apart as if it were all an illusion, her father no longer her hero and her brothers no longer untouchable. With no sense of how long she had spent wearing the carpet thin, Riya suddenly looked up when a movement at her door caught her eye.

Harry Ryker stood in the doorway looking like a shell of his former self. The usually suave, put-together businessman, was standing with a disheveled suit, scruff on his chin and a haunted look in his eye. He flicked his gaze to his son's face and immediately shut his eyes in horror, it had not been a dream. He had regressed to the angry beast he kept hidden within. What was worse, his daughter was now looking at him as if he were a stranger!

"Riya…" Harry began tentatively, but in response all she did was to shake her head, sit down at her desk and pretend he wasn't in the room. In an act of pure desperation Harry looked for support from his son, only to be greeted with dead eyes and a shake of the head. Sloping off to nowhere in particular, Harry wondered if his family could ever be the same again.

Chapter Fifty-Seven

"Three days, Melinda. You're going to have to talk to me at some point," Ruby cajoled the resistant patient in front of her. After what the doctors considered an attempted suicide, Melinda had been moved to the psychiatric ward of St John's hospital. No longer bound to the small bed by restraints, the woman drifted between complete denial and hysteria but was no longer able to hurt herself in the small padded room. The vacant eyes staring back at her worried Ruby the most. After first watching Melinda in an interview setting, Ruby, despite her many years of experience, was astounded at the change in the confident and self-assured woman.

As was their routine for the last few days, Melinda's response was to slightly turn her head away from the psychologist. "Come on!" Ruby joked. "At this point what have you got to lose?"

Returning to her previous position Melinda slowly looked Ruby up and down and smirked. "I let you mess with my mind and then I get put in some godforsaken prison somewhere with no service and no comfort. I don't think so," said Melinda, rolling her shoulders into the mattress behind her. "However, if I say nothing, I get to serve out whatever time they give me, which won't be a lot given they believe me to be a nutcase, in here. Not necessarily the classiest place on Earth but better than a cell," looking rather pleased with herself, Melinda finished.

"That sounded almost like a confession, Melinda," Ruby stated accusatorily.

"I didn't kill my daughter, Doctor. I understand it's the easy option, so I'm probably going down for it. Why shouldn't I try and make the best of this crappy situation?" Melinda replied plainly.

"If what you're saying is true, a woman in your position wouldn't be this resigned to their fate — not this quickly," Ruby said, trying to prompt an outburst or even a flicker of emotion.

Ruby was not disappointed as Melinda's eyes turned glassy. "I didn't do this crime, but I deserve the punishment for it. We can't all be psychologists with the pensions of four ex-husbands supporting us." Melinda twisted over in bed, stared across at the room, lifted one end of her mouth into a twisted smile and raised one eyebrow, and she muttered the words Ruby had feared for over a decade.

Chapter Fifty-Eight

Nate was sitting at his desk leaning forward with frustration as the person on the other end of the phone continued to give him the run around. Files needed to be found, statements collected, the record room needed to be searched, the same old lines over and over again until his head began to burn. Nate felt wrong, dirty even, he shouldn't be doing this to her, she didn't need him to dredge up the past, but something was telling him he had to, something deep and dark.

The death of Sophia Ryker felt like it could mean more than just a simple tragedy. While most of him still believed that the second Mrs Ryker committed this murder there was a small inkling of doubt that had been keeping him up each night. On the outside, the Ryker clan looked perfect but there was something wrong with the picture-perfect life they presented to the rest of the world that he couldn't quite put his finger on. If his suspicions were correct, Riya had been told some information last night and it had shaken her to her very core. Seeing the look of pain on her face was something Nate didn't want to experience ever again and made him even more determined to unearth the lies that had brought her suffering to the surface. A firm believer that the past shapes a person's future, Nate had decided to find out whatever he could about the events that shaped the Ryker family into the misshapen nightmare that they were today.

The flash of brightly coloured polyester drew his attention away from the drivel being spouted at him from the other end of the phone. Sequin-covered moons adorned the lively purple coat with pink fur lining the edges that moved with every breath the wearer took. Without looking up, Nate gave Ruby a large smile and without so much as a word to his caller he bluntly put the phone down, rescuing his ears from further abuse. "What can a man like me do for a beautiful woman like you today?" said Nate charmingly.

"Don't think you can charm your way around me, Nate. I've been ringing you all morning!" Ruby urged with a flick of her short neon hair.

"You know I'd never willingly ignore you, Ruby." Still trying to work his magic against the scowl that Ruby had been pulling for the last few days.

Ruby tilted her head and looked at him suspiciously. "I've just come back from the hospital," she said with an accompanying look, which lead Nate to believe he'd done something wrong. Feigning an innocent look towards the woman, Nate jutted his chin out, signaling for Ruby to elaborate. "That woman is a mess," whispered Ruby venomously.

"By all accounts, Ruby, she's been that way for years." Not willing to judge this case by his emotions, any more than he already had, Nate remained impassive to Ruby's obvious blind spot for her patient.

"That woman is sick, Nate!" screeched Ruby horrifically. Realising that everybody else in the open office had stopped their own work to watch the station's psychologist fall apart.

"OK," Nate whispered whilst pulling out a chair, settling her down and covering her hands with his. "Tell me what's wrong?"

Satisfied that her concerns were now being listened to, Ruby took a deep breath and composed herself once again. For a therapist, Nate was always shocked at her ability to flipflop her emotions to suit her purpose. Squeezing her hands once more in reassurance, Nate convinced Ruby to explain. "She's broken, Nate. Melinda's past has destroyed any healthy ideals she has about relationships and basic life principles. After the last few days, she's shut down completely believing there is no point in continuing to function."

Struggling to get the point of Ruby's insight, Nate sighed. "Ruby, help me understand here. We know Melinda is damaged but…"

Interrupting Nate mid-sentence, Ruby anxiously gripped his arm and in a whispered voice said, "Melinda didn't do this!"

Briefly squeezing his eyes shut and shifting his head to the left, Nate was at a loss. "Ruby…" he tried to console.

A glare from the woman in front of him told Nate he was doing the wrong thing in trying to convince her of Melinda's guilt. Of course, Nate wasn't sure of the fact himself but the sooner the older woman came to terms with the most likely possibility, the better. "How many times do I have to prove that my methods work for you to believe me? Melinda is innocent, mark my words," Ruby finished.

Watching his slightly eccentric colleague become flustered over a woman who had proved herself to be a master manipulator, Nate wished he hadn't involved Ruby in any of it. The woman was good at deduction, brilliant at reading people and a genius at figuring out minds but she never took prime suspects on as clients and never became this personally involved with them. "What did she say to you?" Nate asked softly.

Shuddering as she clenched her hands underneath his repeatedly. "She knows things... things that she shouldn't be able to know," Ruby said with a single tear running down her cheek.

Using one hand to pull his seat closer to hers, Nate ducked his head to speak. "What does she know?"

A harsh whisper was all that followed. "She could ruin me!" Shocked beyond words, Nate didn't have a chance to respond as Ruby fled from his desk and left in what looked like a cloud of purple haze.

Chapter Fifty-Nine

The sound of a car's horn blaring brought a smile to her face. Outside, the warm summer sun had disappeared to be replaced by a silvery white moon. Squeezing her hand against Logan's left shoulder she stole a crisp from the large bowl in front of him and made her way to the door. Cash in hand, Riya handed over the crisp bank notes and in return carried two large plastic bags back into the kitchen to join her brothers.

"Dinner, boys!" sang Riya jollily. Watching these two men dish out food was like watching the hunters finally find their prey. Food disappeared just as quickly as it was retrieved with barely a word spoken in between bites. After less than forty minutes, all three siblings sat completely overstuffed and unable to move. Logan sat on one end of the sofa with his legs outstretched in front of him, Riya lay horizontally next to him with her head resting on his legs and hers curling over the side acting as Thomas's pillow. Any stranger walking in would be struck by the comical sight, but each of them was thoroughly contented to sit in the afterglow of eating wondrously unhealthy food.

Patting Riya's leg, Thomas leant forward and picked up the remotes in front of him. Flicking through the channels, Thomas could hear the subtle snore of his brother from the other side of the couch. Bouncing her wrist lazily over the edge of her seat, "How did you do it?" Riya asked, only slightly affected by the alcohol that had been consumed before the much-needed food had arrived.

"Do what?" muttered Thomas sleepily.

"Forgive him." Riya stated dramatically. "I know he didn't do anything to me, but I can't forgive him for hurting you!" she shouted, not allowing tears to overcome her this time.

Thomas leant his head back against her knees, looked up to the ceiling and then closed his eyes. "He's not perfect, Riya. Sometimes he lashes out but most of the time he does everything for *US*. He has his problems, but does he really deserve to lose the thing he lives for, over a few mistakes?" Thomas finished quietly.

Riya stared at her brother for what felt like an eternity to gauge how serious he was being. "No. I guess not," she whispered back, closing her own eyes only to be awoken a short time later by the shift of her pillow. Riya scrunched her face together in protest as the same pillow gently nudged her upright.

"Taxi's here, Riya. We've got to go." A hushed voice burst through the fog of doziness she was currently fighting. Not managing to reply in any understandable way, Riya grumbled quietly. The chuckling, to her annoyance, made her eyes slowly blink open to reveal Logan and Thomas both pulling their light jackets over their broad shoulders. Both men kissed her lightly on the head and said their goodbyes as she heard them leave, being content to just sit and watch the mindless late-night shows that were blaring out of the screen in front of her. Sending one quick text, Riya shut down her phone for the night and curled up in her favourite blanket against the arm of her sofa.

Less than an hour later, Riya was in the same position when she heard a deep voice filtering through the doorway. "Want to tell me what's going on in that head of yours?" Nate's soothing presence calmed her, even when she hadn't realised she needed it.

"I didn't see you come in," Riya replied, stretching her arms above her head and giving him a lazy smile.

"Your message said just to let myself in," Nate said cheerfully as he moved over to the sofa where he picked up her legs and lightly laid them out over his own. Leaning his head against the hard back of his seat, Nate looked at her questioningly. "How's your day been?"

Returning his smile with ease, Riya nodded slowly. "Same old, same old. It was nice to see the boys."

"Just the boys? I thought your dad might come along too?" Nate asked, trying but failing not to pry.

"No... not Dad today. He and Thomas had a thing the other day." Riya tried to brush off as if it were nothing. Nate wasn't convinced.

Stroking his hand against her calf slowly, Nate began gently. "You can talk to me, you know. Anything you say to me stays between us and only us."

Looking at him with a gleam in her eyes, hopefully showing how much he had come to mean to her, Riya sat a little straighter and took a deep breath. Starting from the beginning, Riya told him everything that had been spinning around her brain in the last few days. As she disclosed detail after detail, she waited for Nate to make some kind of comment or sound to show he'd had enough, but he just sat and listened intently and allowed her to unburden herself. Riya looked at the clock fleetingly and couldn't believe the time, she'd been speaking with him, or more realistically at him, for the best part of an hour. She'd moved on from relaying the events to rambling through her thoughts and feelings on the subject. Giving one last long breath she looked at his focused eyes and smiled sweetly. "Sorry. You didn't ask for all that."

Nate gave a rumble of laughter and returned her look intently. "Whatever you need, Riya. I'll listen to you for hours if that's what it takes for you to believe that I'm in this. Through and through," said Nate as he swept in for a brief kiss.

It took Riya a minute to recover from his unexpected statement, but she smiled and nodded, reaching for his hand, and squeezing it in agreement and with her own sentiments. "How about you? How was your day?" Riya asked, slightly later than she should have.

Nate groaned and she giggled at his obvious frustration. "Annoyingly boring."

"It goes both ways, Nate. You can talk to me, I know at the moment it's a bit weird given that its Lina's case you're working on, but we've got to be able to trust each other and the safety of these four walls," Riya added wanting to be able to help him as he had helped her.

Nate seemed to consider her words carefully and once again curled his fingers around her own. "Your stepmother is running rings around my people and I have no idea how to handle it."

Riya rolled her eyes to sympathize with him. For years Melinda had been wreaking havoc over her family, it was only right to pass on her knowledge and experience of the deceitful woman, to someone who obviously needed it. "Melinda has her own rules. The only way to beat her is to deny her the attention she wants."

In response to her advice Nate sat forward. "From what I can gather she's taken to blackmailing a sixty-year-old therapist who is desperate to help her," seethed Nate angrily.

Riya was shocked by her lack of surprise and, not for the first time, realised that the woman was deranged and dangerous. "Take her away from the limelight. Give her what she needs but no more." Watching Nate waiting for her to continue, she sat up and swung her legs over his. Straddling him, she looked down into his eyes. "Don't give her any more interviews for the time being. No therapists. It will take away the only attention she can have right now, and it will destroy her into giving you information and dropping her bogus attempts at blackmail. Melinda's biggest problem is that her bark is worse than her bite, she hasn't got the strength, knowledge or connections to follow through on any kind of threat."

Nate laughed and rested his hands on her hips. "You're a genius," he joked, caressing her cheek.

In response Riya shrugged a single shoulder and said, "I know!" with more volume than anticipated as Nate chose that moment to tickle her sides making her squeal in delight. In response she leant forward and kissed him, effectively ending the talking part of their evening.

Chapter Sixty

The ringing on Riya's newly bought doorbell woke him with a start. Convincing himself that it was better just to remain exactly where he was, Nate tightened his arm against Riya's midriff making sure she wouldn't leave the warm cocoon that they had created either. Unfortunately, the ringing persisted, and Riya rubbed her face against the pillow of his arm which stretched beneath her neck. With one long groan she tiptoed out of bed with a single kiss to the inside of his elbow and she grabbed the discarded dressing gown from the floor beneath them.

Nate listened to her bare feet as they slapped along the floor leading to the door. It was Saturday, he wasn't working, and he had really been hoping to spend this weekend the same way as he spent his last. The mumbled voices filtering through the house sounded calm enough that Nate buried his head further into her bed and tried to fall seamlessly back into sleep, but it was no use. Pulling on his jeans that had been carelessly thrown across the floor, Nate followed the delectable woman out of the bedroom.

Greeted with the unwanted sight of Thomas Ryker making himself at home, Riya was nowhere to be seen. It took Thomas a few moments to realise he was no longer alone in the cosy kitchen but as Nate watched the man come to grips with a man standing bare-chested in his sister's kitchen, he couldn't help but smirk. "Mr Ryker," Nate greeted politely.

"Detective," Thomas replied, unable to hide the confusion from his voice and face. The man simply stood unmoving in front of Nate trying to, but not really wanting to, define the connection between the detective he obviously didn't like, and his sister.

Chuckling as he walked over to the stool he had come to think of as his own, Nate decided to play the gentleman for once in his life. "Sorry, I didn't mean to shock you by being here. I didn't know Riya was expecting company." Nate apologetically tried to sound genuine.

Thomas glared daggers at him, and Nate could almost see him jumping to the wrong conclusions. "So, you and my sister..." Thomas tried to finish even as his voice grated out like knives. Nate watched as the other man's gaze darkened and the twisted part of him was enjoying the prospect of the fight brewing with the other man. "Listen here and listen good," Thomas began, viciously low-toned. "If you dare try and manipulate this family by screwing my sister, you will regret it."

Without realising, Nate puffed out his chest and planted his feet more securely on the floor. "It sounded like you just tried to threaten a police officer. Care to elaborate?" Nate said, humorously daring Thomas to continue.

He wasn't disappointed. Thomas took a menacing step towards him and slowly rolled his shoulders back. As Nate braced for the impact, knowing full well, out of respect for the man's sister, he couldn't physically retaliate, Riya breezed her way back into the room and planted herself between the two males, unaware of the simmering tension. "Sorry about that. Nate, you're up!" Obviously trying to sound chipper, rather than awkward, Riya beamed. "Thomas, you know Detective Richards."

Ignoring the last few minutes, Nate reached around Riya's back and extended his hand towards Thomas. "It's good to see you again, Mr Ryker," Nate tried, nodding his head lightly. Without looking at Riya he could feel the daggers she was shooting at her brother, trying to get him to accept the offered hand.

Finally relenting, Thomas grasped his hand and shook it firmly with more force than was needed. "You too," he replied eventually, grimacing slightly as Nate applied equal strength to his own side of the handshake.

"We were going out for breakfast if you wanted to join us?" Riya asked, still blissfully unaware of the testosterone flying through the air. Both men continued staring at each other, daring the other to say something to burst her bubble of happiness.

"No, I'm OK, thanks. I just stopped by to see if you wanted to join the rest of us for Sunday lunch tomorrow. I'd invite you too, Detective, but given the circumstances, I think it would be a touch on the awkward side," Thomas said boldly with a patronizing tone.

"Rest of us?" Riya rasped nervously, pulling Nate's attention away from the other man and onto the woman shaking in front of him.

"Yeah, all of us, at Logan's tomorrow. Are you in?" Thomas asked again, wishing for a quick exit from the current situation.

"Dad will be there?" Riya mumbled, ignoring Thomas's impatience.

"Yes, Riya, Dad will be there," Thomas snapped as he

replied, quickly recoiling at the anger that flickered over Nate's face when he'd registered the tone that Thomas had used when speaking to Riya. "It's the first step. Wouldn't it be easier to see him when we're all there as buffers?" Thomas argued further.

"Fine! I'll be there," Riya relented, annoyed but still moving in to hug her eldest brother goodbye. The siblings parted quickly, and Thomas made his move to leave. Riya said something about getting ready to go but Nate was more concerned with following the man who needed to get a few things straight.

"Ryker!" Nate snapped just as Thomas was reaching for the door handle. Thomas turned and seemed more than happy to pick up where they had left off. Rushing towards Nate with a dangerous stance, Thomas looked ready to kill. With mere centimeters between them, Nate outstretched his arm and gripped the other man's shirt in his fist and brought their faces together. "Let's get one thing straight," Nate growled quietly, "your sister means more to me than anyone. You do not get to accuse me of using her, you do not get to talk to her with anything less than respect and you do not get to be angry at her for trying to be happy with someone other than a Ryker. Hurt her or belittle her in any way and we will have a problem. Do we have an understanding?"

A look that resembled something like respect passed over Thomas's face. The other man sharply nodded and quickly broke his shirt free of Nate's vice-like grip. Not bothering to look back in Nate's direction, Thomas left the house quickly. As if nothing happened, Nate walked back into Riya's bedroom and pulled on the rest of his clothes to prepare for the day. He found her putting on a coat of lipstick in the kitchen and the smile she sent him almost stopped his heart. Popping the tube into her bag she brightly asked, "Ready to go?"

Nothing else mattered to him for the next forty-eight hours except for this woman. "Absolutely!" Nate beamed and linked his fingers through hers.

Chapter Sixty-One

Walking into Logan's house, Thomas paced with his hands clenched around his hips. "Did you know?" Anger was still pumping through his veins. He'd respected the way Richards had defended Riya's honour for all of ten minutes until the reality of what the man had been doing in his sister's house, first thing in the morning, wearing nothing but jeans, kicked in.

Logan looked confused as his older brother barged his way into his home. "Know what?" he asked casually, trying to figure out what had prompted Thomas into his whirlwind of irritability.

"Riya and that *man*," Thomas replied as if his vague statement explained everything.

Logan sat, slouching in the closest chair he could find, deciding it was best just to wait out the storm sweeping through his brother. "What are you talking about?"

"Riya and Richards!" Thomas bellowed, becoming annoyed at his brother's lack of understanding. "He is... using her!"

"Oh." Logan became suddenly evasive, piquing Thomas's interest.

"Oh? That's all you've got to say. She's your sister too!" argued Thomas suspiciously.

"She's a grown woman, Thomas," uttered Logan quietly,

noting Thomas's attitude. It wasn't the first time his brother had tried to wrap their little sister up in cotton wool and, he suspected, it wouldn't be the last. At Thomas's intent stare, Logan looked at him sympathetically. "Riya needs to be able to make her own decisions. God knows I don't like the thought of them… together but it's not my or your business." Seeing the furious expression remain firmly pasted across his brother's rugged face Logan decided to take pity on him. "If it's any consolation I don't think he's using her," he added.

"You knew!" Thomas yelled, enraged at being the last to know and the fact that Logan had neglected to do anything about the new couple.

Logan nodded as he took a sip of his now lukewarm orange juice and grimaced. "Yep. I saw what I believe was their first kiss and then found him at her house a couple of weeks ago."

"And you didn't think to tell me. We could have done something!" Thomas said, not even believing his own outrage at this point.

Logan nodded towards the vacant chair opposite him in the sterile kitchen. Thomas sat down and raked his hands through his hair. "I know you don't like the bloke but she's happy, Thomas," Logan said and continued before his brother managed to interrupt him, "It's true! She's smiled more in the last few weeks, she seems less stressed. We've got to face up to the fact that he might be exactly what she needs."

Groaning into his hands, Thomas rubbed his palms into his eyes. "There's something about him that I don't like," he moaned more quietly than the last few of his statements.

A single laugh bubbled out of Logan's lips as he shook his head. "You know why that is, don't you?" At Thomas's confused expression Logan continued. "You two are very, very similar." His brother looked at him as if he were speaking a different language, but Logan knew his point had hit home.

"I need a drink," Thomas said, hissing a breath out between his teeth.

Laughing whole-heartedly, Logan was forced, yet again, to shake his head in rebellion. "It's not even eleven, Tom."

"When's that ever stopped us before?" Thomas asked, wiggling his eyebrows and signaling to the decanter of whiskey on the raised counter next to them.

"Not for me, but don't let that stop you!" Logan replied to the unanswered question, sarcastically chipper.

"You were a lot more fun before you were heartbroken, little brother," teased Thomas with a smirk. Glaring at his brother, Logan rolled his eyes and moved towards the tempting liquid. Pouring them both a large helping and tilting his glass in a silent salute, Logan swallowed the burning liquid in one swift gulp.

And that was how their father found them hours later, laughing at inconsequential things, not making sense and commiserating about their own versions of broken hearts. Harry walked round the long rectangular table and stood facing his eldest who in response leant back in his chair and raised his empty glass smugly at his father. "Dad," greeted Thomas bluntly.

"Day drinking. Great example you're setting for Rory," Harry said bluntly but closing his eyes as if instantly regretting his tone.

"Ha! You're one to talk, Daddy dearest!" Logan slurred and then hid his face within the rim of his own glass. "Besides, what's wrong with simply following in the footsteps of the great Harry Ryker?" finished Logan whilst still shielding himself behind the thinly cut crystal.

"I'm sorry, I didn't mean…" Harry began but was quickly interrupted.

"Of course, you didn't mean it. You never meant it. Not then. Not now," Thomas added bitterly. "Don't lecture us, Dad. We forgive you and all but don't lecture us about things that you've been doing for the majority of our lives."

Harry's face turned stony with both of his sons' attitudes. "Logan, give us a minute." Firmly stating his authority over his children.

"Sure, why not. It's not like this is my house or anything," Logan said as he moved out of earshot.

As soon as Harry made sure that he was once again on equal footing rather than being outnumbered, he sat down facing the swollen lip of his eldest son. "For what it's worth, I am sorry about the other day," he pleaded remorsefully.

"Yeah, I got that," Thomas snapped, feeling the effects of the alcohol he had coerced himself and his brother into.

"I'm serious, but it was the wakeup call I needed in a weird way." Harry squirmed, desperate for the tension to evaporate between him and his children.

Refilling his glass and taking a sip this time, Thomas tilted up his chin in defiance. "I'm glad my face was able to help you work out your demons," he added scathingly and standing up as if to leave.

Thomas made it halfway to the door before Harry was able to force out the words he needed to say. "I know you're probably too drunk to remember this tomorrow," Harry began saying towards Thomas's back but could feel his son losing interest. "I joined AA," Harry said quickly, relieved to see the statement had stopped Thomas in his tracks.

Turning his head slightly towards his father, Thomas's glassy eyes flickered with hope for a moment. "Good for you," came the choked response.

"I just thought I should let you know," whispered Harry nervously. Never in the whole of Thomas's life had he seen his father like this. Could it be that Harry Ryker had realised that his children were now grown and capable of walking away or fighting back? Or was it simply because this latest episode had finally taught the old man that him and drink did not mix? Thomas had no clue of the answer but whatever the reason he was hoping it stuck for all their sakes.

Harry had stood watching his son for a long while, praying for some kind of response. Silence continued to fill the room and Harry decided to give up, at least for today. He turned around to retreat back into the spare bedroom he was calling home, when he heard a small voice, similar to that of the small boy's voice that he used to know, speak up out of the metaphorical darkness. "Sunday lunch tomorrow at three. We'll all be here if you fancy it?" spoke the voice of hope in front of the wide-open door.

"That would be good," Harry replied, struggling to find the breath to speak with, and not for the first time struggling to comprehend the love that almost burst out of his chest, at the sight of his children's unconditional love and forgiveness.

"Tell Logan I headed home, and I'll see him tomorrow." And with that last instruction, Thomas left as quickly as the forgiveness had come. Harry smiled for the first time for what felt like years and headed towards the sleek stairs behind him. This was a new start, a chance to prove himself to the world he'd hurt so badly.

Chapter Sixty-Two

Balancing on her three-inch heels, Riya waited on the step outside Logan's home. Not one to usually wait for an official invitation to walk through the door, Riya felt the tension in the air increase as she waited to face her father for the first time in a week. For the last twenty-four hours, since Thomas's visit, she had been considering her position on recent revelations. After taking some time to objectively talk through her issues, Riya had realised one thing, she wasn't the one who should be hurt by this. In reality her father's actions had made no impact on her life until recently, and she had suffered none of the abuse.

The slight creaking of the door brought Riya out from within her mind. Logan's smiling face released some of her inner tension and she greeted him with equal affection. Heels clicking as she walked into the familiar room, Riya faltered in her movements as she came face to face with her father. Knowing she was responsible for how awkward this day had become, Riya shyly smiled at the man who had raised her. "Hi," she tried.

"Riya," Harry responded in awe, "I... It's good to see you." Trying to bring back the ease of conversation that usually hugged father and daughter the minute they saw one another.

"You too," Riya replied cautiously as the silence engulfed

the room. Seconds ticked by and the air thrummed around the family in conflict and Riya had had enough and loudly clapped her hands against one another. "Right!" she began, looking towards Logan who was busily shuffling around the kitchen. "Do you need a hand with anything?" Asking while simultaneously walking around her father, ruffling her hands in Rory's short hair, and making her way into the kitchen to join her brother, she ended the tight conversation.

The preparation of dinner took up most of the conversation for the next forty minutes. A calm settled amongst the five people surrounding the table. Riya looked to her left and smiled down at the small boy next to her. He was being quieter than normal, some might say subdued, but still dominated most of the dinner conversation and she had never been more grateful for that fact. The small boy rattled on about the things he'd watched on the television over the last few days and Riya realised that since Lina's death Rory had become a shut-in, he'd vanished from the outside world and had been forced to grieve in the silence of a home that wasn't even his. "Rory!" Riya exclaimed, desperate to solve at least one tragedy. With the mention of his name, Rory looked up with curious eyes in an unspoken question. "How about a walk to the park after lunch?" she asked hopefully. Rory didn't respond but the gleam that made its way into the little boy's eyes was all the answer Riya needed to voice the next stage of their afternoon with the others at the table.

Walking hand-in-hand with Rory relaxed her more than she could explain, and it seemed to have the same effect on the rest of her family as they moved in unison down Logan's Street, towards the small park. Conversation flowed, jokes were told at each other's expense and the past was seemingly forgotten. The boys played with Rory by running around pretending he was faster than them both, Harry laughed, and Riya just basked in the happiness.

Harry moved to sit next to his daughter on the tattered wooden bench that ran along one side of the enclosed park. Neither said anything for minutes, happy to just sit in comfortable silence. Riya spoke first as she looked at her father in the afternoon sun. "When's he leaving?" she asked, focusing on a neutral subject that wouldn't cause awkwardness.

Harry sighed as he followed Rory around the park with his eyes. "I'm not sure yet. Dominic wants him back as soon as, but I don't know." Harry spoke confidently even though his words obviously confused his daughter.

"But with Melinda in hospital for the foreseeable, surely…" Riya began to argue but was quickly shut down.

"I'm not ready for him to go!" Harry growled but shook his head forcefully at the sight of Riya's widened eyes as they reacted to his aggressive tone. "I'm sorry, I didn't mean to snap. It's just, after Lina, I feel like he needs me."

Softly responding to her father, Riya shuffled her way closer to him across the bench. "He needs you. Or you need him?" In response to her tenderly spoken words Harry absent-mindedly patter her hand that rested on her legs to which Riya replied by resting her head on his shoulder. "He's a great kid," Riya said mindlessly.

"Yes, he is." Harry agreed and smiled to himself about the joy that the little boy could bring to this family without his mother hovering around. It would be hard convincing Dominic that Rory should spend time with him after Melinda was charged, or even sectioned, but he was willing to try.

All three of his boys came rushing over to them, pulling Harry out of his thoughts and plans. Three sets of eyes looked at the intimate moment that father and daughter were sharing, breathing heavily from their exhaustion. Rory seemed to be fading fast but even the heavy weight of his eyelids could not stop the grin that spread across his cheeks as he looked on hopefully at his stepfather and sister. No longer content to simply be a bystander to the people on the bench staring at him, Rory climbed onto Riya's lap and laid his head back against her chest. "Home?" she asked the small boy who was slowly becoming dead weight as he lost his battle with the looming exhaustion. A small nod was the only hint that Rory had heard the question, but it was good enough for the rest of the family. Thomas reached forward and lifted Rory into his arms as the group of newly forgiven family members made their way back home.

Sitting with her legs curled up beneath her on Logan's sofa, Riya was well aware of the Cheshire cat grin that covered her face as she listened to her brothers and father chat amongst themselves. After returning from the park Rory had been put to bed, already fast asleep and from the look of relief on her father's face, that had been a rare occurrence for little Rory in the last few weeks. "What are you smiling about?" Logan asked from the other end of the couch.

"It's been a great day, that's all," said Riya contentedly.

"Here we go. She's getting all sentimental on us again!" Thomas joked from the other side of the room.

"Shut up, you idiot. You know what I mean!" Riya chastised, giggling. "We haven't been like this since Lina. It's just nice to know we can still be a normal family," supposed Riya hopefully.

Three sets of agreements came from around the room and Riya gave them all a small smile. The sun had gone down outside and there was a large sweep of pink highlighting the evening's long dusk. Not long after the clock reached ten their father made his excuses and headed towards his bed. Harry patted both his sons on the shoulders and kissed the top of Riya's head as he made his way up the stairs to hopefully get some rest himself. The man looked wretchedly tired.

"Another?" Logan asked, offering to pour another helping of wine into Riya's glass.

"I really shouldn't. I need to get home," Riya said disappointedly.

"Just stay. Sofa's comfortable enough," Logan said as if it was obvious.

Smirking at her brother she offered him her glass. "Go on then!" Winking at the laughing man. "I just need to make a call." Riya excused herself, not listening to the over-exaggerated whistling coming from her brothers. Picking up her phone Riya dialed the now memorized number. She didn't have to wait long for an answer.

"So how was it?" Nate asked through the phone, making Riya smile at his concern.

"Better than I thought it would be!" Riya practically yelled down the phone.

A deep chuckle vibrated through the phone making her go slightly weak at the knees. "I told you," teased Nate in a rumble.

"I know. I'm starting to think you're the genius!" joked Riya, thrilled with the easiness of talking to him. They were in sync and she felt she had known him for far longer than just a month. "I'm going to stay here tonight if that's OK with you?"

"What! Spend a night with your family instead of me? How could you be so heartless!" Nate chided humorously. "Of course, it's OK. Not that you need my permission," he said with a chuckle. "I've got some work to do anyway. Fancy ordering in something tomorrow night instead?"

"Sounds like a plan!" Riya bounced enthusiastically.

"Great. I'll message you tomorrow. Go have a good night, Riya, and I'll try not to miss you too much," Nate finished and Riya could feel the wink that came with the last part of his sentence. She laughed and said her own goodbye before hanging up and heading back in to join her brothers.

Chapter Sixty-Three

Hanging up the phone, Nate wiped his mind of thoughts of the illustrious Riya Ryker and tried to focus on the task in hand. Sam sat at his smaller desk opposite and both men were trying to figure out a twenty-year-old mystery. Turning over the page to reveal another set of photos, Nate caught a glance of Sam's questioning look. "What?" he asked distractedly.

"You know if the big boys upstairs find out you'll be screwed," Sam said and Nate couldn't bring himself to pretend like he didn't know what his partner was talking about.

"I know. Problem is I don't know if I care," Nate said, still focusing on the crime scene photos in front of him, so much so he missed the shocked expression that graced Sam's face. Before the other man could make comment on his boss's unexpected amount of emotion toward a person of interest in their murder investigation, Nate passed him the sheet of paper he had been studiously studying, silently asking him what he thought. "Look at the tyre marks on the road."

"There are none," Sam stated, muddled.

"Exactly," Nate replied somberly. "Every report about Sophia Ryker's death said it was just another fatal car accident."

"I'm sensing a but coming," Sam said, resting his hand on his chin.

"In what kind of accident does a person not try and brake

at least once? It doesn't make sense unless somebody has tried to cover up what really happened," Nate explained, working his way through the puzzle in his mind's eye.

Sam whistled. "A lot of people would have had to have been persuaded. A person would have had to have a lot of powerful connections to pull something like that off," he finished, sounding skeptical.

"Someone like Harry Ryker?" Nate asked, raising his eyebrows. "He's a big fish in the business world, giving him the connections. He's got more than enough money to pay numerous people off and was the closest living adult relative she had," stated Nate, agreeing with himself more by the second.

"So, what exactly are you saying?" Sam asked, still not grasping the point Nate was trying to make.

"Maybe the wife's death wasn't an accident after all," uttered Nate thoughtfully.

"You want to talk to him?" Sam asked, assuming that they'd be carrying on as usual.

"No. I'll go with you, but I want you to take the lead in the interview," Nate declared without explanation. Sam became instantly surprised and his shock transferred to his face, but Nate refused to take pity on the man. He didn't want his partner seeing him face Harry Ryker. The man had upset Riya in a way that he couldn't forget, neither could he trust that he'd be able to remain calm when thinking about the man hurting his own children. It was better if he watched from afar to judge the man's body actions and to see if his guard of politeness dropped when faced with a less senior officer.

"Right. OK," Sam stammered nervously, having rarely taken the lead in interviews especially in a high-profile case like this.

"Let's call it a night. Go home, get some rest. We've got a big day tomorrow," Nate ordered, not having to tell Sam twice as his colleague quickly rose from his chair in an attempt to rush home to prep for the following day. Leaning back in his swivel chair, Nate considered his options, he could either go home, turn in for the night without Riya by his side or, he could stay and try and figure out the many messes that were following him around these days. Choosing the latter, Nate settled himself in for the night, coffee in one hand and change for the vending machine in the other. It was going to be a long night.

Chapter Sixty-Four

Nate gave the go ahead for Sam to knock on the door with a tip of his head. The loud rap didn't make the strong door shake but it should have, given the force his partner had used. The door opened revealing a sleep-touched and comfy-looking Riya Ryker and Nate had never been surer of a decision in his life. This woman was worth the risk of his career and then some. "Detectives," whispered Riya, taken aback by their presence at such an early hour of the morning.

"Good morning, Miss Ryker," Sam began, remaining the absolute gentleman while Nate remained stoic. "We were wondering if we could have a word with your father?" asked Sam politely. Riya replied with a nod as she opened the door wider for both men to enter.

Sam moved past her without incident but as Nate brushed past her, he froze. "Just a few questions. That's all," he whispered into the shell of her ear.

She touched his arm briefly to show her understanding. "It's your job, Nate, I get it," assured Riya sympathetically, offering a small encouraging smile.

Riya made her excuses and went in search of her father while simultaneously gesturing them to make themselves comfortable. Nate and Sam took seats on either end of the sofa lying in wait. Both men looked at each other and Nate raised both his eyebrows at his partner as a silent gesture of support.

All too quickly a shuffling noise behind them indicated they were no longer alone in the open-plan room. Turning their heads in unison, Sam and Nate were shocked by the small person staring back at them with wide innocent eyes.

"Who are you?" the child asked shyly, shuffling from foot to foot on the hardwood floors.

"You must be Rory. Your stepsister has told me a lot about you," Nate said, rising from his seat and crouching in front of the youngest member of the Ryker clan.

At the mention of Riya, Rory's eyes brightened and looked up the stairs in recognition of where said woman had gone. "She's my sister," Rory said confidently. "We don't have the same Mummy and Daddy, but Harry said that doesn't matter. We're a family," stated Rory in a surprisingly mature way. The little man in front of him was startlingly self-assured and clear on the values the Ryker family seemed to pretend to live by.

"That you are," Nate said in an assuring voice. Rory had been through so much, it was good he could take comfort in the people around him. The clearing of a throat brought Nate out of his pleasant talk with the small boy. Harry Ryker stood directly behind his stepson looking like the business royalty that he was.

"Detective. My daughter tells me you wish to ask some more questions. Shall we have a seat?" Harry asked, waving his arm towards the sofa that Nate had only recently vacated. "Rory, why don't you go and find Logan?" directed Harry in a stern voice, telling the child that it was not a question that was open for discussion.

Nate rose from his squatting position and smiled down at the boy to say goodbye and then moved himself back into position. Harry sat opposite in a large chair that looked like it could have been used as a throne at one time and waited for himself or Sam to speak. Nate gave Sam a reassuring nod and sat back to give him the lead. "Mr Ryker, we have come here today to ask you a few questions about some information that has come to light in the process of our investigation," Sam strongly began. "And before we begin, I would like to remind you that this is a murder enquiry, so us getting the absolute truth is vital."

"Yes, Detective. There is no need to remind me of the importance of this case, in case you forgot it is MY stepdaughter that was killed," the eldest Ryker mocked. Luckily footsteps coming down the central staircase gave Sam time to pull himself together. Rory in arms, Riya made her way into the room with a look of confusion and lack of recognition as she looked at her father. It was clear to everyone in the room that she had overheard his rather rude statement to the police. Surprisingly, when Harry saw the look in his daughter's eyes, he immediately closed his eyes of shame and pasted on a more pleasant and seemingly helpful expression. "I'm sorry, Detective, that was rude of me. Please ask me anything you need to know." Reassured, Harry looked towards Riya, who, in response, simply walked out of the house with Rory in tow intent on playing in the small front garden lining the outside of Logan's house.

"Can you tell us about what happened to the first Mrs Ryker?" prompted Sam softly.

"I don't see how that's relevant," Harry replied, his eyes darkening immediately at the mere mention of his first wife.

Nate smirked at the textbook response. "Why don't you indulge us, Mr Ryker?" Joining the interview momentarily.

221

"She died. Almost twenty years ago," bluntly responded Harry, lowering his eyebrows so they acted as shields. Noticing the prying expressions on the detectives' faces, Harry continued. "She lost control of her car and crashed headfirst into a tree. She died instantly," muttered Harry, lost in thought.

"I'm very sorry to hear that, sir," Sam said sympathetically. "We've had recent cause to look into that accident and we believe that it quite possibly wasn't an accident at all," mused Sam, looking at Nate when both men realised the tension that had just worked its way into Harry Ryker's spine. "Any ideas, Mr Ryker?" Sam continued to press.

"I don't know what you're talking about," whispered Harry heartbreakingly.

Sam coughed into his own hand breaking some of the silenced tension. "I think you do, Mr Ryker. See, I think you might have had something to do with your wife's death, Mr Ryker," teased Sam relentlessly. Harry began vehemently shaking his head and denying any involvement in the would-be suspicious death. The cool, calm, and collected Harry Ryker fell apart in front of their very eyes. "Unburden yourself, Mr Ryker. You'll feel better for it," Sam hammered in but Harry remained shocked into silence. "Did your wife try and leave? Did you find out she was seeing someone else and snapped?" asked Sam tauntingly.

"What? You think I killed her?" Harry yelped, appalled at the insinuation.

"It's what it looks like from our point of view," Sam said, pulling out a wedge of paper from his bag. "Your bank records for the few months after Sophia's death. Money going out of your account to the accounts of your wife's pathologist, crime scene investigator and inquest judge," confidently stated Sam as he pointed at each important payment.

"Doesn't look good, Harry," Nate chimed in, shaking his head sarcastically.

"I didn't kill her!" shouted Harry which prompted both Riya and Logan to come crashing into the room from different directions at the sign of their father's distress.

"Dad?" the uniformed voices spoke out. Both adults looked frantically between Harry and the detectives trying to gauge what was going on between the three men. Riya moved to crouch next to Harry's side and Logan perched on the identical chair next to his father, bracing his hands on his knees. Taking a minute to look between his children, Harry Ryker seemed to resign himself to his fate. "OK. Fine I'll tell you." Harry nodded in agreement with himself. "Just remember that I did it for you two and Thomas," he said, patting Riya's outstretched hand and staring intently at Logan.

"Go on, Mr Ryker," encouraged Sam, ending the moment of perfect silence between the three relatives.

"I didn't kill her. You have to believe that," Harry said, pleading with Nate and Sam. "A year or so before she died, Sophia found out that she was pregnant again." All eyes in the room snapped towards Harry at his confession but he kept his eyes glued to the wall behind the couch. "We were so excited, but the doctors had said after Riya that it was unlikely that Sophia would be able to carry any more babies to term. We were on edge. We didn't tell anyone even after she passed twenty-four weeks, but everything seemed fine," tearfully spoke Harry.

"But it wasn't," Riya whispered jarringly.

Harry shook his head from side to side and gripped his

eyes between his thumb and forefinger. "I was at work one day when the phone rang. It was Sophia and she was screaming down the phone in pain. There was blood everywhere when I met her at the hospital. She looked so pale, so scared." Harry spoke as if he was reliving every painful moment. "She'd suffered a major placental abruption, the baby, a little girl, didn't survive for more than half an hour. We held her as she took her last breaths." Shuddering uncontrollably, Harry looked as if he were dying himself.

"Why didn't you tell us?" Logan asked, looking haunted.

"We couldn't risk having you three feeling that kind of pain," stuttered Harry without looking up. "After she'd recovered physically, she tried to put on a brave face. I found her a few months later crying over a photograph of the three of you. She said she couldn't bring herself to love you any more. That it hurt too much." Stopping when he looked down at Riya's tear-streaked face, Harry couldn't stop spilling the secrets of the past. "Your mother didn't mean it, of course, she was just so confused! I got her help, put her through counselling but nothing made a difference. It was like she just checked out of her own day-to-day life. She kept disappearing for hours on end and coming back filthy or breathing heavily. I don't know where she'd been to this day, it was like she'd been in a trance."

"What about the day she died, Mr Ryker? Can you tell us how it came about?" Sam said softly, fearing the answer for the sake of the woman's children.

"She went for a drive, turned into a tree going eighty miles per hour. She didn't try to brake, just let go of the steering wheel and closed her eyes," finished Harry somberly. "I'm so sorry!" he rasped to the room in agony.

Sam looked at Nate who nodded his head slightly towards his partner, both agreeing that they had all the information they needed. "We'll leave you to it, Mr Ryker. We'll be in touch," Nate quietly uttered. Harry didn't respond, just continued to sob. Riya stood and walked them to the door. Following Sam out, Nate inconspicuously wrapped his fingers around hers and leant forward, brushing a small kiss to her forehead. "Call me later, OK?" he asked, looking straight into her eyes. Riya gave him a tentative smile and nodded.

Chapter Sixty-Five

Riya shut the door behind Nate and made her way back over to her father. The man had not moved an inch but was still sobbing uncontrollably. Returning to her crouching position, Riya stroked her father's hand. What he had said broke her heart but in an odd way it explained a few things. His actions towards the boys after her mother's death for one. It didn't condone it, but it certainly explained his guilt that caused it. "Why don't you go upstairs and get some rest? It doesn't look like you got much sleep last night," Riya asked her father, stroking the small bits of hair hanging across his head. Harry nodded and sloped off.

Logan looked haunted as he sat still as stone. "Well, that... explains a lot," he mused quietly before looking up at her. "You OK?" he asked concerned.

"I don't know. Knowing that she killed herself is upsetting, I know, but..." Riya trailed off, frightened of his reactions towards her thoughts.

"But?" Logan prompted, looking at her expectantly.

Taking a deep breath, Riya uttered the words that had followed her throughout her life. "I didn't know her, Logan!"

The whispered cry made Logan look up, startled. Finally understanding his sister's indifference, Logan pulled her into a hug and buried his face in her hair. Riya began to quietly weep, and Logan allowed himself to shed a few tears for the mother he once knew. "We're going to sit here for a while, have a coffee and in a few hours have some lunch. Then when you're ready you're going to go home, call Nate and get some rest, OK?" Logan said quietly in her ear. Riya's small nod was the only communication that he needed.

Chapter Sixty-Six

Logan knocked on Thomas's door roughly, not wanting him to answer. Telling your brother that his mother willingly left him was something he'd never wanted to deal with. Unfortunately, Logan's luck was not in as Thomas's front door opened widely. "Hi," Logan said, shuffling on the front stoop.

"You all right?" Thomas said, instantly concerned by the lack of eye contact coming from his brother. When Logan didn't respond Thomas ushered him into the building. "Logan, you're starting to scare me," joked Thomas, trying to bring some humour into the room.

"I've got to tell you something, Tom," rigidly said Logan. He felt the room beginning to shrink and swallow him whole. Throat tightening, palms sweating, Logan had no choice but to just bite the bullet. Thomas needed to know, and he had to be the one to tell him before the news came from elsewhere. Thomas was unpredictable at the best of times, Logan could only imagine what his elder brother's reaction could be. "Dad was talking to the detectives earlier and he told them something, something that we didn't know," babbled Logan, unaware of the countless words sprouting out of his mouth in an effort to calm his own fried nerves.

"Spit it out, Logan," snapped Thomas, becoming increasingly more anxious.

Ripping off the verbal plaster, Logan spat out the horrific truth. "Mum killed herself." Logan waited for Thomas's anger, shock, grief, or horror but nothing came. His brother stood looking at him unmoving. No emotion crossed his face, it seemed as if his brother had simply been put on pause waiting for someone to either fast forward or even rewind the last few moments. Ever so slowly a spark of recognition filtered into Thomas's irises and Logan felt as if someone had punched him the gut. "You knew?" he asked, stringing out the words like they were dirty and untouchable.

Thomas nodded at his brother, it hadn't been a secret he had wanted to keep but it was something that he felt he must do to protect the hearts of his siblings. He'd been the eldest, the one that was relied on by his parents to protect Logan and Riya. At the age of fourteen he had years on the other two and apparently that was enough to qualify him to know the barely buried secrets that his parents had kept hidden from most of the world. "She told me," Thomas stated plainly.

Glaring at Thomas, Logan looked at him skeptically as if he were going mad. "Thomas. Make sense," he growled.

"I didn't know what she was telling me until after it happened. She told me that she wanted to love us, but she couldn't any more, and that's why she had to leave," Thomas explained against his painstakingly raw throat. "Next thing I knew the police were knocking at our door telling Dad that her body had been found," he finished.

"Why didn't you tell us?" asked Logan soberly.

Thomas looked crestfallen. "At the beginning I couldn't really make sense of it all. What she'd said just wouldn't make sense!" Becoming angry with the painful past running on repeat through his mind, Thomas banged his fist into the wall beside him as he continued. "A year or so after she died some man came to the house. He was strung out, mumbling about some woman who'd died and that he needed more money to keep it a secret." Explaining the events that had morphed themselves into a life of anger and feeling of inferiority. "He carried on, spouting mumbled sentence after mumbled sentence until they all strung themselves together into the truth. Mum died. She killed herself because she lost a baby." Thomas paused at Logan's surprised expression. Obviously, his little brother was startled to find out that he did indeed know the whole truth. "At fourteen I knew what a pregnant woman looked like, even if they tried to hide it," added Thomas, incredulously at his parents' past naivety.

Logan swore under his breath and began pacing. It often occurred to Thomas that himself and his brother dealt with feelings of anguish in completely different ways, Logan preferred to wear the carpet away with his incessant pacing and Thomas generally lost his self-control through violence in one form or another. "I couldn't tell you. It turned my head into mush, I couldn't do it to you as well, couldn't ruin your childhood like that."

Logan didn't move for a few minutes. Thomas was unsure whether or not this most recent revelation would cause an unfixable rift between him and his family. Eventually Logan moved and did the unexpected. He moved forward and embraced his brother in a tight hug. Thomas returned the hug with equal feeling and slapped his brother on the back in a show of support.

Both men took a deep, steadying breath and released the other. "Food?" Logan asked, still with a slight tremble in his voice. Thomas chuckled, nodding in return as he made a move to grab the phone, thinking there was no point in souring the day even more by attempting to cook themselves.

Chapter Sixty-Seven

Grabbing everything she might need for the day, Riya was rushing through Nate's sparse house in an effort to be somewhat on time. The quiet laughter was not helping her endeavors. Riya flipped her hair over her shoulder to glare in Nate's direction as he stood, annoyingly handsomely, against the door frame of his bedroom's entrance. "You could help, you know," she grumbled distractedly.

"Why would I do that when watching is so much fun?" winked Nate teasingly. Once the second and third glare followed each other in quick succession, Nate decided to take pity on her. Looking for less than a minute, Nate returned to Riya's side victorious. Holding up the keys directly in front of her eyes he chuckled again at her irritated facial features. Avoiding her attempt at snatching the keys off of him, Nate grabbed her around the waist and pulled her tightly against him. With her hands trapped between her chest and his, Riya looked up into his eyes and gave him a sultry smile, tilting her mouth higher. Taking the open invitation, Nate swooped in and kissed her firmly. After kissing her for far less time than he'd have wanted to, Nate pulled back but kept her close. "You OK?" he asked, concerned that the emotional rollercoaster of the day before would catch up with her again today.

"I'm fine, Nate. Stop worrying!" Riya replied, swooning at the concern he was showing her. "I'm spending the day with

Rory. Nothing will upset me, I promise," she exclaimed. Nate's eyes went from looking at her curiously to taking on a look of reluctant acceptance. He nodded his head and kissed her once again in an effort to say goodbye. Riya accepted fully and then pranced out of his arms with a sparkling smile across her face. "I'll call you later." Winking at him this time as she walked towards the door.

The drive to Logan's house was a familiar and short one. Stepping into the room that her father had fallen apart in yesterday, Riya overlooked the band of pain that wrapped around her stomach at the thought of her mother in so much desolation that death was the only peace she could find. Hearing a noise from Logan's downstairs bedroom, Riya swept through the room as if she had not a care in the world. Seeing Logan standing tall and proud as he fussed over his cufflink's exact placement, Riya was able to see the man he once was. Then his somber expression crashed into her like a tidal wave. "Are you sure you're ready to go back to work?" she asked, knowing that Logan was hiding more feelings inside him than most people felt in a lifetime.

"Riya…" Logan began, trying not to argue but wanting something normal, something routinely to take his mind off of his gaping heart.

"OK, OK, I won't ask," Riya stammered, allowing Logan his mask of indifference, for now at least. "Where's Rory?" she asked, trying very hard not to look at him worryingly.

"Still sleeping. He'll be awake in the next hour or so," Logan said, cursing at his cuffs as they, once again, refused to do what he was telling them to.

Walking over to him and taking Logan's wrist in her hands, Riya easily threaded the metal through the small hole in his sleeve. "Anything I need to know before you leave?" she asked but paused when Logan looked at her tiredly. "About Rory," Riya confirmed, doing her best to take his mind off his impending trip to work. Of course, she had been left to care for her stepbrother on more than a few occasions before.

Logan looked at her suspiciously, obviously seeing through her ruse of distraction but didn't say anything to contradict her. "No. Everything should be fine. Dad's brought everything that he may need, you've just got to look for it." He spoke calmly as he pulled on his jacket.

Logan left quickly with a kiss to the top of her head and a promise to call her if he needed anything. With time to kill, Riya began channel surfing to pass the time until the little man upstairs decided to keep her company. Normally she would have sat and watched one of the morning news programs but recently her life had had enough bad news in it for her to hear any more through a television set.

Sometime later she heard a sharp beeping noise from the back of the house. Riya rolled her eyes and thought that it was just like Logan to start a job, not finish it and leave it for her to fix. However, disorganised her brother may sometimes have been, she was relieved to have something to fill the unexpected boredom that was sitting on her own in an empty house. Living on her own was not new to Riya, so why was her own company all of a sudden so desolate?

Shaking herself out of questions with no immediate answers, Riya grabbed the clothing inside the tumble dryer and neatly folded them up, smiling at each small t-shirt that had a different cartoon character gracing the front. She turned off the machine and left the spotless clothes precisely in the basket on top of the dryer they had just come out of. As she walked back into the kitchen come living area, Riya was surprised to see Rory perched on one of the island's high stools. Moving around the work bench in the centre of the room, Riya moved closer to Rory with her back towards the door. The closer she got the more she could tell that Rory was not himself. His tiny shoulders were slumped, his head hung, and his body shuddering. Riya had a startling realisation that he was crying uncontrollably.

Rushing over the last few steps, Riya hugged Rory for all it was worth. There was no point in trying to talk to him when his words would not make any sense, so Riya simply held the boy while he cried and whispered soothing words into his delicate ears. She had no idea how long they stood there, his skinny arms gripping at hers in an effort to keep her from leaving him alone, but Riya didn't care. In the weeks that had passed since Lina's death she had never heard talk of how Rory had been coping, everybody had either been too busy to care or too frightened to ask.

Rory's body stilled slightly, and Riya watched as his breathing pattern mimicked her own. Stroking her hand across his back, Riya leant away from the small boy to look into his adorable face. "Rory, sweetie, what's going on?" she asked in a soothing and gentle voice.

Rory seemed to debate on whether or not to open up to her but eventually his eyes filled with trust. "Lina," he croaked, lip wobbling.

"What about Lina, Rory?" Riya questioned, feeling it important that he say it aloud to be able to start healing. With the attention fully focused on her stepbrother, Riya didn't hear the modern door open slightly and footsteps entering the house.

"Lina…" was the last thing Riya heard as a shadow cast over her from behind. She felt the air move as something came down forcibly down onto the back of her head. For a moment she felt the gut-wrenching pain but then everything went numb. Riya couldn't move or even scream for help as her eyes snapped shut and everything went dark.

Chapter Sixty-Eight

Gripping his sister's hands between his, Logan couldn't fathom what had happened in-between him leaving the house that morning, and the moment he had walked into his kitchen and seen Riya's blood pooling out beneath her. In the back of his mind, he could hear the sound of the sirens that adorned the top of the ambulance he was currently riding in. There was too much to do, so many things he had to take care of, but he was stuck. Arguably the closest person in his life was hanging onto life by a thread. Logan couldn't understand the medical language that was being thrown about around him, but the paramedics' expressions said it all, she'd been left too long, she'd lost too much blood, she was dying.

"Come on, Riya, just come on," Logan chanted over and over again, holding her hand firmly and pulling it towards his lips so she could feel, as well as hear, his plea. The ambulance came to an abrupt halt and Logan looked up from his position of hopelessness. Paramedics swarmed him and shoved him out of the way. They lifted Riya onto an awaiting stretcher and burst out of the back doors. As swiftly as they had ripped her hand away from his, Riya disappeared from his sight completely.

Logan ran through the automatic doors and whipped his head from left to right, trying to get a clear understanding on the whereabouts of his sister. The tell-tale noise of metal wheels squeaking along a harshly polished floor gave Logan a clue. Racing towards the frantic team of doctors talking about pulse and blood loss, Logan was halted by a stern-looking nurse wearing trademark scrubs. "You can't go back there, sir," the woman commanded.

"I have to — she's my sister!" Logan roared, trying to barge his way past his formidable opponent.

The nurse blocked him effectively and put her hands on his shoulders, turning him towards the melancholy waiting room. "They are doing all they can. It is best for you to stay in here. They will give you an update as soon as they can. Just sit down," the nurse said softly but her tone gave no room for argument. She walked away leaving Logan sat motionless staring at the ugly white floor that had small flecks of every colour running through it. Twice in as many months, Logan had felt this kind of terror, first the woman he loved, then his sister. Although Lina dying had destroyed any part of him that had been looking for a happily-ever-after, Logan knew that if he lost his sister, it would destroy him.

Reaching for his phone, no longer comfortable with the possibilities roaming his mind, he called Thomas first then his father, not giving them any chance to ask questions or to panic. He told them the basic facts of what happened and where he was, hoping they'd already be en route. Logan's leg began bouncing of its own accord as he waited. In the blink of an eye his sister's life had been passed into the responsibility of strangers and he was in the dark, torn away from his own kin.

Logan must have been buried in his own turmoil because before he knew it Thomas was standing over him with a ghostly look in his eye. "What happened?" he queried with a slight tremble.

"I found her on the floor. They said she'd been hit in the back of the head. She was so cold, Tom," Logan choked out, blinking rapidly which didn't help. Every time his eyes closed, he saw her lying in her own halo of blood.

"What have they said? Have we had an update? I'll go and find someone, I'll…" Thomas heaved as the panic started to set in.

"The nurse said that they'd give us an update as soon as they can," Logan explained, surprised at his level of calm now that someone else was with him and panicking. "There's something else," he added frankly. Thomas looked at him expectantly, obviously in no mood to wait for information. "Rory was with her when I left and now, he's… We can't find him. He's gone."

Chapter Sixty-Nine

"The Simon's murder is still our number one priority. I need you all to go over witness statements, door-to-door enquiries and forensics. There has to be something we're missing. We may have Melinda Ryker in custody with evidence to support her as the murderer, but it doesn't feel right. Something's missing. I want us to find it," Nate instructed his team who were currently gathered around a large conference room table with their pens moving quickly across their notepads. Dismissing them with a wave and a nod, Nate leant back in his chair and looked frustratedly at Sam.

"What are you thinking?" Sam asked as he leant almost horizontally in his chair throwing a ball of elastic bands into the air repeatedly.

"I think it's one of the men," Nate thought aloud.

Sam nodded slowly. "Logan?" he asked.

"No. Whatever happened between them I believe Logan did actually love her. I don't think he had it in him to kill her and then move her body cold-heartedly," Nate murmured, still playing with possibilities in his mind. "Thomas Ryker can't stand authority. Hates those he believes beneath him. Maybe he decided to take out his frustration over his father's re-marrying on Lina."

Sam's grunt in response got Nate's attention. "I put Haversham on him a few days ago," admitted Sam, noticing

Nate's surprise. "All he's done for the last few days is work, see his family and…" trailing off like he'd finished his sentence.

"And?" Nate prompted.

"He's been to see a registered therapist twice in two days. I might be wrong but if I killed someone, I wouldn't go straight into a therapist's office to explain my troubles. Especially if I tended to lose my temper the way Thomas Ryker does," Sam said convincingly. Nate had to give the other man credit, he had a point. Perhaps Thomas wasn't the killer, perhaps Melinda wasn't either. Nate's gut was telling him that something deeper was at play here, something more complicated than one person killing another. Harry Ryker had form for hurting his children, but the man seemed to have spent years trying to make up for it. Would he really have killed a girl he treated like his own?

In the distance Nate could hear a phone ringing but paid no attention to it. Spit-balling with Sam was helping to clear his head, it could get them somewhere. No phone was going to stop the progress he could feel coming just around the corner. The door opened suddenly, and Sam's desk sergeant girlfriend peered into the room. "Sir, there's a phone call for you. It's the hospital. They said there seems to be an attempted murder on one of your persons of interest." At her words Nate's heartbeat doubled and his breathing became hesitant. Unaware of her boss's fear, the desk sergeant continued. "They said it was blunt force trauma to the back of her head."

"Her?" Nate rasped suddenly more than terrified, not taking note of the way Sam was watching him warily.

Taken aback by Nate's question, the desk sergeant nodded her head slowly. "Yes, sir. Victim is a Miss Riya Ryker."

Before the woman had a chance to finish speaking, Nate had already made a beeline for the door. Not caring about the strange looks he was receiving, Nate grabbed his car keys and made his way towards the hospital.

Chapter Seventy

All three of them sat silently with their elbows braced on their knees and lips touching their white-knuckled hands. If they hadn't been waiting on news of life or death, Thomas was sure he would have found the scene funny. No news, no doctor, no nothing. Riya was lying in a room somewhere surrounded by strangers who were making decisions about her life. Everything felt wrong and looking at his brother and father they felt the same way.

The movement of the large white doors against each other made all three men look up instantaneously. A woman wearing dark green scrubs and a blue cap walked into the waiting room and Thomas knew she was the person they had been waiting for. "Ryker family?" the woman bellowed. In unison the men stood up and took frighteningly large steps towards the beckoning woman. "I'm Doctor Garcia. I'm Riya's neurosurgeon," the doctor spoke, holding out her hand in a formal greeting. Thomas outstretched his own and shook her hand introducing themselves as he did. "Riya sustained an injury to the back of her head which caused a nasty laceration," Doctor Garcia explained, her eyes darting towards her patient's father as he loudly gasped and turned away from her.

"Please, Doctor. Go on," Thomas prompted, needing to know how he was supposed to be feeling.

"The force of the blow caused a massive swelling in

Riya's brain. The pressure was too much and that caused her to lose consciousness. That coupled with severe blood loss were our main concerns to begin with," Garcia continued to divulge.

"*Were* your main concerns?" Thomas asked, fearing the worst.

Realising his concerns, the doctor was quick to respond. "Yes, were. We managed to control the bleeding and are monitoring the swelling very closely. Your sister is a fighter, Mr Ryker," tentatively smiling, Doctor Garcia confirmed.

"So, she's alive?" For the first time, since he'd entered the hospital's waiting room, Harry spoke up in a whisper. It looked as if his father was holding his breath in hope as he waited for the doctor's remarks.

"Yes, Mr Ryker. She is still in critical condition and we have her in a medically induced coma in order to help the swelling, but she is very much alive," the doctor spoke patiently. It was amazing to Thomas that this woman had more than enough to do but she still took the time to provide support and reassurance to a family she didn't know.

A loud exhale from his father told him it was safe to relax. "Can we see her?" Harry asked impatiently.

"Yes, I can let you see her but only one at a time and not for very long. She's still quite delicate so it's best to keep visits short," Doctor Garcia instructed with just the right mix of authority and sympathy.

All three men moved behind the doctor, each as eager as the others to see for themselves that Riya was still breathing. Walking around the maze-like hospital took longer than Thomas thought possible. It was baffling to Thomas that in a building where speed was literally the difference between life and death, the hallways seemed to go on for days. Each second they travelled felt like hours. He had felt fear before, felt loss before but never to this extent, never to the extent that each second felt like his heart was being cut with a sharp knife over and over again. As Doctor Garcia indicated that they had reached the room in which Riya had been placed, his father didn't give either of his sons the option of seeing their sister first as he flew swiftly into the room. The large window on the wall beside him gave them a view into the touching moment between father and daughter.

Thomas leaning on one side and Logan on the other, both men stared at their sister who was attached to every kind of wire and tube imaginable, the rhythmic sound of her heartbeat being their only source of comfort for the time being. "What about Rory? Do we need to call anyone?" Thomas asked, finally being able to think about something other than finding his sister.

"I called the police as soon as I finished calling for an ambulance. They said they'd meet us here," Logan said, eyes never leaving Riya's still form.

Taking a moment, not for the first time, to admire Logan's ability to do what needed to be done, even under extreme circumstances, Thomas followed his younger brother's gaze. "What about Dominic? Should we try calling him?" Thomas asked during the lull of panic, needing to do something to make himself feel useful.

"Dad's the only one with his contact info," Logan replied distractedly. Thomas, satisfied that they had done all they could for the time being, went back to simply watching as his father stroked Riya's cheek and kept talking to her as if she could understand every word. What use were sweet sentiments to a woman whose brain function had essentially been put on a back burner anyway? Of course, in saying that Thomas was probably going to walk into that sparse unfeeling room and do much the same.

The large sweep of the doors drew Thomas's attention away. Rolling his eyes and stepping forward, in an effort to subconsciously protect his, more than ever, vulnerable sister. His anger towards the man had calmed down since the initial shock but that didn't mean he had to share these fragile moments with him. "Where is she?" Detective Richards demanded, moving at a startling pace.

"Family only, Detective," Thomas uttered, not bothering to give the other man any look or words of disdain.

"Where. Is. She," Nate said dangerously low. Logan took pity on the man and nodded towards the large windows. The detective walked over to the opening and seemed to be at a loss for words. Ever so slowly he rested his palms against the glass and let out a long sigh of relief.

"She's lost a lot of blood. They've put her in a medically induced coma. Apparently, there's some swelling on the brain," Logan explained in a more generous tone than Thomas thought himself capable.

"She's going to be OK though. Right?" Nate asked jaggedly.

Thomas laughed ironically. "She's been hit over the head by someone who also took our stepbrother captive. So, no, Detective, I think she'll be far from OK." Venom dripping through his words.

"They said the swelling needs to go down, then we'll know more," Logan said, looking like the angel to Thomas's devil.

"Thank you," Nate mumbled quietly. "I need to see the doctor," Nate added, sounding more confident and professional than he had since walking through the door minutes earlier.

With that statement, Thomas decided it was time to draw the line. "You are not family. This has nothing to do with you!" he yelled, stepping between Nate and the open hallway in front of them.

"I am a detective on your stepsister's murder case. This is more than likely connected so that MAKES it my business. Now get out of my way or I'll arrest you for interfering with an active investigation," Nate threatened with an overriding stance that would shrink many men down to half their size. Thomas was not one of those men.

As he stepped forward to release some of his pent-up anger on the unsuspecting detective, Logan placed himself between the two men. "Tom. Let the man do his job," his brother insisted, looking for support from Thomas in diminishing the tension that was rising at his sister's bedside. Thomas started to argue but Logan stopped him. "He means something to her. Don't make him leave, she wouldn't want that," he finished.

"Detective Richards!" a voice called from the darkness of the hallway that went off into the distance behind them. As Doctor Garcia appeared smiling at Richards, Thomas was surprised at the jealously that resonated in his stomach at the doctor's warm welcome to the man Thomas was just about to punch.

The detective turned towards the attractive doctor in order to speak with her privately which did nothing but further Thomas's abhorrent mood. What was it about this man that irked him so badly? His sister was lying unconscious and all he could think about was causing pain to the annoying yet thorough detective that hadn't really done anything to him other than do his job. As the doctor and detective left with whispering voices, Harry exited the room with tear-stains down his eyes. Expression clearing, Thomas suspected, for the sake of his sons, Harry gave a sorry half smile and looked towards them both. "Who's next?"

Chapter Seventy-One

"Any chance you can tell me something about the person that did this to her?" Nate asked Gabby, barely containing his fury at the thought of someone harming Riya in such a barbaric, unimaginative way.

Gabby looked at Nate. Their two professions overlapped more than either of them liked to admit but over the years they had become a team to be reckoned with. Gabby was a beautiful woman, no one could deny it, but since the very moment he'd met her, the doctor had done nothing for him. The complete opposite was true of Riya. It was true that there had once been a misunderstanding after a high amount of drinking, but that was all water under the bridge and since then they had become a good team when they needed to be. "To be honest, Nate, she hasn't been here long enough. When she first came in, we had more pressing things to deal with than helping the likes of you," Gabby tried to tease but it quickly fell on deaf ears. The grimace across Nate's face was not a usual sight for the normally easy-going detective.

"Anything, Gabby?" Nate tried to say, sounding less agitated than he really was.

Squinting her large eyes at Nate, looking at him like she'd never seen him before, Gabby rolled her eyes. "The angle of the injury suggests the person that attacked Riya was at least four inches taller than her."

"Ha! That narrows it down then." Nate seethed, turning

from her and pacing slightly with his hands firmly on his hips.

Not one to suffer fools lightly, Gabby gave him a displeased look. "What's got you so wound up?" she asked snappishly. Nate's distant look as he gazed towards the room Riya occupied. "Is it her?" Gabby asked, tilting her head towards the direction to which he was staring. Nate looked startled at Gabby's question, but the truth behind his eyes betrayed him.

"It wasn't meant to happen," Nate confirmed in an unapologetic tone.

"Nate! If they find out... You shouldn't be on this case. I'll call Sam and see..." Gabby said, seemingly believing that the world really was that black and white.

"No." Nate cut her off. "I will finish this. I will find out who did this to her." Vowing with all of his feeling.

"The dead girl? Or your recent flavour of the month?" snidely Gabby argued. She wasn't disappointed by his reaction.

For the first time in minutes Nate stopped pacing tensely and shot daggers towards her. It was clear to the young doctor that her 'friend', and she used that term lightly given his current attitude, was more than just testing the waters with the female Ryker. "Do what you do best and just stay the hell out my way," Nate seethed at Gabby.

"I'll have more information in the next couple of hours. I call you when I know more," she finished, admitting defeat to Nate's feelings for an inappropriate woman currently at the centre of his murder investigation. In all the years she had been associated with the local police station, Gabby had never seen Nate Richards out of control. She didn't know whether to be hurt or just plain angry.

Chapter Seventy-Two

Sam was overseeing the forensic team that had begun sweeping through Logan Ryker's house in the hope of finding something that pointed towards the person who attacked Riya. The hustle and bustle of the team who were fully within their element of sampling and microfibers, impaired his ability to realise the shift in the room as Nate entered.

The man stood still as he surveyed the room around him. The usually larger than life man was vacant and in his place was a shell that seemed to be barely holding it together. "You sure you're OK to be here?" Sam tried softly if only to spare his partner for the next few minutes.

"I'm fine," Nate said, closing his eyes to mentally pull himself together. "Sorry, Sam. Just feel like I need to be doing something right now. I need to be here," he finished, awkwardly thinking that out of everybody, Sam would understand about his feelings on this latest incident. Nate cleared his throat and forced himself back into his work. "Talk me through what we've got."

Sam seemed to look at his superior with a mix of uncertainty and pity but thought better of it and began walking towards the crime scene. "So, we've already tried dusting the door handle for prints, but it seems to have been wiped," Sam explained, trying to fill the painful silence that was still emanating from his boss. "As far as we can tell, Riya was standing facing away from the front door as the assailant entered. They then picked up one of the kitchen island stools and used the base to hit her over the head. Blood spatter indicates that she was hit from a distance of about a metre," Sam finished, still darting his eyes carefully between Nate and the dark red stain of blood on the floor.

Eyes lingering towards the ground, Nate cleared his throat. "How heavy are the stools? Could anybody simply lift one up and use it as a weapon?" slowly Nate asked.

"Surprisingly, they're quite light, wouldn't take much strength to be able to pick them up," Sam said, indicating the lightness of the weapon by picking up its twin that remained blissfully unaware of the heinous acts its pair had been forced to commit. "The main focus at the moment is the whereabouts of the boy. Neighbours saw nothing and the attacker either covered up the struggle before leaving or… Rory knew them."

"Make sure there are continuous news blasts showing Rory's face. Someone must have seen something, we've just got to make them realise it," Nate said confidently.

"You got it. What are you thinking?" Sam asked, eager to hear Nate's first impression on the crime scene in front of them.

"I think someone has tried very hard to make this look like a random attack and nothing to do with the initial murder. At this point I think that's highly unlikely. Whoever hurt Lina hurt Riya and then took Rory because he saw something," Nate thought aloud.

"You think one of them hurt Riya?" Sam asked unsure. From what they'd both witnessed, every single one of the Ryker men treated Riya as if they worshipped the ground she walked on. It made no sense for one of them to have hurt her like she was no better than an animal.

"I can't see it being anybody else. Who else would hurt Riya and then have a need to take Rory? It only makes sense if Rory knew the person that hit Riya, nobody else would need to worry about him recognising them as they left," Nate said, working the puzzle out within his mind.

"But why bother getting Riya here? Surely it would make sense to get her when she was alone," Sam queried, confused.

"Unless Rory was the target all along," Nate said, finally clocking onto the motive of this most recent crime. "Riya was just standing in the way of their actual goal."

"Does this mean Melinda's innocent?" Sam questioned, struggling to understand the stringing together of facts and suspicion in Nate's head.

"She's secure at the hospital. She couldn't've done this. But Lina... that's another story," Nate said, not even believing his own words. All the evidence was in place, it was a clear-cut answer to the murder of Lina Simons so why was Nate still adamant that the murderer was at large and that it was the same person who had hurt the woman that meant so much to him? Melinda Ryker was damaged, hated her daughter and seemed to drift into different people on an almost daily basis. But a murderer? He thought not. "We've got Melinda on a psychiatric hold for at least another week according to Ruby, so let's just see how things play out," Nate said firmly, taking back his control after realising he had momentarily misplaced it in the whirlpool of emotion that was the last few hours. Working was good. Working kept the demons at bay.

Chapter Seventy-Three

Control. He'd strived for it all day and where had that got him? Back to where the day had begun, standing outside a hospital room feeling like the most helpless person in the room. The graveyard shift at the hospital meant that nobody was there, no Ryker clan to avoid, no nursing staff to annoy and no doctors to not understand.

Nate opened the door as quietly as he could and was immediately greeted by the high-pitch beep of Riya's heart rate. Her usually vibrant eyes were glued shut and her usual endearing smile was nowhere to be seen. Nate had tried to go home and get some rest, but no solace had come as he pictured her lying on the small sterile bed alone and cold. His thoughts had led him here to her and he wasn't leaving until he had to.

Nate pulled the cheap, poorly lined chair at the side of the room and dragged it as close to his woman as possible. Reclining uncomfortably in the plastic wood chair, Nate lay one of his hands across his stomach and the other beside her own on the paper-thin mattress.

A long time later, Nate awoke as his legs, now stretched out in front of him, were moved roughly by another set of feet's kick. The haunting face of Thomas Ryker was all he was able to see on his awakening. Both men, one standing, the other sitting, stayed locked in the other's stare for what felt like hours as they judged how best to handle the situation before them.

Nate recognised the tired and disturbed look of Thomas Ryker as one he was probably still sporting so decided to forego their usual primitive dance of alpha-maleness. "Sorry. I couldn't sleep," Nate said regretfully. He cared a great deal about Riya, more than cared if he were being honest, but this man was her family, her blood. He had no wish to step on his toes when it came to his sister's close call. Thomas didn't respond so Nate believed him to be either so caught up in anger or sadness it was best to leave him to it. "I'll leave you to it. I'm sorry," Nate said, surprised. Thomas Ryker had annoyed him from the start, had actively wanted to antagonize him at every turn, yet at this moment in time Nate felt akin to this man more than he had to any other soul for as long as he could remember. Thomas was hurting just as much as he was.

"No," Thomas said, surprising them both, "She'd want you here. I shouldn't get in the way of that," He stated in an understanding tone of voice. Thomas then did the unexpected, he pulled a similar chair to Nate's from the opposite side of the room and sat in much the same way as Nate had just hours before. Neither man speaking for minute upon minute joined them in a brotherhood of peaceful waiting. Riya was still sound asleep, and would be for at least a few more days, but still they stayed for any indication that she may need them through the night.

As the small clock beside the hospital bedside ticked over to three a.m., Thomas turned his head and looked directly into Riya's face. He remained looking, thinking, for less than a minute and then hung his head in a singular laugh. "It's strange, she's not awake but I can feel her telling me what to do," Thomas spoke with humour.

Nate himself then looked up from his hand, now entangled with hers, and looked at the other man. "What's she telling you to do?" he asked, wanting to prolong the truce they had silently called.

"Apologise," Thomas stated matter-of-factly with no more explanation. Nate raised both his eyebrows in question and the other man smirked over at him. "I haven't acted the way I should towards you. At the station and then again at Riya's the other morning. It was... indecent of me," he ended trying to sound more gentlemanly than he ever had before.

Nate pursed his lips and bobbed his head up and down in silent agreement. "She's your sister. It's only right that you'd try and protect her," he conceded, understanding that it couldn't be easy for Thomas to admit his faults, on top of being emotionally fractured due to his sister's ill health. "Besides, I'm sure it's not easy being pulled into a police station and having your whole family history aired out in front of strangers."

Thomas was suddenly overwhelmed with respect for this man. Not only had he acted completely out of line when he had been going through some 'routine' questioning, but he had almost hit the man numerous times, purely out of spite. "No, it wasn't but I shouldn't have reacted that way anyway. I know you're only trying to do your job and for that I really am sorry," added Thomas healthily.

"Your whole family are persons of interest in my murder investigation and yet here I am. Sitting beside your sister's hospital bed like I have a God-given right to be here. Perhaps you're not the only one who should be apologising," Nate said and Thomas could not help but believe the man's sincerity. "I need you to know that your sister means... a lot to me. I'd never use her for the job," expanded Nate and his words rang true — Thomas could see it through the expansion of his eyes.

"I believe you, Detective, and while we're on the subject I hope you know I didn't hurt Lina. Or my sister," declared Thomas somberly.

His words ran through Nate's mind and despite all of his professional ethics, on following evidence and leads, he believed Thomas innocent of both crimes. This man had his issues, that much was clear, but he tended to take against those he saw as a threat. Lina Simons may have annoyed him, and her presence may have been an imposition, but she was no threat, and neither was Riya. "It may be a mistake, but I believe you. And whilst we're here, call me Nate. No point in pretending that professional boundaries haven't been crossed already," Nate finished, indicating to Riya with a tip of his head and a guilty smirk of recognition of his own short-comings.

Chapter Seventy-Four

"Melinda, did you hear what I said?" Sam tried and failed yet again. The woman lying half alive in the hospital bed with adorning restraints had barely flinched a muscle upon hearing that her only remaining child had been taken. Ruby stood to the side of the room watching, giving the young detective an encouraging nod of reassurance every now and again but remaining silent. "Your son is missing. I need you to tell me anything that might help us get him back."

Sam was seconds away from turning around and leaving her to her own demons, but Melinda's movement stopped him. "I take it you have spoken to Dominic about this. He is, after all, the one responsible for Rory." The bland reply came as an unwelcome interruption to the silence of the room. "One child dead. The other missing. I'm not sure that qualifies me to be the next of kin to any child. Least of all my own," Melinda stated and then once again resumed her lifeless position against the low-priced pillows.

Looking towards Ruby for help, the therapist signaled for Sam to follow her out into the hallway. Closing the door carefully, he looked toward the duller than normal therapist for guidance. "What's going on with her?" Sam asked, wanting to know if the woman he saw laying helplessly powerless inside the room next to him was capable of murder and possibly helping with the kidnap of her son.

Ruby looked thoughtfully at the closed door to Melinda's hospital room. "She's completely shut down. Hasn't spoken to me since I walked in and called her bluff. She now knows she holds no power and has no connections," Ruby observed, slightly less empathetically than she usually did.

"Do you think she's guilty?" Sam asked carefully. Nate had told him that Melinda had tried to rattle Ruby in the worst possible way. They didn't know what Melinda claimed to know, but whatever it had been had terrified their good-hearted therapist to her core. Since then, Ruby had been closed off, distant and had even stopped dressing and accessorizing in such a colourful way.

"I think it's possible she's involved with both, but she couldn't have handled either of them on her own. She's not mentally strong enough in my opinion." Ruby spoke quietly and succinctly without making eye contact with Sam.

"OK. Thanks for your help, Ruby," Sam said, pleasantly dismissing her. Ruby took note of Sam's words and hurried quickly away. After making sure she was well and truly out of ear shot, Sam dialed his boss's number. Within a couple of rings Nate picked up and casually waited for Sam's findings. "Melinda's shut down, won't talk, won't react, nothing. She says we're better off talking to the ex-husband. Have we heard anything from him yet?" asked Sam.

The sigh wavered through his phone as Nate replied, "No. According to his assistant he should be flying back into the country, and more importantly phone signal, first thing tomorrow. He still doesn't know, I'm told."

"Sir?" questioned Sam hesitantly.

"Uh-oh. You only call me sir when you want something I don't want to give. What is it?" Nate asked with a slight chuckle that gave Sam the confidence that he needed.

"I want to get another psychologist in to examine Melinda," Sam said quickly and to the point. The silence that followed told him that Nate wasn't sure about his idea to cut Ruby out of the loop.

"Why?" asked Nate expectantly. He trusted him and Sam knew it, but even then, Nate needed some sort of evidence to back up the undermining of someone they both considered a friend.

After a large indrawn breath Sam began his reasoning. "Ruby doesn't seem invested in Melinda any more. Seems upset about Melinda's would-be innocence, and what's more, they no longer have a rapport, Melinda's stopped talking to Ruby and vice versa. It's like Ruby's too afraid of Melinda's reaction if she digs too much deeper."

"How is Melinda behaving towards her?" Nate asked as soon as he'd finished.

"She's not. Melinda isn't reacting to anyone with more than a few words," Sam said, not really having noticed any difference between the way Melinda reacted to Ruby and the way she reacted to everybody else.

"OK, if you're sure, I'll make some calls and get someone down there to evaluate Melinda. Maybe they can tell us more," Nate said but Sam could feel his indecision on whether to continue or not. "Sam, try not to mention this to Ruby. Melinda scared her. I still want to understand how."

"You got it, boss," Sam replied, thankful for his superior's backing.

Chapter Seventy-Five

Sitting at his desk taking call after call trying to decipher the bogus tips from the real leads, Nate growled in frustration. A child was missing and yet people seemed to thrive on leading the police down the garden path. The room was alight with claims of sightings and descriptions, but none had come to anything worthwhile. Each phone was chirping away with rings upon rings as the whole station continued the almost country-wide search for a child. That is how it remained until a voice bellowed around them. From where he was sitting, Nate could hear the scuffle of raised voices in reception as they began to get louder and louder until they were too noisy to ignore.

Walking into the main reception area, where the likes of witnesses and criminals overlapped, Nate was presented with a somewhat put-together man who was actively yelling at the desk sergeant on duty. Arms waving and threats blasting, Nate decided it was time to step in. "Excuse me, sir, perhaps I can help you? How about we start with a name?"

The man stopped flapping his arms as Nate spoke. Je turned on his heel and came face to face with him. "I'm Dominic Shaw," he said tersely, obviously in some sort of hurry.

"Ah, Mr Shaw. I'm Detective Richards and I..." Nate began but was immediately interrupted.

"Where the hell is my son?" howled Dominic, stepping forward as if spoiling for a fight with just about anyone.

"Sir, please come and sit down," Nate tried to say calmly. "I can explain everything just as soon as you calm down," he continued, ushering Dominic into the adjoining meeting room where he'd spoken to Riya only a few short weeks ago. Reluctantly, Dominic did as he was asked and shuffled into the small room behind Nate who then offered him a seat. "First of all, Mr Shaw, I want to apologise for you having to come back under these horrific circumstances. I'm sure losing your stepdaughter was hard enough without the pain of finding out your own son is missing."

"I'm sorry, Lina is... she's..." Dominic was in a verbal loop of confusion as he struggled to grasp the truth behind what Nate had just divulged.

"I'd have thought that your ex-wife would've told you. Lina was found dead at her home. Murdered," Nate said, sensing this man was one who appreciated bluntness of truth rather than beating around the bush. Unfortunately, as much as Nate may have been right, he didn't find out. Dominic sat frozen in the moment as time passed by. Nate understood it was a shock, but this was a girl that hadn't spent any time with this man in years, it didn't make sense for Lina's death to be this man's sole focus right now, especially with his child missing.

"How?" Dominic asked. "How did she... how did she die?" he finished on a whispering cry.

"She was pushed down the stairs. She hit her head," Nate said pragmatically trying to gauge the situation he seemed not to be clued in on. "May I ask, sir, when was the last time you saw Miss Simons?"

"About six months ago," Dominic said, suddenly pulling himself together. "I worried about her. Her mother wasn't exactly the maternal type." Even as Dominic spoke Nate could hear the rehearsed speech shattering behind his ears.

"Sorry, Mr Shaw, we didn't realise how close you and your stepdaughter were. If you wouldn't mind, I think it is imperative that we ask you some questions in the interview room. You may have some information that we need," Nate said, standing once again. "It could prove vital to understanding the disappearance of your son," he added for good measure. A single nod of the head was all the confirmation he needed. Nate led Dominic through the station and signaled for Sam to follow them into the well-used interview room.

With the formalities said, Nate relaxed into his normal routine. Dominic was here voluntarily, no lawyer, no emotional walls to dismantle and relative information to gather. "Mr Shaw, you say you last saw Lina Simons six months ago, is that correct?" Nate queried.

"Yes. Sometime in February I think," Dominic replied distractedly.

"And what prompted this meeting?" Nate wondered out loud. Dominic had been in Lina's life quite some time ago, but Lina had already grown, she wouldn't have needed him paternally as Rory had.

"I bumped into her in town and we had some lunch," Dominic explained vaguely. "I'm sorry but what does this have to do with my son's disappearance?" he asked, suddenly concerned for his son's welfare.

"We believe your son's kidnap is linked to Miss Simon's death," Sam explained to the abruptly frustrated father. "Did you often see Lina without your son or ex-wife?" Sam asked after Nate nodded at him to dig further.

"Sometimes. We grew quite close when I married her mother," Dominic continued to say coldly. Sam began to rise in his seat to prod further but stopped as he watched Dominic's head drop in recognition. "Full disclosure?"

"It would help," Nate mumbled from his position slightly aback from the conversation.

"We slept together," Dominic said, looking like he would rather swallow glass than expand any further. "It was only the once. We ran into each other and she kept pushing for it and it just happened." Taking in a large gulp of air, Dominic paused for the judgement he suspected was coming his way.

"Lina was in a relationship through the whole of February, however new it may have been. Did she tell you that?" Nate said retaking the lead.

"Yes. She said that he wanted more from her than she was willing to give. Apparently, he wanted commitment, a future. Lina said she didn't want to give up the opportunity of other exciting things she'd always wanted to try," Dominic muttered, closing his eyes and shaking his head once again like he was mentally chastising himself for his actions.

"You think she purposely seduced you?" Nate asked skeptically, not sure whether to believe the man's subtle hint that Lina had been the aggressor and not the other way round. Dominic was in good shape for his age but not in good enough shape to compare to the flawless youth Lina's body displayed.

"All I know is, Lina was upset, well not even upset, I'd say she was angry. Practically vibratingly angry. She muttered something under her breath about Melinda and the next thing I knew she was grabbing at my thigh," Dominic said, gradually dulling his voice down to a whisper. "Can we please move on. I need to start looking for my son."

"What was Melinda's relationship like with Lina?" Nate asked casually, already knowing the answer.

"Ha! They didn't have one. Melinda lives her life barely acknowledging the fact she has children let alone caring enough to have a proper relationship with either of them," Dominic said, ruefully describing his ex-wife in the same manner that everyone else had.

"Is there anyone you can think of that would want to hurt your son and stepdaughter?" Sam asked in a casual way. Ticking off the formal questions that they had to ask.

"He's six years old! Nobody wants to hurt him!" exploded Dominic.

"We understand your frustration, Mr Shaw, just please bear with us a few more minutes and then we'll give you all the information you need," Sam said, ever the peacekeeper. "Have there been any unusual new additions to your son's life recently?" he enquired.

"No. I don't think so. He spends the summer holidays with Melinda and Harry being left with God knows who. Maybe they can tell you something I don't know," Dominic said with a scowl.

Nate looked at Sam and then back to Dominic. "You sound resentful of the fact," he prodded, needing for some unprofessional reason to find out all the skeletons that lurked in the Rykers' closets.

"Melinda took six weeks every year of Rory's life for pointless reasons. She didn't want him, just wanted to keep some sort of leverage over me and my money," Dominic said, referring to Melinda in harsh lighting yet again.

"What about Harry?" Nate asked carefully. He could almost feel the unspoken words of dislike oozing from the other man.

"Harry Ryker seemed to be more interested in re-doing his shot at parenting than he did about Melinda. Rory was just a means to an end for him." Shrugging in his response, Dominic seemed to find humour in Harry Ryker's desperation.

"By all accounts Harry Ryker didn't need another go around on his parenting. He seemed to be the perfect father," Nate said, embellishing slightly to see where the line of questioning ended up.

For the first time since Dominic Shaw walked into the building, he looked smug. "I have been in the same business circles as Harry Ryker for many years. I have seen his children walk into rooms with bruises on their face and fear in their eyes. Harry Ryker is not the man everybody thinks he is," he finished, leaning back in his chair, amused with himself for unmasking the would-be angel Harry Ryker in devils play. "Will that be all? I'd really like to start looking for my son now."

Nate sat and looked at the man incredulously. He could feel Sam's shock at both Dominic's statement and Nate's lack of reaction. "Yes, of course. We'll be in touch with any new developments that come up." Dismissing Dominic quickly and ushering him to the door, Nate breathed a sigh of relief and turned to extinguish another fire that had been lit following this case.

"You knew. Didn't you?" Sam uttered in a dropped voice. It was a rare thing for Nate to keep case secrets from his partner, but he'd needed to keep his promise to Riya. The truth had destroyed her. Who knew what the public finding out would do?

"Yep," Nate said, briskly bobbing his head, bracing himself for the hurt or anger that Sam would hurl his way any second later. It didn't come. Sam simply patted Nate on the shoulder in some kind of consolation and chuckled as he made his way out of the room.

Chapter Seventy-Six

"Just open your eyes, honey, please. Just one look, that's all I'm asking," Harry Ryker whispered into the ear of his only daughter as Logan looked on blankly. His father began stroking the side of her face and Logan had to turn away. His wife had died. He'd survived. Lina was killed. He'd survived. Riya could never wake up. Logan doubted that Harry would survive let alone thrive. Logan walked out of the room quietly and leant against the first wall he found. The thump that his head made as he lay backwards was the only thing that resonated in the otherwise empty hallway. Where had it all gone wrong?

"I'm sorry, Mr Ryker, are you all right?" Dr Garcia spoke softly when she approached from the corner of his eye. The woman had shown herself to be an outstanding doctor in the short time that he had been in her company but even she didn't have all the answers. Riya was out cold, and the doctors had already taken her off the drugs. She should be waking up, but she wasn't showing any sign of doing so and it was breaking each and every one of them apart.

"Can I ask you something, Doctor?" Logan asked, still staring up towards the poorly lit ceiling.

"Of course," the doctor said politely in a fully rehearsed way. Logan couldn't help but think that she must be sick of this part, the part that made her have to be there through all the emotional ups and downs.

Hoping that she took his question to heart and answered honestly, rather than with the same optimistic babble he'd been hearing from every nurse that had come their way, Logan posed a question to the female doctor. "What are my sister's chances of waking up?"

Doctor Garcia appeared shocked at his frankness but on further scrutiny she obviously saw his need to know the realistic prognosis. "Each day that she doesn't wake up limits her chances. At the moment I'd say you shouldn't panic — it's early. It just takes certain people longer to shake off the drugs," the currently un-emotional doctor stated confidently.

"You hear about people waking up weeks, even months after and being absolutely fine, though?" Logan asked suddenly in the need of some comfort. Unfortunately, the doctor had already started on the path to painful truths and nothing seemed to be stopping her.

"The chances of someone waking up like that without having some kind of permanent brain damage are so low there's no point in even considering that as an option," she replied coldly. Her eyes sparkled with medical knowledge and Logan could tell she loved what she did, this was of no help to him in his feelings of helplessness. Doctor Garcia looked up at him and recognition flashed through her eyes. "Your sister is young and strong. As I said, it's early days. No need to panic yet."

Opening his mouth to respond, Logan stopped short as he watched his brother swiftly walking down towards them. He had no idea how Thomas managed to do it, but he managed to exert dominance in the most basic parts of life. Thomas was a man people looked up to, even if they didn't know him. People paid attention to him the minute his presence was felt in a room. Surprisingly, even the doctor seemed to notice his brother's ever-present aura. "How is she?" Thomas asked before he reached where they were standing.

"No change," Logan answered in a blunt murmur and then watched in utter shock as Thomas's gaze and attention remained solely on Doctor Garcia. Nothing moved, nothing happened they just stood. Thomas looking at the doctor, the doctor looking at Thomas as if there were nobody else in the world. "Tom?" he prompted when the tension increased.

Thomas blinked roughly and cleared his throat. "Where's Dad?" he asked in half a whisper and half a growl of frustration.

"In with Riya. He's been in there for hours," replied Logan solemnly. "Might need a hand getting him to leave," he not so subtly hinted to his brother. Getting Harry home resting, and hopefully fed, was next on their agenda and Logan was anxious to get started on the task.

Thomas nodded, still not taking his eyes off of Doctor Garcia, who in turn was locked in his dark gaze. "Yeah. I'll follow you in," his brother said, finally bringing his gaze to Logan's. It was easy to understand that Thomas was asking for a moment alone with the doctor and Logan didn't need to be told twice, he was happy to escape the building tension that had surrounded the hallway.

Logan stepped back into the dim hospital room and was not surprised that his father hadn't moved. Taking the seat next to him, Logan sat in the small, badly lined chair and rested his elbows against the arm rests. Sat in the chair, Logan was closer to his father than he had been since Riya had arrived in A and E, and he could hear the hushed whispers that his father was uttering into his own hands. Not a religious man, Harry Ryker never prayed and yet there he was speaking to a higher power, begging for his daughter to be returned to him. Logan felt the unfamiliar sting of tears well in his eyes. If Riya didn't come through this, Harry Ryker wouldn't be the only one whose world was destroyed.

Rubbing his hand over the lower part of his face, Thomas entered the room. His older brother stepped across to stand behind him and their father. Thomas preceded to gently squeeze Harry's shoulder, and in recognition of his presence their father responded by patting Thomas's hand. "Dad. It's time to go home. You need some rest," his brother tried to reason with the frail man hunched by Riya's bedside but both younger men could feel the resistance before it was spoken.

Harry began actively shaking his head continuously as he gripped the side of the bed in a show of refusal. "No. I'm not leaving," growled their father lowly. "I won't have her left alone," he added more brokenly than he had spoken before.

"I'll stay," Logan heard himself say distantly. Since the moment he had let go of her hand as she'd been wheeled away on a gurney, Logan had not sat alone with his sister. He craved that time now. "Dad, go back with Thomas. Get some food and then get some sleep. You can come back tomorrow morning," Logan said empathetically. Harry seemed to yield to Logan's statement as he began rising slowly out of his chair.

Thomas and Harry left, whispering small goodbyes with Thomas following their father with a hand stretched close to his back in support. The door clicked shut behind them and Logan was left in a gradually darkening room with only his sister for company. He felt better simply being able to sit in her presence. For so many years they had been each other's rock, the one person they could turn to in times of need. Logan wasn't his brother, he wouldn't remain by her bedside all night waiting for small signs of life. He would sit for a while in a show of support and then follow suit of his brother and father.

Hanging his head against the cool metal bar that lined the bed, Logan screwed his eyes shut. He whispered into the darkness, "Please, Riya. Don't do this to us."

Chapter Seventy-Seven

Nate slipped through the now familiar door. His makeshift bed come chair was not at all appealing, but he believed there was more chance of rest there, close to her, than there was at home alone, in his own bed. This had become his routine. Working through the day, trying not to think about this room and the person inside it and then sneaking back in each night for a few restless hours of sleep before starting the whole cycle over again.

Nate flipped over his case notes that were currently clutched in his hand and began procrastinating intently. A deep breath emanating from Riya pulled his gaze to her stilly lain body. Nate tucked a stray strand of hair behind her ear as best he could and hunched forward to grasp her hand in his, the action being very familiar after days of needing the slightest sense of her touch to get by. "What do you think?" he asked the woman who was unable to respond. "Everything, says it was Melinda, the evidence is all there but then you get attacked. They have to be linked and Melinda's been locked away for almost a month." Nate felt ridiculous talking to Riya when he wasn't even sure she could hear him, but in some strange way he felt he could breathe easier the more he said. "I don't think it was her. But if it's not her then it really only leaves your family as suspects. Would you be able to forgive me if I had to do what my job needs me to do? Because I will have to, Riya. Whichever one it was I will have to arrest them. Could you deal with that? Would you be able to stay with me afterwards?" finished Nate, fully aware that he had begun to delve deeper into his mental spin. "I just... need you with me, Riya."

Snapping awake, Nate hadn't meant to fall asleep so quickly but it was like a weight had been lifted. The air around him felt different somehow, more hopeful. He stretched his back and sighed into the dull room. Half intending to just pick up his, now fallen on the floor, case file, Nate casually stood but then came to a halt. Afraid to move, Nate held his eyes on the sight he was afraid to believe.

Riya's eyes were locked on his. Was this the tiredness? Was his mind playing tricks on him? Nate didn't know the answer to his wonderings but was terrified of using the spark of happiness that had just come into his soul. He remained still, not altering his gaze, not moving his body, not feeling like he was even breathing. Nate watched in awe as Riya took in a deep breath and blinked her eyes. Once. Twice and a third time, bringing hope with every eyelid flutter. "Riya?" he whispered in disbelief to which her only response was to tilt one corner of her mouth up in a charmingly optimistic smile. "You're awake! Hold on, just hold on and I'll go get someone," Nate said already rushing out of the room in hot pursuit.

Nate watched as the doctor on call shone a light into Riya's eyes muttering about pupil function like it was supposed to mean something to either his patient or him as the worried boyfriend. The doctor continued checking vitals and murmuring to himself about stats and all Nate could do was bounce his leg impatiently. He understood that the doctor's job was a difficult one but all he wanted to know was that everything was OK. "Now, Miss Ryker, can you tell me your full name?"

The milliseconds ticked by as Nate waited with bated breath for the voice he had missed so much in just as few short days. Riya opened her mouth, but no sound came out. She tried again and again but nothing. The heart rate monitor increased to show her frustration and she began lifting her upper body off the mattress in an effort to force the words out. Collapsing in exhaustion, Nate watched as tears began rolling down her cheeks. "No need to worry, Miss Ryker, it can sometimes take a while for your body to be fully functional again. Your reflexes are all intact, so you'll be able to move about more freely when you are less tired. Give your brain time to heal and we'll see what comes of your voice," the man he called Doctor, who looked no older than sixteen, said cheerfully. Nate wanted to punch the man. The words held optimism, but his statement was riddled with maybes and unhelpful uncertainties.

The doctor left and Nate hurried across the room to resume his position on the chair. Stroking her cheek, he looked deep into her eyes and softly spoke in positives that were a definite as a contrast from the no-longer-in-the-room doctor's spiel. "You're awake. We didn't think that would happen." Nate raised her hand to lay a kiss across her palm. "Everything else we can deal with. I'm with you no matter what," he finished, making circles with his forefinger against her soft skin. After the minutes ticked by, Nate realised he was being selfish. "I'll go and call your dad and brothers. They'll want to know you're awake." Beginning to stand, Nate was stilled by her hand on his arm. Riya shook her head and tried to pull him back into his chair. Unwilling to go against her silent plea, Nate sat back down as she rolled onto her side and faced him head on. Riya gave him one last smile, this one reaching her travelling eyes, grabbed his hand firmly, placing it under her own head and went limp into, what he hoped would be, a peaceful sleep. He'd meant what he said. He was with her. Nothing else mattered.

Chapter Seventy-Eight

Riya was in hell. Awake yet unable to verbalize how or what she was feeling. Nate had left just before her father and brothers had come crashing into the room and she wasn't sure how to feel about that. She knew he was with her, his whispers into the night and early morning had made her believe that, but what she didn't know was how to process her terror at him leaving and her family entering.

Riya's head pounded painfully. It felt like there were knives trying to cut their way out of her skull. Her eyes pulsed with every movement but even those feelings paled in comparison to her anxiety that came on the moment her family had moved into the room. On entering the room, Thomas had picked up the small whiteboard Nate had tracked down for her to communicate with and looked at it with a mixture of disgust and curiosity, until finally laying it back down across her legs. From her 'talk' with Nate, after she had awoken from a needed but unhelpful sleep, she was more concerned about Rory who had apparently gone missing, than she was about making small talk with the men currently surrounding her.

Logan was quietly standing watching the room as he leant against the back wall. He hadn't said a word simply just stared at her. Uneasiness swept across her and a sudden wave of sadness crept its way into her heart. Never in her life had Riya felt anxious in the company of her family but there she was uncomfortable in her own skin. Her father kissed her on the forehead for what felt like the hundredth time since he'd entered the room and she struggled not to shudder. In her mind, Riya had decided there was nothing worse than not being able to understand your own impulses.

"I'm so glad you're OK, honey. You had us worried there for a second." Harry spoke with a soothing voice.

Breathing heavily out of her nose, Riya tried her best to return the smile but came up horrifically short. Bobbing her head in recognition she tried to pretend everything would work out all right, that everything would return to normal. Instead, she found herself thinking about how strange it was. All her life these people had been her rocks, her comfort but now, in the confines of the increasingly depressing hospital room, the only thing she could draw comfort or happiness from was the idea that Nate would be back in a few short hours.

Hoping to prompt her family's departure, Riya closed her eyes in an effort to pretend to be asleep. All three men began speaking in hushed whispers as one by one they sloped through the, now well used, door. She began opening her eyes slowly to check that the coast was well and truly clear when she heard the door re-open from the outside. Her rapidly beating heart, even to her own mind, seemed ridiculous given how safe a hospital should be but unencumbered by logic, the organ kept fracturing her nerves with every pulse. The subtle hint of perfume made her relax. Of course she knew that women could cause harm too, but her subconscious involuntarily allowed her to relax. Doctor Garcia gently touched her shoulder and Riya opened her eyes to look at her more fully. "I just need to check your vitals again, Riya. If that's all right?" the woman, whom she had only known a short while, implored. Riya trusted her. She didn't know why or how, but nonetheless she did. Knowing this, she nodded willingly in response as the Doctor moved to her pressure points and then her injury site.

Minutes later, Doctor Garcia was finishing up as Nate walked into the room. His bright and cheery smile warmed her in ways that were indescribable. Nate stopped short as she looked between him and the doctor still standing by her bedside. "Doctor," he greeted with a shy, almost roguish smile.

"Detective Richards," Doctor Garcia replied without sparing him a glance. "Miss Ryker is still very weak. I'm afraid you'll have to leave any more questions for another time." The business-like tone the doctor had adopted was unusual for a doctor with such a warm bedside manner, but Riya shrugged it off. They obviously knew each other, and when Riya could be bothered to write the long-winded question on her ever-tiresome whiteboard, she made a mental note to ask Nate exactly what he had done that seemed to have annoyed the doctor so much.

"Ah…" Nate stuttered in a way that gave away his intended secret. He motioned towards the chair that still lay ajar from the side of Riya's bed.

It seemed that Nate's lack of an answer prompted the good doctor to finally look him in the eyes. She shook her head and gave, what Riya interpreted as a, bitter smile and swept out of the room. The pair of them watched as she left, and Nate pointed a finger towards her to tell her he'd be back in a minute. Not for the first time, Riya cursed her lack of voice and tried, but failed, to listen in to the conversation going on behind the door that shielded her from the rest of the world.

Chapter Seventy-Nine

Quietly pulling the door to, Nate turned to face Gabby. It wasn't as if they always agreed on everything but never had she turned on him like this. He'd called her for updates, wanted more information or similarities about the person or people that attacked both Lina and Riya, but it had gotten him nowhere. Gabby had shut him out. "Look. I know I was a bit blunt the other day but there's no reason to ignore me like that or make it obvious in front of…"

"Oh, I see. It's fine to talk to me like shit but the minute I almost harm your boy scout image that you're putting on for the Ryker woman, you get to act all holier than thou," Gabby said with hurt reflecting in her eyes.

The emotions of some people really did confuse Nate. Gabby shouldn't be this angry at his relationship with Riya, surely? "Gabby, what's going on?" Nate asked, deciding it was better to get the facts before risking upsetting or angering her even more.

"Two years ago, you said you'd never mix work relationships with personal ones even though I wanted… And now you're risking everything to what? Have a fling with a suspect. If you didn't want me, didn't find me attractive enough, you should've just told me," Gabby whispered to him with a stony look in her eyes. Gone was the hurt, gone was the anger and in their place were emotions that looked a lot like curiosity and self-doubt.

"Gabby, I think you're an attractive, incredibly intelligent woman but I just didn't see you in that way. I'm sorry if I upset you that night but I couldn't lie to you and just pretend," Nate implored as she held her hand up in an effort for him to stop the emotional trip down memory lane. "You wanted something, you made that clear when you... but I couldn't do that to you. I respect you too much for that."

Gabby nodded her head in an effort to hold the tears at bay. "God, I'm sorry, Nate. I'm over this and up until last week I was fine!" she said, sadly chuckling.

Nate watched her confused. "What happened last week?" he asked softly, sensing that there was something more at play than his rejection of her more than two years ago.

"My dad died," Gabby replied mutedly to which Nate began to offer condolences, but Gabby continued without taking a breath. "I know I shouldn't let it impact my work, but I guess I just... needed someone to be mad at." Smiling sheepishly, Gabby continued, "I'm not really angry at you, Nate, I just needed something to take my mind off... everything."

"I'm so sorry, Gabby," Nate said, gently squeezing her upper arm.

"Thanks, but I think that's my line for today. I'm just not used to seeing you... like this," Gabby replied, waving her arms towards the room where Riya was currently waiting for him. "I'm happy for you, Nate. I am. It feels like you two are heading somewhere." Trying to bring a bit of friendliness back into their conversation, Gabby hinted.

Nate appreciated her attempts at reconciliation but could tell there was more going on behind her eyes but chose to leave it be. For now. Trying to respond in a way that wouldn't risk upsetting her further, Nate looked at the closed door behind him and sighed out a smile. "I think it is. Yeah," Nate said nonchalantly.

Gabby tightly smiled back at him and pulled her white coat around her body like it was a protective shield. "I'll leave you to it then," Gabby said, turning on her heal but stopping before she disappeared from sight. "I really am sorry, Nate," the doctor forced out, not waiting for him to respond before hastening away.

Nate re-entered Riya's room and laughed at the curious expression that was lining her face. Deciding it would be fun to let her stew for a while, Nate took his time bringing himself further into the room and making himself comfortable in the cheap furniture. His teasing had the desired effect as, as much as she could, given her current difficulties, Riya huffed out an irritated puff of air. Flashing her a smile, Nate gave in. "She tried it on once, but I just didn't feel it, you know. Anyway, her dad died this week and she said that she needed someone to be mad at and seeing me and you made her pick me."

It took her a few moments to write her response on her small whiteboard. The scrawled words made him laugh unceremoniously loud. Riya had not so subtly written the words, 'Lucky for me then.' Nate was amazed at her lightheartedness. She believed his words at face value and Nate had never met a person able to do that for him without so much as a question. Riya wiped her board clean and began writing something else but this time her face contorted slightly in unease. 'The boys came over earlier.' A quick wipe and she was off again. 'I'm not sure I want them to come back.' Shocked by her revelation, Nate was heartbroken to see tears hovering on her eyelashes.

He stroked the side of her face and looked deep into her eyes. "Why, Riya?" he whispered quietly, not wanting to stop her from expressing her fears.

Forcibly wiping the tears from her eyes, Riya snatched her pen up yet again and began frantically writing the words he had thought, but never voiced to her. 'It had to be one of them.'

Chapter Eighty

Harry sat watching the small clock next to him as it counted down the seconds until it reached a more sociable hour. A few more hours and he could go back to the hospital, could sit next to his daughter and hope for medical science to do its job and make her better. The minute each of his children had come along, they had captured a special part of his heart, they had enamored him in ways that were incomprehensible to those that had never been blessed with children. Riya had been the same and yet different. Sophia had wanted a third child, but nothing had come of it for years until the 'miracle baby', as Sophia had said, came along.

Harry could remember the night before Riya was born like it was yesterday. He'd returned from work to a dark and quiet house and watched his boys sleep, the kind of sleep that was so deep you were unaware of everything that was going on around you. Vividly, the feelings of uncertainty still lingered in the back of his mind like a bad dream. Harry remembered thinking that he'd never be able to love anything or anyone as much as he loved his sons. Then he held her. Everything had stopped and he was smitten. His daughter, his baby girl had wrapped him around her tiny little finger with his first look into her deep blue eyes and it held more strength than anything he'd ever felt before.

Deciding that sitting there watching the minutes tick by

was a waste of his brain cells, Harry got up and exhaustedly made his way into Logan's still dark kitchen. It had confused him that Logan had been allowed back into his house less than three days after Riya had been hit, but he was still in limbo about when he could go back to his own home. Not that he was sure he ever wanted to go back. Perhaps there was a difference between the crime scene of an attack and the crime scene of a murder.

Coffee in hand, Harry looked down at the countertop where the picture he had been staring at earlier still lay. Rory's smiling face beamed through the thick paper and Harry closed his eyes in remorse. The boy didn't deserve the few months he'd had to go through and there was nothing Harry could do to help him through it. Dominic wasn't answering his calls, as if he had no right to know about the latest developments in Rory's disappearance. Everything had fallen apart, and Harry didn't know if he even wanted to fix the remnants of his forgotten life.

Chapter Eighty-One

"Melinda Ryker is being released from the hospital," Ruby said as she swanned into the harsh lighting of the station, her hair floating it it's small ringlets around the outline of her face. The light shade of blue that highlighted the ends of her curls was only eclipsed by the look of panic that darted from her eyes to the flush of red across her cheeks.

"I know," Nate uttered softly, content with letting hurricane Ruby say her peace before offering an opinion.

"How is that even possible?" Ruby ranted. "She is ill, Nate. She's ill! At the very least she's a murderer. Shouldn't that count for something?" She was in a spin now and Nate was concerned about how long it may take to get her out of it.

"Ruby," Nate said, stopping her in mid flow, "she's out on caution whilst we investigate Riya's attack, and her doctors said she was well enough to go home." Nate tried to explain, much to her confusion.

Ruby looked at him as if he'd grown two heads. "She's not talking, Nate! She tried to kill herself. How is she well enough to be out in public?" she stated with tears running down her face.

Nate stood and ushered her into his chair as he crouched down in front of her. "She is talking, Ruby, just not to us. Melinda has been held for weeks being psychologically assessed and the doctors have decided she's well enough to leave." Even as he spoke Ruby started shaking her head, so he tried calming her down from another angle. "From the start you said you thought she was innocent. Riya's attack changes things. It has to be connected, has to have been an aftershock of the murder but it couldn't have been Melinda."

"But…" Ruby tried to interrupt.

"Melinda is still under caution, she could be guilty, but the prosecution doesn't believe she's a flight risk. Her funds are tied to her husband and so are her connections. Melinda has no power. If she's guilty, she won't get away with it and letting her go might prove useful," Nate tried, but saw darkness lurking beneath her eyes. "What does she have on you, Ruby?" he asked softly.

"Apparently she knew my first husband," Ruby confessed, much to Nate's surprise. He'd never heard a single mention of husband number one. It wasn't that they were so close that Nate would've expected Ruby to divulge her past because of sentiment, but he supposed it to be strange that after the years he had spent working in the station Nate hadn't heard a single rumour, whisper or speculation about Ruby's first attempt at matrimony.

"I don't think I know anything about him," Nate said with a smile, hoping that his face, which was a reminder of their friendship, may prompt her into divulging her secrets.

"I work hard to keep it that way. He's not something I like to think about, let alone talk about," Ruby said as Nate noticed her hands trembling where they lay placed on top of her knees. "She knows, Nate, she knows, and it could ruin everything," she added with tears running down her face looking more desolate than he had ever seen someone of her energy and excitement look.

"She knows what, Ruby?" Nate pushed. "I can only help you if you tell me everything."

"I killed him," Ruby forced out in a hushed whisper and her face crumbled.

Nate looked at her wide-eyed. "Ruby..." he said, trying to think of something useful to say.

Ruby suddenly looked panicked as if she'd only just realised what she'd just confessed to. "I mean... I didn't... I tried to... I didn't mean to," she resolved, looking more frazzled than most murder suspects that had passed through his interrogation room. Ruby looked wide-eyed at him trying not to hyperventilate. Seemingly pulling herself together, she began to explain but not loud enough to attract any more attention. "He liked to knock me about a bit, you know. Over time it got worse and then one day I woke up in the hospital. No idea how I got there and no memory of the day before. I told the police that it must've been him, but they said if I couldn't tell them exactly what happened there was nothing they could do."

Nate nodded along carefully so as not to interrupt her in mid flow, but at her long pause he decided she needed some sort of encouragement. "Keep going, Ruby, it's OK."

"I got discharged and had to go home. He was there and he... he came at me. I grabbed the first thing I could get my hands on. There was so much blood." Ruby shuddered at the thought, but Nate still didn't understand.

"Ruby, if it was self-defense there is nothing she can do," Nate said in his most caring tone of voice.

"I covered it up. It was on my record, Nate. I had to fix it, I had to make sure I could still work, do what I loved," Ruby uttered in a world of her own. "I lied about my name, Nate.

287

They wouldn't let me continue to work with vulnerable adults and children if my record was stained with a murder."

"Self-defense," Nate corrected. No matter what Ruby had done in her past he could see innocence in her soul. She wasn't a cold-blooded killer and the man who had caused her to act in a violent manner had obviously abused her. Mentally and physically.

Ruby strongly shook her head once. "Doesn't matter what it was. I lied to get my degree. I lied to get this job and Melinda knows. I don't know how, but she knows!" Unable to say anything more, Ruby gave in to the sobs that had been brewing in her throat.

Nate engulfed her in a hug and stroked her back softly. "I'm going to take care of this, all right? I will fix this, don't worry," he said between quietly hushing her.

"How? What's going to happen to me? To my job?" Ruby hiccupped.

Nate thought for less than a second before he answered. There was no question in his mind that Ruby didn't deserve her life to ripped apart after everything she'd been through. "As far as I'm concerned nobody else needs to know. This happened a long time ago, if I'm understanding correctly. I'll deal with Melinda. You just carry on doing what you do best," Nate said soothingly while tapping her on the nose like he would a child. His efforts were not in vain as she shone her regular bright smile at him.

"Thank you," Ruby whispered, looking at him gratefully and squeezing his hand. "Now go and see that gorgeous woman of yours," she said with a wink and then quickly leaving. Nate was left there in shock at her last statement. Did everyone see through his, what he thought of as a, closely kept secret that was Riya Ryker? Whatever the case, Nate had one stop to make before doing exactly what Ruby had told him to do. Melinda may have some amount of innocence, the extent of which was still unknown, but he was going to make sure she knew that his team, the people he cared about were completely off limits for her twisted, sick mind games. As a woman who had experienced trauma of her own, Nate couldn't help but think she should be a bit more understanding of Ruby's circumstances. But no. Melinda was a monster. That much was clear.

Chapter Eighty-Two

The subtle click of the door's mechanism was the only sound that could be heard throughout the first floor of the small hotel where Melinda had found herself staying. The impersonal room was bleak and unfeeling but somehow, she felt more at home here than she ever did in the house she'd been living in for the past five years. Whatever that said about the life she had led, Melinda didn't want to dwell on.

Throwing the small bag that held nothing but material things, Melinda perched on the end of the half-sized bed and considered her options. Her head was going stir crazy, she hadn't really spoken more than a few words in days, and she'd not seen anyone besides doctors and detectives in weeks. As if conjuring up a demon, there was a knock on the door with the telltale blow of impatience and indifference.

Melinda sighed into her steps as she made her way towards her borrowed door. Opening the oak panel cautiously, Melinda was surprised that mere hours after her release, Detective Richards was back with more accusations. "May I come in?" he asked as if it were a question and not a demand.

"You're going to no matter what I say," Melinda replied venomously, opening the door further to allow him room to enter. The detective scanned the room as if to inspect the state of her living but didn't relax enough to sit down. "What can I do for you now, Detective?" Melinda questioned, anxious to get the man out of her hotel room.

Nate seemed to consider his next words carefully before looking at her scrupulously. "You've been released," he said, stating the obvious in her opinion, "but in my book, you need to remember that you are still under watch." Melinda could sense that with his last statement the detective was trying to make her read between the lines. She was in no mood.

"Your point being?" Melinda asked, already tired of his attitude and hidden anger. Releasing her meant one thing, they didn't have enough on her to make the charges stick and she was determined to keep it that way.

"My point being that no matter what you think, you have no escape, no leverage and definitely no power." The detective looked at her and accepted that she was still not following his train of thought, so continued. "You do not threaten my team. You do not threaten the livelihoods of people I care about and you shouldn't even think about harming a single hair on their heads. Do I make myself clear?"

The dangerous twang in his voice vibrated around the small room in an effort to intimidate her. After the life she'd had, she was not that easily scared. "The old woman blabbed, did she? A violent woman like that working with mentally scarred people. It's not right." Pretending to be the concerned citizen.

"That woman suffered years of domestic abuse and accidently hurt the man who had tormented her to protect herself. The same woman then dedicates her life to helping those in similar situations. That 'old woman' is worth ten of you and if you follow through on any of your threats, even though I doubt that you actually have the power to do so, I will personally make sure that you are not only called out for being a good for nothing gold digger but I will make sure you are never allowed to make another penny off anybody else in this city. Penniless wouldn't be a good look on you, Melinda. Think carefully about your next move," Detective Richards seethed at her and then started making a move to leave.

"I take it that means I should stay away from my step-daughter then. Last I heard you were spending an awful lot of time sitting at her bedside. Tell me, Detective, do you give the same amount of attention to all your suspects or just the young good-looking ones?" As she spoke the detective froze and half turned to face her. Melinda couldn't fathom her own actions, she was a mystery to herself and all those around her. Why would she, at a time like this, anger the man that could make or break the next twenty years of her life.

"Don't test me, Melinda. You stay away from them or you will live to regret it," Detective Richards quietly growled before slamming his way out of her once again silent hotel room.

Chapter Eighty-Three

Storming through the doors to the hospital room he had become so familiar with, didn't help Nate's mood. Usually the sight of Riya, the mere thought of her cheered him up from whatever darkness he had shrouded himself him. Not this time. Not today. Riya sat still and watched as he paced in front of her. "How can you stand it? How can you stand her? She wants to destroy everything around her, and people just let her get away with it." Nate was aware he was ranting aggressively but something inside him wouldn't allow himself to stop. She was here, she was listening, and she wanted to help with or without a voice. "Melinda tried to get to Ruby. She tried to threaten and terrify a sixty-year-old woman who has done nothing but help people. What kind of a monster is she? How does she keep getting away with it?"

Breathing heavily, Nate placed his hands on his hips and looked up into the pale lifeless ceiling. "I don't think she's a murderer though. She has something to do with Lina's death but there's something telling me she wasn't the one who did the deed. She would have caused it, so why can't I do the world a favour and let her go down for it anyway? Nobody would miss her, nobody would be upset, just relieved," Nate rambled away, shaking his head, not noticing Riya's slow movement towards the edge of the bed. She placed her bare feet on the cold tiled floor and silently stepped towards him.

Nate, in his stupor, didn't hear or feel the movement in the room. Nor did he realise he had begun flexing his hands roughly in his hair until her soft, smaller hands gripped his wrists in an effort to stop him. "Nate," came a whisper that appeared to come from Riya's lips. The single word had made his mind stop still. No longer consumed with anger or confusion, Nate moved his palms across Riya's cheeks in hope and uncertainty.

"Riya?" he whispered, even quieter than she had appeared to speak moments before.

Although the words were husky and raw sounding, Riya replied confidently. "I was wondering how long it was going to take you to let me speak for a change," she said, adding a large grin to convey her point.

At the blissful joke bursting from her previously mute mouth, Nate chuckled out a sound of happiness and tearful joy as he kissed her firmly against her lips and then swiftly buried his face in her hair. Riya was healing physically, which meant he could start functioning properly once more. The woman he loved was safe, she was with him and she was healthy. Through everything, that was all that mattered.

After a reunion of sorts, which was ridiculous given they'd been together each night since she'd been admitted into the hospital, Nate ushered Riya back into her bed much to her annoyance. In her mind all she'd done for the last couple of weeks was sit or lie. Riya was sick of it. "Nate, I got my voice back. I'm not dying," she said in a chuckle.

Satisfied that she was once again resting, Nate returned her laugh with a relaxed smile and he leant back into his chair. "Indulge me," he added, shrugging his shoulders, and lifting his hands, palms face up. "How are you feeling? Really?" Still feeling panic at the thought of her in any kind of pain.

Riya tucked her hair behind her ears and let out a small sigh. In many cases a sigh would be a sign that she was in pain, or at least fed up, but not this time. Riya's sigh was one of contentment and relief. "My throat's still a little raw from the ventilator and this headache I've got going on isn't going away any time soon, but I'm awake so can't complain," she said in a teasing tone, hoping that Nate knew she was grateful to still be breathing let alone being able to speak.

"What've the doctors said?" Nate asked, linking their fingers together and stroking her hand with his thumb.

Riya leant her head back into her pillow and twisted her head to look at him fully. "As far as they can tell there's no lasting damage. The swelling has gone down to practically nothing so as long as I take it easy everything is back to normal."

Before Nate could respond there was a large billow of air from the opening door behind them and Harry Ryker stepped through into the light of the room. Immediately, like he was still a sixteen-year-old boy who had been caught doing something wrong, Nate jumped up and away from Riya's beside. He considered the difficulties he was now facing as both an investigating detective, and also as a man who was facing the father of the woman he had been sleeping with.

"Detective Richards." Harry spoke succinctly looking like he'd rather be anywhere but in front of Nate. "I don't think this is really the time for your questions. My daughter needs rest," he continued to instruct as he opened the door and nodded his head through it in an attempt at dismissing Nate.

"He stays, Dad," Riya said quickly, and by the look in her eyes was meaning to sound confident but the tremble that ricocheted in her voice gave away the emotional roller coaster that was going on within.

"Riya, he's not family. He will leave and..." Harry began.

"He stays!" Riya shouted with conviction. Harry seemed to be taken aback by the suddenly commanding Riya. Whatever the reasons for her sudden attitude change towards her father, Nate knew his decision was to stay by her side unless *she* asked him to leave.

"You've got your voice back?" Harry rasped in response, obviously only just realising the good news. "When did... How did..." He was at a loss for words and couldn't seem to pull a sentence together.

"Happened this morning just after you left," Riya said, managing a weak smile in her father's direction. "I would've called but I thought the surprise would be better." At the skeptical look Harry Ryker shot Riya, Nate knew that her thinly veiled attempts at throwing him off the scent of her anxiety and paranoia were not working. Gabby had told him it was to be expected after an attack like hers and he was damned if he would leave her to her fears in front of her father.

Nate looked into Riya's eyes and understood her silent plea. Her brothers knew about them, but her father did not. Riya wanted to keep it that way. He didn't ask why. "Since the attack, both myself and my colleagues believe it to be in your daughter's best interest to be under some sort of police protection while she's still in hospital. We keep our distance during the day but allow Miss Ryker the comfort of telling her we'll be right outside whilst she sleeps. It also allows us to update her on her case." Surprised at his own ability to lie convincingly, Nate stayed remarkably still as Harry assessed his explanation.

"I see," Harry replied bluntly, taking Nate's words at face value. "I'm more than happy to stay, honey, if you need me to." His eyes returning, lovingly, towards Riya once again.

Riya smiled at him shyly and patted his hand that lay beside her. "Don't worry, Dad. It's their job, they're trained for this. You're not. Besides, I'd feel really guilty making you sleep in one of those god-awful chairs," she explained to her father, who in turn turned around considering his options. As he contemplated his next move, Riya managed to throw a wink in Nate's direction.

Harry seemed to resign himself to leaving and turned back around to say his goodbyes. "You sure?" he asked, kissing her on the top of her head. Riya nodded and pasted on yet another unfeeling smile, and Harry left the room. The drop in tension was almost immediate until Riya broke out in a sob.

The tears rolled down her face in a constant stream. The shudders coursed through her body until she had no energy. Throughout it all Nate held her, whispering comforting sentiments into her hair. It had all come on suddenly, her father had said goodbye and the panic had set in. Not that it was her father's leaving that caused her sudden lack of air, it was the unease at being uncomfortable in her own skin and identity.

She'd locked the door, she knew she had. Whoever had come into Logan's house and hit her had a key, of which there were only four in existence, one was hers and the others belonged to the people she used to trust more than anything. It was terrifying. One of her brothers, or God forbid her father, had done this to her, left her for dead. Everything she had ever been taught or told to hold dear had collapsed into doubt and dread. The secrets were killing the Ryker bond slowly and as brutally as someone had killed Lina. "I'm sorry," Riya muttered into Nate's chest. He quietened her with a finger to her lips and gave her a tilt of his own.

"It might not be them, you know," Nate said, caressing her cheek. "You're upset, exhausted and in shock. Whatever your brain is telling you to think right now, is too jumbled up to really listen to. Get better, get some rest and see how you feel then." Nate seemed to realise she wasn't impressed with his attempt at consolation so continued. "If," he said prolongedly, stopping her impending interruption, "you still feel the same way in a couple of days, I will do everything in my power to make sure you are comfortable and safe."

Satisfied that Nate wasn't just dismissing her concerns, Riya leant back but kept a hold of his hand. With one last look of contentment on her face, Riya asked him a question she already knew the answer to. "Can you stay with me?" And despite knowing the answer she still couldn't stop the hint of anxiety that crept into her question.

"For as long as you'll have me," Nate perfectly replied, allowing her to fall back into a then peaceful and uninterrupted sleep.

Chapter Eighty-Four

Nate sat tapping his pen against his desk as he waited for Sam to arrive. The hospital was closer to the station than his house was, so he was uncharacteristically early to work that morning, making his agitation heightened. The phone rang, breaking his own silence. Nate picked it up, half expecting yet another bogus claim of information proclaiming to know where Rory Shaw was.

"Hello," Nate answered into the phone, already pinching the bridge of his nose with his thumb and forefinger. He half listened to the man on the other end of the phone's opening line. The exhausted detective's interest piqued as the distressed voice rambled through what they had thought they'd seen. "OK, sir, can you tell me where this was?" Nate scribbled down the location on a scrappy piece of torn paper as Sam strolled towards him. The less senior detective opened his mouth as if to speak but was stopped by Nate's outstretched finger. "Right. Can I take a full name and address for you, sir?" he finished asking before the dead silence echoed through the receiver. "Damn!" Nate shouted, smashing the phone back into its cradle. "They hung up." Finally directing his attention to his partner.

"Another nutjob?" Sam queried, still eating his breakfast.

"I don't think so," Nate said, contemplating all he had just heard. "We need to check something out," he said, not waiting for a response before rising and grabbing his jacket from the back of his chair. Passing Sam, Nate slapped him on the arm in an effort to make him follow him out of the door.

The pair made their way through the station and into Nate's car. They slid into their respective seats and Sam turned to look at him expectantly. "Want to tell me where we're going?" he asked jokingly.

Nate scrunched his eyebrows together and let out a large breath of air. "The man on the phone said he saw a small boy matching Rory's description being handed over from one large vehicle to another at some petrol station along the A167," Nate explained, putting his keys keenly into the ignition. The hum of his engine both invigorated and calmed him with the knowledge that they were doing something about the missing child that was slowly stealing the heart of the nation.

The car sped along the road heading towards the possible lead on Rory. Nate gripped the steering wheel in hope that this would be the bread crumb that lead to the feast. This case needed results, he needed some peace and the boy needed to be safe. Sooner than he thought, Nate rolled his car into a parking space and hopped out quickly. Sam followed along behind him as Nate flashed his badge to the cashier standing at the till.

The men were led to the backroom storage area that had been 'converted' into a make-shift office where the manager sat regally. "Good morning. I'm Detective Inspector Richards and this is my partner Detective Sergeant Turner. I understand from one of your workers that you were on duty early evening yesterday."

The woman, who could have been no more than twenty, leapt up from her casual position in the throne-like elderly chair that sat before a rickety desk. The young woman coughed and spluttered the half-chewed doughnut still between her teeth. Realising how she must look, the girl covered her mouth quickly and hurryingly swallowed the remnants of her food. Nate couldn't help but chuckle, no matter how many times he got to see it always amazed him how caught off guard the general public could be. Pulling herself together, the manager dusted her hands against her standard issue work trousers and looked both Detectives in their eyes, darting between the two formidable men. "Yes. My shift started at midday and I ended up working a double until midnight. Is there a reason why you're asking me this?" 'Dianna', according to her name badge, asked suddenly concerned as to why two morbid looking Detectives were after her working schedule.

"Yes. We have reason to believe that a child who has been missing for over a week was seen here yesterday. We need to know if you remember seeing anything in particular or serving someone who appeared nervous or agitated in some way," Nate prompted professionally. He was under no illusion that a service station, like the one he was standing in, got busy at times, especially when situated on a main road such as this one, so the chances of the overworked staff member actually seeing the 'transaction' of the young boy take place was pretty much nil, but he had to try.

"You make it sound like my days aren't surrounded by crazies," the manager said, batting her eyes towards both men and twizzling her hair around her finger. As tactics go it wasn't an uncommon one, the interviewee often favored flirting with two male detectives rather than having to deal with questions they weren't prepared for or interested in.

"A child is missing. He has been gone for more than seven

days. We do not have time for jokes. Did you or did you not see anything untoward?" Sam seethed from behind him. Nate understood Sam's annoyance, the man had a history with children and his particular story did not end well. His partner managed to hide his personal pain well but every so often, in cases like their current one, Sam's feelings were too strong and rose to the surface.

Watching the shock register on the woman's face, Nate decided that, for once, he was to be the more reasonable and approachable police officer out of the two of them. "My colleague is right. Please, if you can think of anything at all it would be very helpful to us," he implored with a kind smile plastered across his face.

Dianna seemed to consider the contrast between the two men in front of her. Making her decision, one Nate didn't think was a particularly hard one given a child's life was at stake, the girl looked at Nate, completely disregarding Sam, and made her move to reply. "I'm sorry, Detective, I really can't remember anything out of the ordinary. I wish I could do more to help." Finishing with a solemn look towards Sam, Dianna gave a sorrowful lift of her lips.

Nodding subtly, Nate waited for Sam to finish his diligent note taking. "Thank you, ma'am," he muttered and made their excuses to leave, turning himself and his partner towards the door.

They barely made it a few small steps out into the quiet shop when Dianna rounded the corner with a shout bursting from her mouth. "Detective!" she squealed, afraid of being too late. Nate span around to face the suddenly anxious woman. "There was something... I'm sorry I didn't think of it before, it just gets so busy sometimes and I hardly have time to pay

302

attention to the customers in the store let alone the ones outside filling up. But it was strange so I couldn't help but keep an eye on them," she finished, looking like she believed her explanation to be done.

"Are you saying you saw someone outside doing something you believed to be out of the ordinary?" Nate asked, trying not to lead the young woman's ramble in any particular way.

"It was so strange, the first car pulled up next to the first pump at about seven, no one got out, nobody moved but the engine kept running and so did the headlights. About fifteen minutes later another car pulled up next to it and a man came out of each. Both were dressed in long trousers, one had a dark blue coat on, and the other a black hoodie with both their hoods pulled up around their faces. The first car's back door opened and a small child hopped out, I couldn't see if it was a boy or a girl, they were too far away for me to really see anything but the kid got straight out from the first car and into the other," Dianna said, closing her eyes as if studying the details of the night before in her mind's eye.

"What happened next?" Nate asked in a commanding voice, no longer concerned with acting as the kindly officer, more bothered about the information they were finally gathering.

The now helpful manager blinked her eyes rapidly to clear the fog. "The men didn't seem to say anything to each other. The child got into the second car and then, straight away, both men moved into their own vehicles and drove off," Dianna said confidently. Sometimes, when walking away from a witness, Nate could feel the credibility around them but for some reason this girl, this woman, gave him the impression that her testimony and her word was finite. This was the lead in finding Rory Shaw that they had been waiting for.

Sam took note of Nate's thoughtful expression and continued without him. "Did you notice anything about the cars? Make, model, colour perhaps." As always, his pen remained poised to write her response word for word.

"I'm sorry, I didn't see the make or model. They were big cars though, very dark, you couldn't see through the windows on either car and the colour looked like it was black, but I couldn't swear by that," Dianna guessed and both men nodded their thanks towards her. Despite earlier appearances, the young manager had proved herself to both detectives standing before her. She gave information when asked and had provided key testimony to Rory's whereabouts.

Sam nodded at him as he left the store to search the front of the shop. The man's process was sometimes a mystery to Nate, but he often brought results and he couldn't fault that. "We'll need copies of your CCTV from last night if you don't mind," Nate rhetorically asked the girl who nodded and hurried away, presumably to gather the evidence he had asked for. Nate had already spotted two cameras at the front of the store, watching the petrol pumps from different vantage points. Hopefully there was more. If the child was indeed Rory, there'd be a surge of new efforts to help find him. The tapes could prove he was still alive and that was imperative. In cases like these people began losing hope after forty-eight hours and assumed the child to be dead and the hunt for them began dwindling.

Dianna returned handing him a small USB stick. She smiled tentatively at him and Nate thanked her genuinely before heading out towards his still wayward partner. To his surprise, Nate found Sam standing looking up and down the busy motorway with questions behind his eyes. Seemed like a pointless endeavor to him but he was determined to give Sam the benefit of the doubt. "What's got you all worked up?" he asked casually, joining Sam in his, feet planted wide apart and hands in his pockets, stance.

Sam surveyed the motorway once more and then gritted his teeth. "There's no way to turn from the other side of the road to get to here, correct?" he asked but Nate wasn't sure he actually wanted the answer. "Even if there was, there's another service station directly opposite for cars travelling in that direction. The cars wouldn't use this particular station unless they were coming from the same direction, the direction of town." Try as he might, Nate knew there was no way he was going to decipher Sam's ramblings without help.

"You're point being?" he asked, only slightly annoyed by the subtle feeling of stupidity flowing in his blood.

"If the CCTV proves that both cars came from that direction," Sam began, pointing to his right, "it shows that both men came from the direction of town." Still not getting Sam's point, Nate nodded for the man to continue. "Which means we can prove that whoever took Rory to begin with and then took him last night are both leaving the town where all of the Rykers are. One of them took him and then handed him off to somebody who, up until last night, was also staying in town." Sam was looking rather pleased with himself and Nate couldn't help but agree with him. The man was on to something, that much was clear.

"We need uniforms to get in touch with traffic control and scour up and down this stretch of road for cameras. You get back to the station and work on the CCTV and make sure it really is Rory, then we can let the media know and get some more traction on this case," Nate said, already picking up his phone to dial in for help.

"On it, boss," Sam praised, walking away to jump into the car and start on his new project. Nate joined him opening the door. "What about you?" Sam asked him before he'd managed to take his seat against the supple leather.

"I've got some alibis to collect," Nate replied agitatedly.

Chapter Eighty-Five

A couple of loud raps against the door was all it took for Harry to open the door impatiently. His stepson was missing, his daughter was in hospital, not acting like herself and he had the hangover from hell. Of all the misfortunes Harry couldn't abide the one that was now waiting expectantly in front of him. Detective Richards stood with a smile playing across his lips wanting to be let in, and of course Harry knew he didn't have a choice. "Detective. Please come on in."

Richards sauntered his way into the house and looked around casually. "I was hoping your son would be here too, Mr Ryker. I have some questions to ask both of you." His words sounded calm and collected but something about the way the man was standing, not moving and yet somehow not still either, told Harry he was not someone to be messed with, let alone be lied to.

Harry leant back against the breakfast bar to mentally prepare himself for whatever new revelation the Detective came up with. "I'm sorry, Detective, my son had to go into work today. He won't be home until this evening. You might want to wait until then for your questions to be answered," Harry stated, not really grasping how pathetic it made him sound, a grown man not wanting to face a singular detective without his son there to support him.

The detective raised his eyebrows which showed Harry how ridiculous he was being. "I will find time to catch him later in the day. I assume you won't mind me asking you a few questions without him?" His teasing tone did nothing to tame the irritation Harry began to feel at the man's joking persona.

Stare going icy, Harry cleared his throat and crossed his arms over his chest. "Of course. Anything I can do to help," he said trying to remember his gentlemanly attributes he'd been taught from an early age.

"Where were you between the hours of seven and nine yesterday evening?" the questioning man asked in a strange tone.

Harry wasn't sure why, but the man didn't seem very interested in whatever his answer would be, more like simply using the question as a means to judge his tension levels. Whatever the reason for the question, Richards was anxious, or was it angry? Harry wasn't sure of either the emotion or the reason behind it. All he could gather was that something had happened. Something had caught the police's attention. "Why? Did something happen? Have you found Rory?" Harry asked in the blink of a second, suddenly on edge with the knowing eyes of the Detective baring down on him. Something, had definitely happened, Harry just didn't know what.

He watched as Detective Richards swallowed heavily and blinked hard. "Yesterday, a child was seen at a petrol station on the A167 matching your stepson's description. We believe this claim to be genuine and are currently reviewing tapes to corroborate our witness's statement. So, I'll ask again. Where. Were. You. Yesterday evening?" the investigator said, taking on a voice of quieted rage and certainty.

"I don't much like your tone, Detective," Harry whispered, defiantly angry.

For seconds after, time slowly ticked by as both men eyed each other ruefully. "My tone is not up for discussion, Mr Ryker. I am trying to solve not only a murder and an assault but a child abduction as well. Your family have been attacked, sir, and I have to ask myself why you aren't willing to help find the person responsible." The younger man spoke coldly. Harry didn't know how to handle a man like this, a man with that much regality. "Some might say it's because you've got something to hide, Mr Ryker. But I'm not so sure," Richards' verbal turmoil continued towards Harry. He turned and walked towards the door once again. "How do you want to be remembered, Harry? A man who lets his family down, or a man who helped catch the person who destroyed them?"

The question echoed through Harry's brain almost shattering his skull. He'd always believed his family was his life. The reason for his actions. Could he be letting them down? "I was here, Detective. From about three o'clock yesterday afternoon," Harry finally divulged.

The ominous detective didn't turn to face him, simply spoke with his head cocked to one side. "Anyone to vouch for that?" the question came out. The question he had been dreading.

"No," Harry muttered mutedly. "Logan was at work. I was alone," he added for good measure, not sure why he wanted to add yet another nail to his own coffin. It seemed everything he did or said implicated himself in all three crimes which was something that could not happen. Not unless the world wanted to watch his family truly fall apart.

"Interesting," Richards said cleverly before stalking out of the door and into the adjoining street. Once again, Harry was left alone in a house that wasn't his. Nothing was going as it should and for once in his life, Harry was unsure of what the future held. The only ones who mattered were the ones that had his name and his protection, the numbers of which were dwindling fast.

Chapter Eighty-Six

Nate closed the door softly behind him, sure of the confusion he had left in his wake. Harry Ryker was a strange soul. Nate believed that the older man loved his family, extending to both his stepchildren, but there was something sinister about the man. It was as if the man saw himself above his sins, his family needed to be kept wholesome no matter the cost. Would Harry be the kind of man to murder his stepdaughter, attack his own child and then kidnap his stepson? Nate didn't know. He'd like to think the man was too respectable, that he'd built a business and family in a respectable way. But what did he know? The more he got to know this family, the more he realised that it was rotten to the core.

The squeal of tyers pulling half into the space behind him was Nate's first indication of an impending Ryker. Logan stepped out of his small convertible with his Italian leather shoes clacking along the pavement. "Richards," he greeted in a pleasant tone of voice. It seemed that his connection to Riya had smoothed his fractured image out for both brothers.

"Good afternoon, Mr Ryker," Nate responded professionally. Logan's eyebrows raised so they were almost touching his hair line.

"Very formal. Must mean you need to ask me some more questions," reacted the youngest male Ryker with a kind of half chuckle. Nate had to give the man one thing, he was the most endearing one of them. He didn't react in anger or irritation, he simply tried to cheek and charm his way in or out of any situation that he deemed necessary.

"Yeah, sorry, just need to know where you were around seven p.m. yesterday evening?" Nate asked casually, taking on another tactic to the one he had just tried to use on the man's father.

Logan narrowed his eyes, Nate knew that the laid-back man in front of him could see through his calm persona. "I was at work. They might be able to vouch for me at the office, but there weren't very many people around," he explained, easily putting Nate at ease. Logan was looking like he was going to be an easy man to deal with, his explanations came easily despite the heartbreak Nate could still see lurking behind the surface. But was that all an act? Nate knew the complications of this case were expanding by the day, especially given his personal relationship to the family. He just had to hope that himself and his team figured out what happened to both Lina and Rory before his world came crashing down around him.

Chapter Eighty-Seven

Stepping through the automatic doors, Nate swept his way through the police station and into the comfortable chair opposite his desk. Sam was busy tapping away at his computer as he sat and spun with the chair's momentum. His partner stared intently at the screen with his retro glasses perched on the tip of his nose as his tongue kept peeking out from the side of his mouth. As if sensing a shift in the room's atmosphere, Sam looked at him through his thick lenses like he'd appeared via a puff of smoke.

"Well? Any possible culprits?" Sam asked, pulling himself from his unwarranted surprise.

"Thomas Ryker is the only one of the three with a solid alibi. The other two have no one to vouch for their whereabouts," Nate said regretfully. Of all the suspects that had followed him around throughout this case, he could've put money on Thomas Ryker being involved, but in the last week he had proved himself to be innocent of the most recent crimes. Thomas had been the big bad wolf to Nate's red riding hood from the offset of the investigation, but now all he could see was how similar he was to the oldest of the Ryker offspring. Maybe that's why the tension between the two alpha males had been so palpable in the beginning.

The silence hung around them like an unwelcome companion until Nate dropped his head and glared at the gawky detective. "What?" asked Nate impatiently, sensing his partners unspoken queries. "Come on, Sam. Seriously," he prompted further as the smaller man continued to remain mute.

Sam returned Nate's stare with equal edginess before he spoke. "I'll check with the hospital to make sure Miss Ryker didn't leave or show any sign of suspicious behaviour," he stated firmly and confidently, which, although not unusual for Sam, was out of the ordinary for him to display his dominance over Nate who was, after all, his superior officer.

Taking the bait as Nate believed his partner had expected, he bristled in retaliation. Not only had Sam thrown down the gauntlet for him to prove his professionalism without a shadow of a doubt, he had also, for all intents and purposes, just accused the woman he loved of being an accessory to child abduction. Or worse. "Sam," he growled in response. Nate in no way wanted to be accused or be seen to be forgetting his ethical duties. "You honestly think she took Rory, faked her own attack and what? Killed Lina as well? She's the only one of them that has an alibi for the murder for God's sake!" shouted Nate defensively.

"I'm not saying that," hushed Sam quietly. Amazingly, Nate's anger diminished somewhat, and his shoulders released some of the sudden tension. "You said so yourself, she's starting to suspect one of her family of killing Lina. Perhaps she orchestrated Rory's kidnapping to, in her own way, save him from the same fate," he continued to explain. Logically Nate knew that all his partner was trying to do was spit ball ideas, but it still stung. It wasn't possible. He refused to even contemplate it.

"Riya then hit herself over the head until she bled out across the floor, did she?" spat Nate sourly across the divide of their desks. He had no idea how unreasonable he may have sounded.

"No," Sam replied patiently. If he wasn't close to breaking point, Nate would have been impressed by his partner's ability not to take offence. "She could have had help, could have paid someone to do it. I know it sounds like a long shot, but these are the questions we NEED to be asking. Everything above board, everything out in the open. I'm not saying she's done anything, but hypothetically she could have. We just need to check it out rather than pretending she is not a Ryker when it comes to this investigation," Sam finished, leaning back in his chair until the unmistakable squeak of metal against leather became unbearable.

Locked together in a staring contest, that Nate knew he couldn't win, both men listened to the hands of the clock move minute by minute until neither could stand it any more. "Fine. You make the call. I want no part of it," he managed to whisper towards his partner. The confused man stilled across from him, not understanding why Nate would let something so close to him out of his control. "If it comes down to it and the evidence said she could have done something, it needs to be seen to be completely legit which means I, the man who's been sleeping with her, cannot go near any witnesses or evidence that may go against her. Understood?" Nate growled out.

Finally taking his boss's anger into account, Sam nodded slowly and uttered, "Yes, boss," quietly. He stood and moved past Nate, head hung in suspense. Sam didn't regret what he had said but hadn't quite comprehended how deep his senior officer's feelings for the Ryker woman really were.

Nate reached out and caught Sam's forearm. "She didn't do this. Check, because I know you have to, but don't expect me to be happy about it." He nodded towards the man who, on more times than he could count, had saved his life.

Sam bobbed his head in acceptance of Nate's dismissal, but the worrier in him couldn't leave without knowing the state of his relationship with his boss. "Nate are we…"

Interrupting Sam before he could finish, "We're OK." Nate nodded soulfully. "Go," he instructed bluntly before Sam left quickly. Rubbing his open palms against his face, Nate looked up at the hole filled ceiling above. Riya was innocent. He knew that. He just needed to find a murderer and a child abductor to be able to move on with his life. Everything he never knew he wanted was in his reach and only a sick-minded fool was standing in his way. Once he could put a face to that shadowy figure, Nate could enjoy the hunt.

Chapter Eighty-Eight

Thomas remained still as he sat beside his sister's bedside. He hadn't visited her alone since his impromptu meeting with Nate. The man and his attitude didn't bring the same wave of anger as it once did, the rage had cleared, and its wake had left the knowledge that his sister would be safe with the detective by her side. Her safety was all that mattered now. Who else could either of them trust? In a few short weeks everything had crumbled down around them. Logan had been sleeping with Lina, their father had relapsed into the shell of the man he maliciously became and Rory, an innocent, some would argue the only innocent amongst them, had been taken. Thomas wasn't sure he could ignore the blindingly obvious any more, a Ryker committed the crimes, but the reality was terrifying.

Riya stirred against the creaking bed and fluttered her eyelids open towards him. Her sleepy look took Thomas back to days of childish antics and a once loving family. "Hi," she uttered, the single word dripping in sleepiness.

"Hi yourself." Thomas tried, but failed, to appear cheery and hopeful. His sister was the only one of his so-called family members he could trust. There was no sentimental reason for this, he wasn't that kind of a man. His opinion was based on fact. Himself and his sister were the only ones who could say, with absolute certainty, where they had been during recent events. Of course, Thomas understood that his alibi for Lina's murder was unverified in the eyes of the law, but as harsh as it sounded, why would he make the effort to kill someone he cared absolutely nothing for? Some could say that his lack of interest was a motive in itself, that it showed his hatred for the girl, but they needed to understand the difference between hate and indifference.

Sitting up in bed slowly, Riya had taken the time, which he had spent internalizing his own thoughts, to shift herself upright. "Why aren't you at work?" she asked casually but with something else, that Thomas couldn't determine, lurking underneath.

Thomas sensed, more than he saw the trepidation in his sister's eyes. "I couldn't concentrate so thought I'd come see you instead." Freezing at the vacant stare Riya gave him Thomas continued, "I needed to make sure you were safe and that look in your eyes tells me you don't feel very safe right now. What's going on, Riya? Richards has this place surrounded, no one apart from us is allowed inside," Thomas asked and pleaded his sister to speak but still no words came. Silence when she couldn't talk was rough but the lack of words, knowing full well she could use them, was painful. Then a lightbulb went off within Thomas's mind. "It's us, isn't it? You're scared of us," he managed to whisper.

A few tears escaped down Riya's cheeks and Thomas knew he had hit the nail on the head. He leant over and used the pad of his thumb to wipe the drops of water from her porcelain-skinned face. "I don't know what's wrong with me," rasped Riya ungracefully allowing the tears to flow more freely.

"Talk to me. Whatever you are thinking, trust me, you're not the only one to have thought it," Thomas implored. Riya couldn't fall apart. Not now. Not ever. He wouldn't be able to bear having her slip away from him too. "What's got you so scared, Riya?"

Four seconds was all it took for Riya to speak the words that he had been thinking for the last few days. "It had to be one of you," she said as if it pained her to speak the words. "All my life you're all I've known. Please don't be the ones doing this to me, to them!" Riya shrieked laying backwards forcibly, placing her hands over her eyes so her fingers could also grab at her hair. The machine beeped faster around them signaling her rising anxiety and Thomas knew he had to calm her before a nurse, or the good doctor rushed in to help.

"Shhhh, Riya, listen to me." Thomas tried to console her by stroking her arms, still raised in front of her face, gently. She stopped struggling and looked at him through the small gaps in her fingers. "I think you're right," he said, deciding it would be best to be upfront and blunt rather than caring and slow. "I think one of them did this." The relief he saw from his words was instant. It was almost as if she had been scared of her own thoughts, thinking that they were misled and fanciful, and on hearing someone else felt the same, she was set free of the fear she felt in her own mind. Riya questioned him through wide eyes, and he responded with a slow nod of his head, confirming his agreement.

Riya gave a relieved smile, lowered her arms, and pushed herself back up into a sitting position. "I'm scared," she stated more in line with her usual tone of voice.

"I've got you, and I dare say that annoyance of a detective you've got hanging around you is in the wings waiting to protect you. Whatever happens next, we will handle it," Thomas promised. He had no idea if his father or Logan were actually the ones responsible, but the evidence was saying it could only be one of them. Whichever one was left at the end would be part of his sister's healing, but for now, Thomas was resigned to the fact that he was his sister's family, he was her safety net.

Chapter Eighty-Nine

Hunched over the small table in front of him, Nate surveyed the large whiteboard which held a timeline and numerous pictures of the people he had brought in or questioned in regard to all three of the active cases. The station was a buzz with activity, men and women running at twice the normal speed while the motivation for Rory Shaw's search continued to rise. It somewhat restored his faith in the police force to see their dedication and renewed purpose, but the fact that the station's finery had to have proof of life to give it their all, irked him more than his glimmer of hope for his colleagues.

The thick red and blue drawn arrows running to and from each profile of a suspect mocked him prolifically. Every one of the people smiling tauntingly at him, had hidden something. Nobody in this investigation was innocent, they had all in one way or another caused harm to another person, another loved one, including him.

If Logan killed Lina, why would he take Rory when his motive had nothing to do with the boy? If Harry had killed Lina, he'd have a reason to take the small child, he loved him, but the problem is Harry also loved Lina so why would he have killed her? Thomas would have made sense as the offender but for the life of him Nate couldn't see Rory's abduction and Riya's attack being separate to the murder case. If Thomas had killed Lina, Riya would have remained happy and healthy and

Rory would still be in the comfort of his own home.

"Boss!" Sam's yell resonated into Nate's conscious mind. It pulled him from the knotted strings that were holding his brain waves together. He turned to watch the slightly younger man rush his way into the busy room. Sam knocked the side of his leg against one desk while catching his jacket on the corner of another.

"Whoa. Slow down, Sam. Tell me what you've got," Nate said, determined to be the more pulled-together detective of the two.

"We can't get hold of Shaw," Sam replied, out of breath as if he had just run a marathon instead of a couple hundred metres at most. "I've tried calling his house, his hotel, his mobile, his work. Nothing. Even tried to get local uniforms to check in on his registered address but they said it's been completely emptied out," the out-of-breath detective rasped out, looking skeptically at the busy white note board in front of them.

"Doesn't make sense," Nate mumbled under his breath to no one in particular. He slapped the table in front of him with his opened palm and swore tentatively. "He couldn't have taken Rory to begin with. Melinda's out of the picture, no judge would allow her any kind of custody. He had his son, there was no need to take him, let alone pay someone else to do it." Rambling on like the puzzle was missing the most vital pieces.

"You think all this," Sam started waving his hand in a large circle through the air, "is about custody for the kid?" Sam asked, but Nate could tell the other man didn't believe that was the case either.

"No. He alibis out for both Lina's death and Rory's

abduction but it's possible he was the man collecting Rory from the service station. But even still. Why would he do it? There's no reason for it," Nate mused aloud without wanting a response. Dominic had struck him as a complicated man but a devout father. After their initial meeting, the man had rung twice daily to check on the progress of finding his son.

"What if..." Sam began to say but trailed off like his words were a pocket in the wind.

"What if what?" Nate snapped impatiently. Any idea, any hunch was a welcome distraction. They had suspects who were remaining squeaky clean, people who were like victims acting like criminals and a whole lot of unanswered questions.

Sam looked at his boss with wide eyes that flickered from side to side. It looked as if the slightly disheveled man was mentally putting his thoughts into a neat order before voicing them. "Say, you're Dominic. Your son is taken, and you rush over to try and find him. Someone gets in contact with you, outside of our tracked calls and phone taps. They say they have your son. They don't want money, they want nothing but the boy's safety. The person on the other end of the phone says that the only condition is that you have to leave, you have to take your son and disappear for a while. Would you do it?" Sam finished.

"It's a good story," Nate said, running his hands through his hair yet again and slumping back into an old chair beside him. "But what kind of kidnapper takes someone for the good of the victim and their family?" he asked, trying, but failing, not to succumb to the sharp, stabbing migraine that was looming behind his eyelids.

"A kidnapper who had been living as part of Rory's family. Loved Rory," Sam said blatantly. His mind, as always, remaining one step ahead of everybody else's in the room.

Nate groaned into the air and looked up in frustration. "And... we're back to the Rykers again. How can one seemingly perfect family cause so much trouble?" he grumbled.

"What's the next step, boss?" Sam asked, ignoring the emotional response his superior had adopted and moving onto the factual and listed duties.

Nate considered his options. Sam's theory proved to be their only lead and the only thing that made sense. "Call the CPS and see if we can get a search warrant for Shaw's calls and financial records. If he's gone with Rory, he would have got a call or message and then he would have needed to get his hands on some money and fast," Nate explained, even as Sam picked up his phone to call through for the information that could break this case wide open.

Chapter Ninety

The wail of police cars echoed throughout the dark night and Nate's chiseled face was highlighted by a thin layer of neon blue. There was a slight chill in the air as the world cooled down into the darkness of the evening. Nate resisted the need to zip his windbreaker up against the slight harshness of the breeze. The screeching sound of a woman's voice was higher than Nate thought possible. Smashed glass and hurried hospital staff were gathered around and shouting at one another as his target sat hunched over with handcuffs around her wrists.

Strongly walking towards the woman, Nate was filled with anger. What had she been thinking? What had she thought to accomplish? Realising he was now toe to toe with the woman, who looked like a shell of her former self, Nate raised his head to speak. "Melinda," he greeted sourly as the woman before him became smaller and smaller in a ball of her own despair. With no response to bounce off of, Nate stood in a kind of torturous limbo. "Melinda, tell me what happened?" he finally asked in a softer tone than he was feeling. The hospital's strong windows lay shattered and broken across the gritted street and the large pieces of flint that had been used to cause the unforeseen breakage were scattered beside Melinda like a badge of guilt.

The shivers ricocheting throughout her body were evident

in the way her body began to jump uncontrollably. "I don't know. I was at the hotel and then everything goes dark," she eventually replied while closing her eyes.

Nate opened his mouth to speak but was stopped by a stern-looking doctor in a pristine white lab coat. "I'm Doctor Robson. I've spoken to Mrs Ryker's doctors and have decided that it'll be best if she stays here. We need to take her inside and clean her up to assess the damage. Your questions will have to wait," the male doctor said as if his words were the absolute law. Nate rose to argue against the hindrance, but the older man stopped him with a hand halting him in the air. "Any questions you have, ask the nurse who discovered my patient, otherwise please allow me to do my job without any interference," the medical professional said blatantly before assisting Melinda to her feet and dragging her towards the large automatic doors that lined the entrance to the imposing hospital.

Pacing his way quickly to where the male nurse stood talking to other medical staff that happened to find themselves in the wrong place at the wrong time, Nate flashed his badge, effectively diminishing the small crowd to all but one person, and stood before the man who had, rather heroically, talked Melinda down and restrained her until reinforcements had arrived. "Good evening, sir, I'm Detective Richards. I was told you were the one to first approach Mrs Ryker after the initial incident. Is that correct?" Nate asked and was relieved to see the nod that the nervous man gave him in response. "Could you describe, in as much detail as you can, what you saw after Mrs Ryker arrived?" he questioned, opening his notebook to jot down the particulars in Sam's absence.

"Um... She came and um... she." The man fumbled with

his words and Nate could see the unmistakable of sheen of anxiety in the eyes of the heroic nurse.

"It's OK. It's normal to feel some shock. Take your time and whenever you're ready we'll go at your pace," Nate tried to console. He placed a comforting hand on the other man's shoulder. "Start at the beginning. What happened first?"

The younger man scrunched his eyelids together before taking a long deep breath. "I was in the front lobby and I heard her screech first. I ran out, thinking she was hurt and that's when it happened. She threw these large rocks towards the bottom floor windows with enough force that I remember thinking she must be on something. I tried to talk to her, tried to ask her questions but all she kept saying was that she, I don't know who 'she' is because she never said a name, was in there and that she was one of them and 'they' had to pay," the man said, adding to Nate's small amount of information gathered.

Taking a mental note of Melinda's cryptic words, that he understood more than he wanted to, Nate focused once again on the man reliving the nights events. "So, after she'd thrown the rocks, that's when you restrained her?" he asked, needing to complete the sequence of events for his superiors, if not for anybody else.

"Um… Yes, Yvonne, the receptionist, rushed out and handed me some medical restraints and then phoned the police. I talked to Mrs Ryker for a few more seconds and then when she lowered her arms, I managed to wrap the restraint around her," the nurse said as if it were a normal event for a normal day.

"And then what happened? You waited for her doctors and the police to arrive?" Nate asked, ready to wrap up this conversation so he could try and pry more information out of

327

Melinda herself.

Nodding his head, the nurse agreed with Nate's assumption. "Yes. I talked to her, she stopped screaming and then we sat on the curb until you arrived," the youthful hospital staffer finished, looking suddenly more tired than he had done in the last five minutes of conversation.

Nate smiled lightly. "That's great. Thanks for your help, you've been brilliant. Get some rest," he instructed, patting his witness on the shoulder once again. Quickly making his way through the front doors, Nate made his way into the hospital's busy A and E and over to the large fake marble reception desk. "Melinda Ryker, where is she?" he asked a woman, whom he assumed was Yvonne.

The woman, who was currently rushed off her feet, was moving papers around as if there was an impending fire following her every move. As Nate's voice registered in her brain the woman stopped and cast him a skeptical look. "I can only give that kind of information out to the family, sir," she said briskly before turning away.

Following her around the circular desk, Nate pulled his badge out of his back pocket. The wide-eyed receptionist looked knowingly at the warrant card. "Now. Tell me which room Melinda Ryker is in," he demanded, taking on the harsh persona that he was so comfortable in. As the woman rambled out the number and floor of Melinda's new home, Nate grabbed his phone and dialed Sam's number. He nodded his thanks to Yvonne and was relieved when he heard his partner's casual greeting. "Sam, I need you down at the hospital. Melinda Ryker has just had an episode. I need to question her and we both know I'm more tolerable when I've got the good cop to my bad cop," Nate said with a glint of humour, trying to tempt Sam out from what he assumed was sleep.

It worked. "Hang on. I'll be there in ten," Sam said quickly and Nate could hear the rustling of bed sheets as his partner readied himself for a much earlier start than expected. The soft sound of a female's voice in the background surprised him. He knew of Sam's office romance, but he had no idea how serious it may have become. He was happy for him, which was something he couldn't remember feeling before. If any of his friends had gotten married, moved in together or popped a sprog or two out, he'd said the necessary congratulatory remarks but deep down not really cared one way or another. Was it all because he had someone now? Was it all because of Riya that he could now delight in other people's happiness and good fortune? He didn't know, but it felt good to allow some semblance of joy into his otherwise murder- and- crime-filled life.

Deciding he had some time to kill, Nate knew he wouldn't be able to sit still without checking on the woman that was staying only a few floors away. Walking confidently through the familiar door, Nate smiled a greeting at Riya who was sitting delicately on her hospital bed with a book in hand. "Hi," he said with more relief in his voice than he was comfortable with at the sight of her, unharmed and as he'd left her. Placing what was supposed to be a gentle kiss on her lips, Nate felt his desire grow as Riya deepened the kiss.

Breaths mingling, hands roaming, Nate had no idea how long they remained like that, embraced and locked together. Like a bucket of ice water, they both seemed to realise exactly where they were at the same moment and gradually pulled away from each other. Nate rested his forehead against Riya's and gave her a confident smirk. "You seem to be feeling better," he said with a laugh. Looking into her deep eyes, he realised he could lose himself quite easily into their blue depths and not give a damn.

Riya grinned at Nate's words and stroked his face with one of her hands. "What brings you here this early in the day, Detective?" she said light-heartedly. Nate could see that Riya recognised the shadow of anger that passed across his face. She straightened and plastered on a more serious expression and tilted her head to the side. "What's going on?" she asked.

Nate considered giving her a white lie instead of the truth but decided against it and let out a deep sigh. "Melinda tried to break into the hospital today. I had to come and talk to her and get some statements," he said, trying to gauge her reaction.

She looked unsure of herself, which was not like Riya Ryker at all. "Why would she do that? She wasn't here... She wouldn't be... Was she here for me?" Riya asked him and the vulnerability in her voice almost broke him.

Nate reluctantly bobbed his head up and down. "I don't know but it's a possibility. Has Garcia told you when you can go home?" he asked, hoping he would be able to protect her somewhere other than the hospital very soon.

Pulling herself back into some semblance of happiness, Riya smiled. "Actually, Doctor Garcia said I'm good to go any time today. I was going to wait until I saw you later but now, you're here..."

"Pack your bag and I'll be back for you in less than half an hour," Nate instructed, finishing with one last firm kiss before going in search of Sam and Melinda.

Chapter Ninety-One

By the time Sam arrived, Nate was leaning against the wall next to Melinda's hospital room holding two cups of terrible coffee. "Hey," Nate said gruffly, greeting his partner. "The doctor's just finishing up and then we can go in and see her," he explained whilst outstretching one of the steaming paper cups, full of black liquid, towards the other man.

"Any idea what caused her to flip out like that?" Sam asked, more than a little curious about Melinda's psyche.

Shaking his head, Nate looked up at the young detective. "No. But apparently she was blaming 'them'," Nate depicted, air quoting at Sam to convey Melinda's fragile state of mind. "I'm working on the assumption that 'they'" air quoting again, "is referring to the Rykers," he finished with a pessimistic scowl.

"Really?" Sam asked skeptically. "Seems like a bit of a stretch. As far as our people are concerned Melinda has had no contact with any member of the family, let alone enough to cause that kind of reaction," Sam said and Nate couldn't help but think that he may just be the only impartial person associated with this case.

The opening of the light brown door prevented Nate from responding to his partner's musings. The unforgettable Doctor Robson made his way into the corridor without so much as a glance towards either police official. "Excuse me, Doctor,"

Nate said, stopping the older man in his retreating strides. "We were wondering whether it's not too much hassle for us to speak with our suspect now?" he asked with only a hint of sarcasm dripping from his words.

The doctor froze and looked both Nate and Sam up and down judgmentally. "In case you haven't noticed, *sir,* this is a hospital, and I do not have time to molly coddle the local bobby. Speak to her if you must but if it impedes my future work with her, you will be hearing from our lawyers," Doctor Robson said sternly before turning away.

Letting out a slow whistle, Sam motioned for Nate to lead them into Melinda's lair. Nate could hear as the latch clicked open and the wood moved to show them the small form of Melinda in a bed very similar to Riya's. The only noticeable difference was the addition of the familiar restraints that were strapped tightly around the guilty woman's wrists. "Here we are again, Mrs Ryker," Sam said in humour, mixed with a touch of kindness. Nate could never understand how his partner managed to charm everyone. No matter how rigid or tense their conversation companion had become, one word, one look from Sam and they were put at ease.

In that moment, with that thought at the front of his mind, Nate made the decision to leave the conversation in the capable hands of his friend. Nodding towards Sam, hoping he got the message, Nate sat himself in the corner of the room so he could become a simple observer rather than the leading man.

Sam stepped forward and placed his hands on the plastic end rails attached to Melinda's bed. "Melinda, what happened?" he asked gently but with no response he continued to try and convince the mentally fragile woman to divulge her plight. "Who upset you?" Sam finally said, more softly than Nate believed himself capable.

Melinda stared blankly to the side of her bed and heavily blinked a few times before looking directly at Sam. Nate wasn't sure if she was simply ignoring him or hadn't noticed his presence in her state of confusion. "Who," she whispered quietly to no one in particular. "Funny question. Who else would it be, Detective? What else would it be?" she asked rhetorically. "For years I have sat in that house and waited. Waited for something to happen, for something to change. But the Rykers made sure I would never be anything but a gold-digging unfit mother," Melinda said in a daze. Nothing she was saying made sense, she was reliving her past and her present at the same time and the lines were becoming more and more muddled as the seconds went by.

"Did you come looking for Riya?" Sam asked, still remaining calm. With his words, Melinda's eyes flickered towards Nate for the first time since they had arrived in the room.

"I had to make the pain stop. She's the only one I could get to. The weak link," Melinda said still in a whisper. Her words bristled Nate as she described Riya so inadequately. "If it wasn't for them, things wouldn't have gone so wrong," she added, dropping her elevated head back into the thin pillow.

Nate and Sam exchanged a glance. "What do you mean, Melinda? How did things go wrong?" Sam prodded. They could feel the words Melinda was trying to hold back.

"Lina," Melinda grated in response. "She tried to best me. Tried to make things hers. I had to stop her," she finished.

Sam's shoulder tightened and his stance strengthened. "How did you stop her, Melinda? Did you kill her?" Sam

333

asked, still slightly comfortingly but with an edge of command to his voice.

At his question Melinda began screaming. Her pitch was loud enough that Nate feared for the windows. Tears rolled down her cheeks and her hands gripped at the magnolia blanket covering her legs. The room was a rush of activity as nurses bustled in and began trying to console the shrieking woman. Thinking the room was crowded enough, Nate and Sam began moving towards the exit walking straight into an irritated Doctor Robson. The growl directed at him almost made Nate stand up to the obnoxious man, but it wasn't the time. Melinda was now actively fighting against the hospital staff and Nate couldn't watch the destructive scene any more so made his way to leave.

"I didn't do it! I asked him... I didn't know he was listening to me. He did it. I told him to," Melinda screeched towards the room but then immediately fell brutely silent. With her words hanging in the air, everything had changed. They didn't know who she was talking about and, given her current state of terror, they weren't going to find out from Melinda, but her outburst had put one major piece of the puzzle in place.

Chapter Ninety-Two

The first thing that struck her when Nate quickly swept her up and into his car, was that he was on edge. The second thing was that he was in a terrible rush. The minute the door closed behind him and he placed the keys into the ignition they were off, speeding through the scattering of other cars that lined roads, heading in the opposite direction to which she expected. Riya looked behind them through her window and then turned to Nate questioningly. "Nate, we're going the wrong way." She stated laughing under her breath. Living with two brothers and a father had taught her to approach tension and possible anger with as little of either emotion from her direction as possible.

"You're staying with me for the next couple days," Nate responded and both his tone and stature indicated he wasn't looking for any arguments.

That, however, was not his decision to make. "What do you mean? I want to go home. I need my stuff, I've got work, I've got…"

"Riya!" Nate shouted loudly in the small confines of the sleek car. For what felt like minutes they sat silently in the cab just absorbing the elephant in the room. Nate seemed to fully digest her look of terror and confusion and softened. With one hand left on the steering wheel, his other hand reached over and affectionately squeezed her knee. "Look, something's about to go down. I can't give you the details, but this mess will be over soon. I just... I need to know you're safe while we catch the bastard who did this," Nate finished with a heartfelt look.

In response, Riya placed her hand of his and smiled. "OK. I'll go," she said quietly. "I just need some stuff to wear and some other bits and pieces," she said, hoping his rush and anxiety would at least allow her a few niceties.

Visually relaxing at her agreement, Nate bobbed his head. "I've got some work to do but then I'll swing by your house and pick some stuff up for you. Text me everything you need, and I'll grab it," he compromised, giving her one more sincere smile. She nodded and they spent the rest of the journey in comfortable silence. In less than half an hour they were pulling up outside of Nate's neatly kept front door. She hopped out expecting to wave him off, but instead he followed her all the way into the house, checking both the windows and doors for possible entry points. After checking every lock, seemingly twice, Nate span around and let out a large sigh of relief as he rubbed his flat hands against each other. "Right, I'll leave you to it," Nate said, swaggering his way over to her and to the door. "I'll let you know when it looks like I'll be heading home," he finished, kissing her on the top of her head. "Send me that list!" he yelled as the door swung closed behind him.

Riya watched as he jogged back down the small, hilled driveway back to his car. She turned into the empty kitchen and living area. Nate had told her this would all be over soon, and she believed him, but part of her couldn't help but expect the worse to happen in the coming days.

Chapter Ninety-Three

Sliding out of the car, Nate came face to face with Sam who was still busy writing down whatever thoughts were whirling around in his ever-busy head. "Anything?" Nate asked as he brushed past his partner, and made a beeline for the station to grab whatever it was he needed, in order to get on the road and start their final search.

"I got a list of all properties in the country that the Rykers either own or have shares in. There's a few dotted around the place but one sticks out. The company owns a cabin in Kieldar Forest Park, very secluded, no neighbours or main roads within thirty miles," Sam said, flipping from page to page for each minute detail. As the two men continued verbally brainstorming ideas, they had reached their joined desks and grabbed both jackets that always remained over the backs of their chairs for incidents such as these. They grabbed their radios, then went to check in with the rest of the team.

"OK, people, the working theory is that Rory Shaw was taken by one of two people," Nate explained to the roomful of hard-working detectives. "Logan or Harry Ryker are the main suspects. It could be one of them, could be both of them or someone else. We don't know. All we do know is that Rory Shaw was handed over from one car to another less than forty-eight hours ago and since then his father has gone off the grid," Nate said, stopping when he saw an outstretched arm raised in the air. "Yes. Daniels."

"You think the kidnappers made contact, boss? Asked for a ransom?" Detective Constable Daniels asked. He was the newest member of the team and had proved himself to be an eager, ambitious young hopeful.

Nate nodded once, firmly. "Detective Turner and I believe the abductors did not want money or favours from Shaw, instead we believe that they took Rory to protect him and themselves. It's likely Rory is currently with his father and they've gone to ground after being reunited. Rory could have seen Lina being killed and been told to keep quiet by either Harry or Logan, who then subsequently attacked Riya Ryker to stop her finding out more," Nate continued to explain. "Melinda Ryker has just told us that she told 'him' to do it, that she instructed someone to hurt or kill Lina," Nate finished, nodding for Sam to continue.

"Of course, we can't take what Melinda has said at face value. Her mental state will be called to question and will affect her credibility, but her confession makes sense," Sam said, pointing to Melinda's picture that remained plastered across their large whiteboard. "We think Shaw has taken Rory somewhere out of the way," he continued by sticking an overhead image of a large log cabin in the centre of the board, "The Rykers own, or rather the company owns, a cabin in the Northumberland forests. It's quiet and completely off the grid. Our intel says that someone has visited the tracks that lead to the cabin in the last few days," Sam finished, looking over the room. All the eager faces of the officers made the space feel stronger and more hopeful.

"We are moving in on the cabin today. Our aim is to find Rory Shaw and his father both unharmed. If needs be, we will bring Mr Shaw in under caution but the CPS has no desire to charge him if he was simply running to protect his child," Nate added.

"But sir…" another constable tried to interrupt.

"He has done nothing illegal. The man thought it was in the best interest of the child. I won't be part of prosecuting him for that," Nate retorted decisively. "We wait until this evening then drive up towards the cabin, shouldn't take more than a couple of hours. Sam and I will be in the lead car and we will be followed by three teams of two. I want a complete sweep of the place while I bring back both Shaw and Rory for questioning. Is that clear to everyone?" Nate asked, watching a sea of nodding heads fill his vision. "All right then." Nate finished by assigning teams and orders.

Hours later, Nate preoccupied himself with his driving and watching the trees pass them by. The quickly approaching dusk lingered on the horizon as a calling card to a new beginning. "You think they'll be there?" Sam asked quietly, pondering the case that had been engulfing them both for many weeks.

"I don't know. If our theory's right, Shaw would have taken Rory somewhere exactly like this," Nate said, answering his partner honestly.

"And if our theory's wrong?" Sam asked, voicing Nate's own fears.

Nate responded with the truth, however desolate it sounded. "If it's wrong we've wasted time in finding a child that might not even be alive any more."

Chapter Ninety-Four

The leaves moved with the gentle breeze that moved through the air as Nate's team moved quietly up to the edge of the perimeter. They'd parked down the road so that their arrival was a surprise and they had begun traipsing through the wooded forest in a synchronised military fashion. The darkly covered men and women formed two symmetrical lines on either side of the mahogany door as Nate signalled for the team to move forward with pushing their way through the only barrier in their way.

Warrants had been issued, force had been sanctioned. Any officer or government official were on edge with the threat of a missing child still looming. The battering ram slammed against the thick wood and Nate could hear the splintering of metal and timber giving way as they moved forward as one unstoppable unit.

The lights in the front of the house were off so silence remained among the officers as they flashed torches towards any possible hiding places a child, or man, could find. As the eery house continued to remain mute, Sam and Nate felt, rather than heard, the movement from above. The creaking of the floorboards echoed down the spines of every officer in sight as they crept up the flawless, short staircase.

Unlike the downstairs of the luxury cabin, the upstairs was completely alight with soft lamps and decorations hanging from every nook. Only the slight whispering of a digital voice could be heard as a clock ticked by from an unknown location. The team moved forward, kicking the door open forcefully. A short scream sounded, and a child's cry filled the room. Nate's eyes adjusted to the now bright lighting and he scanned the room in its entirety. To his surprise the people in the room were the last thing he noted in his visual inspection of the room that held many answers. The room looked like it had been designed immaculately but had been recently turned into a bunker of sorts. Sleeping bags lined the floors, the curtains had been drawn and the TV was playing at the minimum volume like it was only meant to serve as a small distraction to a child.

Dominic Shaw stood rigidly in the middle of the room, it was like everybody was waiting with bated breath in hopes of more movement. At last, the small shimmer of a tiny hand, curling its way round its father's leg, captured the attention of everyone crowding the small alcove. Rory Shaw's head popped out next as he stared wide-eyed at Nate and then up to his father. In that moment Nate knew that the man had taken his son for protection and no other reason. Nothing sinister had taken place and the boy had managed to remain with the only stable parent he had ever had. Even still, as a detective, Nate had a job to do. "Mr Shaw, you need to come with us. We have some questions to ask you," he directed at the usually suave gentleman. To his credit, Dominic simply nodded, picked up Rory, who wrapped his arms securely around his father's neck, and moved to follow Nate out of his borrowed hidey hole.

The drive back to the station was uneventful. Nate kept one eye on the road and the other on his review mirror. He could see Dominic Shaw murmuring soothing words into his son's ear and decided to give him the benefit of the doubt by placing trust and kindness into the man's palms. "When we arrive, I'll get uniforms to take you to a nearby hotel for the night. We can talk in the morning so you can both get some rest," Nate heard himself saying softly as not to wake the young boy.

Dominic sat in shock for a moment. Apparently in the world of international business, human beings didn't offer kindness to each other, especially not to Dominic Shaw. "Thank you," the older man muttered, and Nate could see the sincerity lining his face.

Chapter Ninety-Five

The latch clicked shut and Riya's eyes flew open. Nate didn't live in a shoebox but the large bed that occupied the bedroom wasn't too far away from the noise-inducing door. A shadow moved through the house and made its way into the dimly lit room and over to where she lay sleepily. She forced her eyes to open and took in the man standing before her with softness in his gaze. "Sorry, I didn't mean to wake you," Nate said, moving a strand of her hair behind her ear.

Riya shrugged. "I wasn't really asleep anyway." Murmuring as she bunched the feather pillow up behind her and hugged it as if it were a lifeline. "You're back late," she finished with a large yawn.

Nate seemed to freeze at her remark, and she could tell that he'd been hit with something. The man, who was still touching her face, let out a long indrawn breath. "We found Rory," he said definitively like it was a fact only, and not a massive emotional relief to him and everybody else who cared one bit about that newly found little boy.

Riya sat up quickly, sweeping her own hand through her mop of hair. "You found him? Is he OK?" She was panicking and she knew it but still couldn't help the palpitations of her heart as it beat erratically inside her chest. Rory was found, but she still didn't know to what extent his 'trip' had harmed him physically or mentally.

Nate quietly chuckled and her tension eased ever so

slightly. "He's fine. He's with Dominic. I'll know more tomorrow when I talk to them," he stated, removing most of his clothes and sliding down into the covers next to her.

Riya snuggled into, what she had started considering as, her safe place and let out a deep contented sigh. She began nuzzling her face into his ever-warm neck and laid a gentle kiss into the groove of his shoulder. Nate's hands stroked her back for a while and then slowly moved them towards her face. His index finger tipped her head back and his mouth came down onto hers. There they lay, entwined as Nate rolled them over so that he was poised above her. He kissed her mouth, her cheek, her neck, and everything in between before lifting her legs so they wrapped more firmly around him. Nate paused before entering her and looked into her lust filled eyes, he rubbed the tip of his nose against hers and froze. "I love you," he whispered to her in the dawn's light. Everything that had been milling around in her head stopped still, she felt peace wash over her and brought her arms up to circle his neck and her fingers dug into his soft hair.

"I love you too," she responded as he moved forward into her, the feeling of which was nothing like she'd ever experienced. Riya had never felt this in sync with someone, never felt that every fibre of her being was connected so forcibly to someone else. It began slow but the desire grew, it became more heated, more ferocious. They moved together, finished together, and lay tangled up in each other for the hours that followed. There was no doubt in Riya's mind, this man was her saving grace. The family to replace the one that was broken. Nate was more than that to her, it just helped knowing that she had something else besides the slowly fading light of the Ryker clan.

Chapter Ninety-Six

The loud buzz that grated against Nate's skin sounded to show that the interview was being recorded. A nervous-looking Dominic Shaw sat across from him, clenching, and then unclenching his hands over and over again in a vicious cycle as Nate rattled off the information that was legally necessary for the tape. "Mr Shaw..." Nate began, only to be stopped by a small lifting of the tense father's hand.

"Dominic. Please," he said pleasantly. The man may have been tense in many ways, but he wasn't angry. If anything, Nate got the feeling that Dominic Shaw was nervous simply because he believed that he'd done something seriously wrong. He knew it was wrong to keep the other man on the edge like this but for the time being, it would help their line of enquiry to keep him guessing as to what his future might hold. If Dominic felt like he owed the case something in exchange for his actions, who was Nate to stop him?

Thinking that the show of good faith by Dominic deserved some recognition, Nate continued with a small smile of gratitude. "Dominic then. Could you tell us what happened after we last spoke? It was our understanding that you didn't know where your son was, and yet we find you hidden away with him in the middle of nowhere," Nate asked. Despite Dominic showing willing, he couldn't take it easy on the other man. For Lina's sake.

"I didn't!" Shaw responded loudly before remembering where he was. "Sorry. I didn't mean to shout," he apologised, pinching the bridge of his nose. "When we last saw each other, I swear I didn't know where Rory was but that night I... I got a call."

"A call from who?" Sam asked, chiming in.

"I didn't know. His voice was muffled. All he said was that he had my son and that, provided I didn't go to the police, I could have him back for nothing. I just had to lay low for a while," Dominic explained, showing an admirable amount of regret over his conduct. "They gave me a time and a place and said I'd see my son soon. Then the line went dead."

Nate leant forward and clasped his hands together. "So, then what?" he asked in a frighteningly low tone.

"I waited until the agreed time and drove down to the ser..." Dominic stopped when he saw Nate's smirk. The accomplished detective knew it was childish, but he needed the other man to know he had no legs to stand on. The word 'agreed' implied that Dominic had some sort of say in the matter, which he did not.

Nate considered his options. Dominic was trying to be up front about everything and he would thank him for his information. Just not yet. "Who was at the service station Dominic? Who had Rory?" Nate asked, knowing he was only a few pushes away from cracking whatever walls Dominic Shaw had decided to erect.

Vehemently shaking his head, Dominic began speaking. "You have to know that he was unharmed, he was safe. Rory was never in any danger. He cared for him. He loves him, and yes, I disliked that my son had to spend any time with *that* family, but they love him." Dominic stopped but saw Nate's wide-eyed expression and realised the detective was waiting for more. "He did it for his own good. Apparently, he was protecting Rory from something. He wouldn't tell me what, but I believed him."

"A name, Dominic," Nate commanded sternly, yet again using his persona as the rough and burly police detective to his advantage.

Dominic hung his head and growled. "I don't know what happened with Lina, if he had anything to do with it. I don't know. I can't tell you anything about her death, I swear."

"A name," Nate repeated, his voice barely above a whisper.

The air was heavy as it circulated the room. It felt like the three men were all holding their breath. This was it. The key to the crime and Dominic Shaw was the man on the door. The man in their hot seat exhaled loudly and tapped one hand against the shiny table. One word, one sentence, that's all they were waiting for and it felt like the hardest few moments to have ever crossed the Earth's timeline. One more sigh and the can of worms would be opened. The whisper ricocheted off the walls as the name seeped into the detectives' heads. "Harry Ryker."

Chapter Ninety-Seven

Something wasn't right. The atmosphere was… off. It was like the world was preparing for something to happen, something bad. Harry couldn't stop the nervous bounce of his leg as he sat in the plush sofa that rested in the middle of Logan's front room. It was like time had stopped. Harry couldn't put his finger on what was about to happen, but something was imminent.

Like it had been conjured up from the darkest depths of his mind, the door to the condo burst open. Uniformed police officers came swarming into the open-plan room. The shouts echoed throughout his ears, but he couldn't understand them. Harry wasn't sure whether it was because they were all speaking at once or because of the shock and surprise of their unwarranted entry. All of the sudden the sea of Hi-Viz-covered policemen and women parted to reveal a face that Harry did recognise. Detective Inspector Nathan Richards.

"Harry Ryker, you are under arrest for the abduction and illegal containment of Rory Shaw. You do not have to say anything, but it may harm your defense if you do not mention, when questioned something which you later rely on in court. Anything you do say may be given in evidence." The detective spoke clearly as if he were being understood but Harry couldn't comprehend what was happening until he felt cool metal tighten around his wrists in front of him. He looked down at his now bound hands and reality came crashing down around him.

Chapter Ninety-Eight

For the second time that day, Nate sat in his interview room surrounded by silence. Harry Ryker looked broken. His usually put-together self was now disheveled and tatty. The man was sitting cowering, trying not to hyperventilate but Nate couldn't bring himself to feel any sympathy for the man. Against all his training, all his instincts, Nate had already sent a text to Riya with all the basic information about her father's arrest and the reason for it. He knew it was unethical, but she needed to know where her father was and after last night, he couldn't keep anything from her. It just didn't feel right. He loved her. It was as simple as that.

"Mr Ryker, we can sit here all day if that's what it takes. The more you say. The less time you'll do," Nate prompted. Harry still refused to meet neither his nor Sam's gaze. "Dominic Shaw has gone on record, stating that you dropped Rory off, with him, at a service station along this A road," Nate started, laying a map under Harry Ryker's nose and pointing towards a long red line that showed the track in question. "This means that unless you start talking, I will charge you for both Rory's abduction and Lina's murder. Am I making myself clear?"

"What do you want me to say?" shouted Harry suddenly. "You already think I'm guilty. What more is there?" he seconded, looking even more haunted than he had, when he realised he was trapped by the confines of a pair of handcuffs.

"Harry! You need to say something! You have had something to do with kidnapping a child. That much is clear. If you get charged with this, right now, people will talk, people will assume things about you that won't sound pretty. The minute you get taken to prison the inmates will come for you," Nate said angrily. It didn't feel right, Harry Ryker was a man who fought back, he would not simply sit back and accept the kind of fate he'd brought upon himself. "I'm not saying this to scare you. I can see it in your eyes, there's more to this story." Nate could see the cogs turning inside Harry's brain, so he pressed on. "Tell us. Give your children a reason to keep believing in you."

The one thing Nate was not expecting was for Harry Ryker to succumb to shuddering sobs. It was the ugly kind of crying that made faces contort and puff up. "I can't," Harry finally whispered defeatedly.

"You took Rory," Nate stated. It wasn't a question, that much they knew. Harry took the hint and nodded. "Did you kill Lina?" Nate asked, fearing the answer, either way. On one hand he had the means and opportunity to do so, but on the other hand the man seemed to have no motive. So why?

Instead of denying his question violently, Harry Ryker shook his head almost regretfully. The older man didn't seem to want to be innocent. "No. I loved Lina, like she was my own." Another sob racked his body. "It just…"

Nate could sense Harry's reluctance in explaining any further. The older man let the words hang in the air without finishing the sentence. "Tell us, Mr Ryker. Help us understand all this," he urged. Harry shrank into to himself even more and shriveled into his pain.

"I can't," he silently cried, finishing on a shudder. "I can't tell you what you want to hear!" he finished more loudly than he had managed to speak in the last few days, let alone the last few minutes.

Nate's patience snapped. "You kidnapped a six-year-old child! Any sympathy, any chance at mercy you have is controlled by us. This is your only chance. After this I will let them throw the book at you without a backward glance!" Screaming his displeasure at the older man, waiting for all the answers he'd been craving. "Talk to us!" Nate commanded, slapping his hands against the steel table and then pacing across the room.

Harry sniffled once more and then stilled. It took minutes but the older man wiped his face and slowly put on a mask of strength. There he sat, his face like stone, unflinching and cold. It was like he had become someone else entirely. He said nothing, but Nate could tell that Harry Ryker was thinking of his next move, what he was going to say and how he was going spin his involvement in this case, were the questions Nate could see whirling around Harry's head like a storm waiting to be released. "Fine. I did it," he finally responded very succinctly.

Nate stopped dead in his tracks and slowly turned his head toward the man who had uttered the few words he had been waiting for. "Did what exactly?" he queried skeptically. Something didn't feel right.

Harry rolled his eyes impatiently. "Took Rory, killed Lina. Everything," he stated firmly, with no sign of remorse or emotion.

Nate narrowed his eyes. The old man's demeanor had changed and nothing about the situation himself and his

351

partner had found themselves in made sense. In the space of half an hour the outpour of emotion had turned into a sort of sociopathy. This wasn't Harry Ryker speaking. "I don't buy it," he said, surprising both himself, Sam, and Harry.

"I'm sorry?" Harry replied, tilting his head to the side as if he were from another planet.

Nate shook his head. "You didn't do it," he stated confidently.

"I did," Harry said humorously, Nate could tell he was simply trying to mask his discomfort with a subtle snort.

Breathing in air between his clasped-together teeth, Nate scrunched up his nose and shook his head. "You want to know what it looks like to me?" Nate asked, not waiting for an answer. "It looks like you are a very desperate man. A man who, by all accounts, does everything and anything to protect his family. I think you're doing that now, you're protecting one of them," Nate surmised, finally siting down in his designated metal chair, identical to the one Sam sat in a few feet away.

"Harry. Tell us what happened the night Lina died, for her sake if not for your own," Sam said, leaning forward juxtaposing Nate's confrontational stance with one of care.

Tears formed once again along Harry's lower eyelid and he began running one thumb across the top of the opposite one. His knuckles had become almost translucent white in the process of gripping his fists together. He began to murmur into himself and then spoke more loudly as the seconds went by, remembering that he was not alone in the room after all. "I heard her scream, the kind of scream that only a parent knows. I could tell she was hurt so I rushed out of the bedroom and down through the landing," Harry said, his eyes glazed over as if he were no longer present in the room. "It was like everything was going in slow motion. I watched her fall! She fell and I did nothing! Her head bounced against the marble floor and then this red liquid started pooling around her head. That's what I thought it was. Just liquid. Then it hit me all at once. It was blood, it was *her* blood," a now crying Harry Ryker disclosed.

Looking at each other, Nate and Sam raised their eyebrows at each other in recognition of the breakthrough. "Who was at the top of the stairs, Harry?" Nate asked, mimicking Sam's concerned stare.

A haunted man sat opposite them. "I couldn't let... I couldn't leave her there. The questions, the assumptions," Harry started, obviously on his own timeline of events rather than the case's. As far as Sam and Nate were concerned, who pushed Lina was the key information here. Harry's involvement could come after in their eyes, but if Harry needed to go through everything to make himself feel better, then who were they to stop him? "I went down the stairs, I didn't think, just lifted her into my arms and carried her into the laundry room. Using the shirt I was wearing, I cleaned up the blood and managed to mop most of it up. Then I closed the house down for the night and went to bed," Harry finished, believing himself to be done.

Nate leant back in his chair and folded his arms across his chest. "What did you do with the shirt?" he asked quietly.

Harry looked off to his left and pursed his lips. "It was part of a set." He laughed cynically. "A wedding gift for me and my *wife*. She has a matching one, same size so she didn't have to wear bottoms." He stopped to nod at the detectives slowly. "I put the shirt under the loose floorboard in Melinda's room. I watched her leave earlier that night and I knew she kept keepsakes and what have you in there, so thought it was the best place for it."

Nate interrupted him, needing to know if he was genuine. "The DNA on the shirt…"

"There was everything under that floorboard, detective. Hairbands, jewelry, the lot," Harry explained and Nate couldn't fault the man's pragmatism. It made sense. DNA transferred between items of clothing and surfaces all the time, no reason why that couldn't have happened with the shirt. "I know it was wrong, but I couldn't let her get away with what she'd done," he whispered, his voice dropping again now that they were back onto the subject of murder.

Nate looked at him heavily. "Are you saying that Melinda Ryker killed Lina?" he asked, already becoming suspicious of Harry's sudden change in story.

The devastated father considered his options for a moment and then smirked sadly. "I'd say yes. But you wouldn't believe me. She is to blame, though," he made sure to add before ending his response.

"How?" Sam uttered softly, not wanting to disrupt Harry's flow.

Harry seemed to force his next words out of his mouth, "She told him to do it." He froze after the pained words slipped out and Nate could see the shutters come down in the man's mind. In that moment both himself and Sam knew that any more information they wanted out of Harry Ryker would be like drawing blood from a stone.

"Who, Harry? Who pushed Lina down the stairs?" Nate prompted, needing to go in hard to get some sort clue into who had committed the deadly act. Harry shook his head violently, convincing himself and Nate that he was determined to speak no more. "Fine. You don't want to tell us, that's fine. Tell me something though, Harry," Nate said firmly and confidently, enough to draw a rouse out of an otherwise frozen Harry Ryker. Nate knew that his moment had come, so he asked the one question that was designed to break the frail man. "How did it feel to bludgeon your own daughter to near death?" Recoiling, Harry began shaking. It was true. Harry Ryker had hurt Riya and Nate wanted to kill him.

"I didn't mean to," the undeserving father sobbed. "It had to be done. I'd worked so hard to keep it hidden but she was going to find out. I couldn't let that happen." Another shudder racked his body and a small amount of sympathy for the man coiled into Nate's heart.

Shaking himself out of his moment of weakened emotion, Nate began his attack. "You don't give us a name," he began, growling at the destroyed man, "and I will make sure you rot in prison for abduction and attempted murder. Your choice." Nate finished by spreading his arms wide, signaling that Harry now had the floor.

"I can't," annoyingly, Harry repeated with conviction.

"One of your sons did this. They are the only ones who have means, motive and opportunity to kill Lina. She broke Logan's heart and Thomas hated her for ruining his perfect family. The more you tell us, the better it will be for them," Nate said, the penny finally dropping that although Thomas Ryker was alibied out for the attack on Riya, he was still in the frame for the murder of Lina Simons.

Nate stood up, his chair scraping against the rough floor. He raised one eyebrow silently asking his questions again. When Harry remained silent, Nate knew he did not have the patience to just wait the man out. So, he did the one thing that

Harry feared the most, he threatened his family. "OK then, I guess we'll have to go and find out for ourselves. Seems like we'll be seeing both Logan and Thomas very soon, in rooms exactly like this one." Nate knew it was a cheap shot. One of the men was guilty, that was evident, but the other was innocent and he was praying that the thought of his innocent son being punished for a crime he didn't commit was enough to prompt Harry Ryker into action.

He was right. "He didn't know what he was doing! He didn't mean it! You can't ruin his life because of this!" Harry shouted distraughtly.

Roughly rubbing his forehead with his open palm, Nate responded, moving further away from the hyper alert man. "I'm sorry, sir, but your sons are grown men, they need to pay for their crimes whatever you may think."

"I'll confess!" Harry burst out. The man continued, not paying any attention to the wide-eyed, disbelieving detectives. "I'll say I did it and you can take me in. Prosecute me. You'd be the men that sent Harry Ryker to prison. It'll make your careers. Just let him be," he finished on a heartfelt whisper that almost tugged on Nate's heartstrings.

Detective Nathan Richards was a professional, his emotions had no place in the interview room. Looking down towards the ground for brief moment, Nate sighed. "I'm afraid that's not how it works, Mr Ryker." And with that Nate turned and headed for the door, Sam right on his heels. Harry's pleas faded into the distance until a thought passed through Nate's head. The man protected his family but felt the need to almost kill his daughter to protect a grown man and his mistake? That didn't make sense. The only way it made sense was if the person making said mistake, wasn't capable of taking full responsibility...

Nate froze at the thought. His hand stilled, halfway between his body and the doorknob. Without turning around Nate whispered the words that no man, woman or detective would ever want to deal with. "Rory."

Looking back at the broken man, Nate watched as Harry hung his head in submission. The truth was out. Question was, how would they move forward from here?

Chapter Ninety-Nine

"No," Dominic Shaw stated firmly, unable to comprehend the truth that was being laid out in front of him. "Whatever you think happened, my son was not involved!" the man rasped, turning away from the guilty detectives, who had just burst his perfect son's perfect bubble. "She was his sister! He loved her. He wouldn't hurt her. Not for anything."

"Not even for his mother?" Nate asked quietly. He didn't want to add to Dominic's pain but watching his reaction could prove vital in getting someone to pay for ending a life and ruining the future of a small child.

"What?" Dominic spat out. His suspicion and pain evident throughout his whole body.

Sam stepped forward. "We need your permission to talk to him. If he did this, there has to be a reason. We just want to help," he tried to argue softly with the falling apart father.

Dominic continued to shake his head in protest and Nate could tell they were losing whatever battle they were fighting him against. "Mr Shaw, we are both trained in interviewing children. Nothing we will say will scare Rory. There'll be a trained child psychologist behind the glass just in case," Nate factually said with only one thing missing. "Please. Help us find some justice for Lina." He spoke sincerely which proved to be enough to convince the still anxious man to allow them access to his son. Dominic nodded and walked into the softly furnished room they used for cases such as these, where a minor needed to be interviewed without being scared into silence.

Nate and Sam followed the protective papa bear into the room and were immediately struck by Rory's small form that played quietly in the corner. The reflective mirror that doubled as a viewing window lined the entirety of one wall as it loomed over them, ever reminding the men that this was not simply a place for a child to freely play without fear of being incarcerated. "Hi, Rory. Remember me?" Nate asked softly, kneeling towards the plastic toys that the boy had gripped in his small little fists.

A noncommittal sound was all the response he received. The child who, for the most part, had shown himself to be resilient and ever cheery was gone, replaced with a shy nervous being who didn't know which way was up. "Rory, the detectives just need to talk to you for minute. Is that OK?" Dominic asked his son in a tone that told Nate that if the boy said no, that would be the end to any conversation in the docile little room.

Rory spent a moment considering. He looked at his father questioningly but nodded all the same. "OK," he said, his voice a much higher pitch than anybody else's in the room.

Nate moved so he was sitting Indian style on the not-so-soft carpet next to him. "Tell me about Lina," he asked tentatively, not wanting to rush the point on a mind that was so fragile.

Rory placed a large red block onto a blue one and responded, not looking up from his great architectural feat. "She's my sister. I don't see her very much," he said as if it were a natural thing.

Nate nodded. "It must be nice having a sister. I always wanted one. Is it hard not seeing her a lot?" he added, placing another brightly coloured block to the now unstable structure.

"I want her to come live with me and Daddy, but he said she was happy staying with Harry," Rory continued. His use of present tense showed Nate just how unaware the boy was of his possible actions.

Judging by the warmth that invaded Rory's voice on the mention of his stepfather, Nate decided to follow through on that thought. "You like Harry, huh?" he queried flippantly as if it weren't a gateway to the truth.

For the first time since Nate and Sam had entered the room Rory Shaw smiled. "He helps me," the boy said, shrugging his minute shoulders.

Nate sensed Dominic lean forward in the cushy sofa he sat on and rest his face against his hands in a kind of pain. This was it, all three men could feel it. "How does he help you?" Nate asked, making sure to keep his and Rory's focus on the building masterpiece in front of them.

Rory giggled as the tower he'd been painstakingly working on crumbled down to the floor. Once the laughing fit subsided Rory looked at Nate more seriously than he could imagine a six-year-old ever needing to look and answered him. "He fixed Lina for me."

"Fixed?" Dominic questioned before Nate had a chance to form a response.

Rory's eyes widened as he looked at his father. It was a look that children get when they've been caught doing something wrong. Rory stood on his small legs and wobbled from side to side. "It was an accident, Daddy," he pleaded across the room towards his one responsible parent.

"What was an accident, bud?" Dominic asked him, his voice breaking as he looked at the should-be-innocent small boy. The heartbreak was enough to make a grown man want to bury his head in the sand.

"I pushed Lina at the wall and then down the stairs, but Harry made her better," Rory said simply and quietly.

Understanding dawned on Nate. Harry Ryker had watched Rory push Lina down the stairs and then moved her body, not only to throw investigators but also to create the illusion to a frightened little boy that he wasn't a murderer. The only thing left to know was why Rory had taken it upon himself to commit such a final act. "Why did you push Lina? Did she do something to upset you?" he asked casually. The last thing that they needed was for Rory to shut down because he thought that they were angry at him.

Rory's face contorted at his question and his little nose scrunched up in confusion. "Mummy said she needed to go. That Lina was bad, and I was good. She said she'd love me if I helped her," Rory said barely above a whisper. With his final confession Rory curled up into a ball on the floor and wept. Dominic crawled across the floor towards him and enveloped him into a huge embrace as sobs overcame them both.

Deciding that it was best to give the small family some time, Nate and Sam retreated from the room. Both men rested against the wall outside and leant their heads back in defeat. "Wow," Nate said exhaustedly. They had their answers, their murderer, but it didn't feel like a win. It felt like a worst-case scenario.

Chapter One Hundred

"What happens now?" Riya asked as they sat on the stone steps outside the police station. Her legs were comfortably hugged in front of her chest as her cheek lay on her bare knee, making it the perfect position for her wide eyes to stare up at him in question.

Nate was in a similar position to her as they contemplated the last few days. Thomas and Logan had been and gone after a de-brief of the situation, but Riya had remained. One look at her and Nate had wanted everything to just go away. Her head was healed, the doctors had given her the all clear, but it didn't mean that she'd be over recent events any time soon. "That depends," he answered honestly.

Her shock showed that she was expecting him to have all the answers and it pained him that he didn't. "What do you mean?" she asked, still searching his face as if the solution to all of the day's problems were hidden behind it.

Furrowing his eyebrows, Nate took a moment. It was her decision and he didn't like the idea of her having to choose the fate of someone she held dear. "Well, Melinda will be charged, I'm not sure with what yet but she'll be charged with something. Rory will have to go through a load of psychological evaluations before they decide what's best for him. It's likely he won't have to be locked up. CPS have no intention of sending a six-year-old to prison. Besides, they're

362

pretty certain that the real cause of death was surprise. If Lina had seen him coming, he never would have had the strength to cause that much damage and she'd still be here," Nate explained, fully aware he was boycotting the real answers she wanted.

Riya tilted her head to look at him more directly. "What about us?" she asked and Nate became alarmed. He hadn't even considered that these case results affected their relationship. She shook her head, realising what she'd just implied and clarified her question further. "What about my family? Me, Thomas, Logan." She paused and he waited for the last person on the list to escape her lips. "Dad. What happens now?"

"You and your brothers have done nothing wrong," Nate started with, squeezing her hand with his. "You three can start to heal. Can start to move on," he said, watching her lips smirk in response. "They need you, Riya. Logan lost the woman he loved and Thomas... Thomas is on his own journey," he thoughtfully continued. "Your dad, however..."

"Is he going to prison?" she asked before he could finish. Her anxiety was evident by the frown lines running across her forehead.

Leaning forward, Nate let go of her hand and rested his elbows on his thighs. "He'll be cautioned for his actions towards Lina's body. Given his position in the community, your board of directors will have to ask him to stand down. He'll lose his job for sure but we're not sure what else," he said pointedly to prepare her for the next few days, weeks, or months.

"And the assault?" she asked, uncharacteristically quiet.

Nate looked at her and turned his body as if to shield her.

"It's up to you. You can press charges…"

"No," she sharply interrupted. "I don't want to see him, I don't want to talk to him, but I don't want him to rot in prison either. Let him go," she finished definitively. Nate had to admire her courage not to seek vengeance. Her reluctance to see him was understandable and whether or not it stayed that way was up to her. All he knew was that he would be there, throughout it all to support her with whatever she needed.

"Come here," Nate said, standing up and pulling her to her feet so she was standing opposite him with her hands hugged by his larger ones. Stroking his thumbs across the tops of her dainty fingers Nate sighed. "I love you. You know that right?" he asked as she shot him a bright-eyed smile that lit her whole face up in a beautiful glow. Riya nodded and moved forward as if to kiss him, but he held firm and stepped slightly away. "I want to move forward. I want us to be a normal couple now this mess is over." The always astute Riya didn't answer, knowing that there was more to come from his declaration. "I want you to move in with me," he said, more nervous about asking the woman he loved such a big question than he was about looking killers in the eyes.

He needn't have worried. Another smile spread across Riya's face and this time he didn't stop the impending kiss but encouraged it. The woman in his arms had quickly become his reason for existence and he'd be damned if he let her slip though his fingers. It was a new beginning. One he couldn't wait to be a part of.